Inside Out Girl

ALSO BY TISH COHEN

Town House

Inside Out Girl

A NOVEL

TISH COHEN

HARPER ● PERENNIAL

NEW YORK ● LONDON ● TORONTO ● SYDNEY ● NEW DELHI ● AUCKLAND

HARPER ● PERENNIAL

P.S.™ is a trademark of HarperCollins Publishers.

HarperCollins books may be purchased for educational, business, or sales promotional use. For information please write: Special Markets Department, HarperCollins Publishers, 10 East 53rd Street, New York, NY 10022.

FIRST EDITION

Designed by Justin Dodd

Library of Congress Cataloging-in-Publication Data

Cohen, Tish.
    Inside out girl : a novel / Tish Cohen.— 1st Harper Perennial ed.
        p.   cm.
    ISBN 978-0-06-145295-6
        1. Single parents—Fiction. 2. Stepfamilies—Fiction.
    3. Learning disabled children—Fiction. 4. Teenage girls—
    Fiction. I. Title.
    PR9199.4.C644I57 2008
    813'.6—dc22   2007042326

08   09   10   11   12   OV/RRD   10 9 8 7 6 5 4 3 2 1

To Gillian

PART I

CHAPTER 1

Four Days of Stink

The stench in his daughter's darkened room nearly brought Len to his knees. Nothing quite pierced the nostrils like the harsh tang of death. Especially death four days later. Len held his breath as he threw back the curtains and leaned down over the bed.

"Olivia," he said, shaking the sweaty ten-year-old's shoulder. "Time to get up and get ready for school, princess. It's Thursday. Drama and music class."

Olivia groaned. Tangled in a mass of *The Incredibles* bedsheets and twisted pajamas, she rolled over—long, reddish-brown snarls strewn across her pale face like a net; doughy stomach, with impossibly deep belly button, luminous in the morning sun. Half of a bandage dangled uselessly over a scratch nearly healed on her forearm. As usual, she'd refused to allow her father to count to three and yank.

She rubbed her eyes and stretched. Squinting into the daylight, she grumbled, "Wish it was Saturday," and slithered off the bed, knocking to the floor her beloved Birthday Wishes Barbie, who, like Olivia's other Barbies, had long been stripped of the finery she arrived in—sky-blue gown, wrist-length gloves, dainty shoes—and been obliged to endure a perpetual state of nakedness ever since.

The child stumbled across the room to her gerbil cage, the

source of the rotting stench. "Need to feed Georgie Boy." Yawning, she reached her hand inside and unclipped the water bottle, holding it up in the sun. She groaned. "Empty? The pet store lady said we should access to water him daily."

"*Give him* access to clean water," Len said. "But it's a little late for that." He could see the gerbil on its back, stiff as Indian rubber. The concept of death was not coming easily to his daughter. Her mother died when she was too young to understand, and this gerbil was Olivia's first conscious experience dealing with the intangible reality of someone, something, being there one minute and gone the next. So when they'd found the little rodent claws-up on Sunday afternoon, Olivia flatly refused to bury him.

In the supposed five stages of grief, the child was besotted by the first—denial—and her fidelity showed no signs of waning.

Len moved closer, sank into her desk chair, and wondered if the air might actually be alive with stink. A soupy fog of putrefaction so strong he was near certain he could taste it.

He glanced at his watch. He wasn't late for anything in particular. The senior partners of Standish, Bean and Roche could, theoretically, stroll in when they pleased. Trouble was, they didn't. By the time Len jogged in at nine thirty each morning, desperate for a coffee, the other partners were already elbow-deep in divorce and custody files, calling out to their assistants or mollifying jilted spouses on the phone.

There had been a time when Len prided himself on being the one to flick on the office lights each morning. He'd arranged his life in such a way that dedication to his family and his career were perfectly balanced. Until his wife died. A widowed parent loses the luxury of balance. And on this particular morning, confronted with a festering rodent, family won.

Taking Olivia's free hand, Len said, "It's never easy to say good-bye to our loved ones. Do you remember that song that used to make you cry? What was it called . . . 'The Circle of Life'?"

Her silver eyes, far too big for her delicate face, shone. She nodded. "From *The Lion King*."

Good. We're getting somewhere, he thought. "Yes. *The Lion King*. Do you know what that means?"

Blinking furiously, Olivia looked up to the ceiling and concentrated. "It means he was king of the jungle."

"No. I mean, yes," Len said. "But, do you know about the circle of life?"

Olivia had already lost interest. She poked Georgie Boy in the stiffened haunch and watched him rock like a tiny, stuffed, upside-down moose. Then she stopped. "Hey!" she squeaked. "I can see his vagina."

"Where did you learn that word?"

"From Callie Corbin and Samantha. I tell them stuff about rodents, they tell me stuff about vaginas."

He'd have to speak to Olivia's teacher. Again. "Do me a favor, sweetheart, stay away from those girls. They're bullies."

Olivia reached for the chipped antique milk bottle on her dresser and, squinting, held it up to the window. Pebbles shimmered in the morning sun—some smooth and round, some pitted and veined, others pure black—filling the bottle by more than a third. "Callie Corbin called me 'Inside Out Girl' again. Everybody laughed. I *hate* her."

"Where was Jeremy?" Jeremy Knight, the scruffy-faced teacher's aide in Olivia's classroom, had made it his personal objective to shield her, as best he could, from the taunts of other children. He'd come up with a way for Olivia to stand up for herself, if only in private, by encouraging her to write the bully's name on the chalkboard when the other kids were at recess, then erase it with all her might. By the time she'd wiped out any trace of the offender, Olivia was usually giggling, drunk with power. Ineffectual, after-the-fact power—not much more than an expired salve, really—never quite soothing the underlying pain, but doing a decent job of drying the tears.

She called Jeremy her "special person."

"He wasn't at school that day," she said. "Is Jeremy going to be there today?"

"I'm sure he will, sweetheart. You know, I'm wondering if maybe I could help you get dressed before school each day . . ."

"I DON'T need help!"

What was better—derailing his special-needs daughter's critical attempts at independence or watching her march toward her classroom wearing her T-shirt backward, knowing full well the kids would eat her alive? It was a question for her therapist, Dr. Kate.

"I'm only inviting nice kids to my birthday party," Olivia said. "No Callie Corbins."

Len sucked in a deep breath. "I thought we'd do something extra special for your birthday this year, something even better than a party."

"No, I want a party. You never let me have a party!"

When Olivia was very young, at the age when kids attended anyone and everyone's birthday parties, she'd had a few successful showings. But that was back when the parents called the shots. Things changed once the children got older and realized Olivia Bean's social skills weren't evolving in quite the same way as their own. Eventually, it became social suicide to be caught *speaking* to Olivia, let alone attending her parties. Len never stopped trying to throw birthday parties—he simply sent out invitations without the child's knowledge. That way, when every parent RSVP'd with a "conflicting engagement," Olivia didn't have to bury herself under her covers and cry. Year after year, the child blew out her birthday candles with only her father and grandparents huddled over the cake.

"It's only April. Your birthday isn't for another eight months," said Len. "We'll discuss it later."

The girl seemed to wilt. Her narrow shoulders sagged and her stomach jutted out further. "I thought it was tomorrow." She turned back to her lifeless pet. "Come on, Georgie Boy. Time for breakfast." Olivia's voice had always had a lilting, singsong quality. It rose and fell like a happy little train chugging across hilly terrain.

"What the circle of life means," Len continued, "is that, as living, breathing beings on this planet, we're born, we live and we die. Do you understand me, Olivia?"

She nodded. "Sure. The earth's round. Like a circle."

"No. Well, yes. What I mean is, Georgie Boy died. It wasn't your fault, or mine. His circle of life was complete."

Olivia waved a shriveled carrot strip in front of the animal's nose. "Circles have no end, Dad. They just keep going and going. And going." She pulled the carrot out of the cage, tore it in half, and held the fresher end in front of Georgie Boy. "Anyway, I *know* he died. I'm not stupid. But it's time for him to wake up and eat so he doesn't die again."

"When we die, there is no waking up. Georgie Boy is gone."

"He's not gone!" Olivia shouted, her face pressed against the bars of the cage. "He's right here!"

"His body is here, but his soul is gone. We need to bury him." Len leaned back in the chair, hoping to catch a fresh breeze. "Soon."

"No. You can't bury my gerbil. It'll kill him!"

Len couldn't take the odor anymore, he pulled his tie up over his nose. "Olivia . . ."

She turned and looked at her father. With no warning, the girl sucked in a jagged breath and screamed the scream that, without fail, scrabbled up Len's spine and caught him in the throat. It was impossible to grow accustomed to such a sound.

Dropping the tie, Len pulled her onto his lap and tried to hush her. "Shh. See my mouth now? It's just Daddy, it's just me!"

Twisting away from Len, Olivia burrowed into the farthest corner of her bed and heaved with sobs. "Why did you hide your mouth?"

"I know, I forgot. See me now?"

She jumped from the bed and ran out of the room. Sighing, Len rubbed his face. He needed help. His time and patience were stretched to the limit and the last day of school was quickly approaching—eight weeks away. The two weeks of rodent camp at the local zoo would help in a tiny way, but Olivia would not be pleased to hear she'd be spending her summer at KidFun, the after-hours program run out of the staff room at school. Asking Len's parents for assistance was out of the question; they'd only suggest he try hiring another nanny and that he should offer top dollar so the next one wouldn't quit.

If only money were the issue.

The last nanny, some two years prior, a hardworking grad student from NYU looking for a summer job that allowed for quiet evenings to work on her thesis, had arrived with two overstuffed suitcases and a sleek silver laptop. Len prepared Kimmie as he did all the others. He explained that Olivia's needs were tremendous. That his daughter had to be ready for a life fraught with obstacles, so her self-esteem needed to be more than solid. For Olivia, navigating an ordinary day was akin to traversing the rainforest.

Like the others, Kimmie was impressed first with Olivia's extraordinary beauty. Behind an avalanche of auburn hair that seemed to crinkle itself up in knots moments after being brushed, was the wide-eyed face of an angel. Other than the odd smear of dirt from the garden or jam from her bagel, Olivia's skin was almost chaste in its creaminess, untouched by so much as a freckle.

Like the others, Kimmie made myriad attempts to dress Olivia in a manner befitting such a face. Summer frocks and matching Alice headbands were pulled from the closet with great hopes of transforming the child into an elegant young lady. But while the dresses made it over Olivia's head, they would be promptly tucked into tattered SpongeBob sweatpants, which, in turn, would be tucked into the musty woolen liners of her winter boots.

The Alice headbands went straight into Georgie Boy's cage to make a corral.

Right away, Kimmie discovered Olivia was enormously knowl-edgeable—gifted, even—in reading, the rules of certain sports, and all things rodentia, and despite Len's warnings, she lulled herself into thinking the child's competence spread to other things, like brushing her teeth, dressing herself, or even walking up the stairs while carrying on a conversation. But it didn't.

By the end of the first week, Len steeled himself for Kimmie's complaints: "Olivia doesn't listen; she won't stop talking; you aren't paying me enough; she steps on my feet; she's 'lost in space'; I need a day off; she's like a four-year-old; I need a raise" and the definitive "she screams bloody murder, too bloody often."

Week Two typically brought some kind of catastrophe. In Kim-mie's case, she'd run Olivia a bath and gone down to the laundry room for fresh towels. She came back to find the child in the tub, fully dressed, humming the Beatles's "Eleanor Rigby." Between great mountains of bubbles, Olivia's naked Barbie dolls executed synchronized loop-de-loops and freefall drops, navigating the most perilous of acrobatic maneuvers onto a partially submerged make-shift stage.

Kimmie's silver laptop.

Len heard the scream over the sound of the lawnmower from the very back of the yard. Tearing upstairs, he imagined every possible catastrophe except what he found in the bathroom: Kimmie on the floor, crying into the clean towels, and Olivia sitting in the tub, her T-shirt covered in bubbles. Len tried everything: apologies, offers of financial compensation, but nothing could soothe Kimmie, who'd never before seen the point of backing up her work.

"Daddy, help!" Olivia called now from the hallway. Her voice sounded strained. "I can't reach the soap that smells like Mommy . . ."

Len raced from the room to find his daughter shoulder-deep in the linen closet, teetering atop a wobbly, three-legged barstool she'd obviously dragged in from the kitchen. Just as he scooped his little girl into his arms, one of the stool legs snapped and the whole thing crashed to the floor.

CHAPTER 2

Accidents Can Happen

When dealing with sensitive parenting issues, ask yourself two simple questions: What do I want my child to take away from this experience and is that what I am accomplishing?

—RACHEL BERMAN, *Perfect Parent* magazine

Rachel set her coffee on the rickety nightstand and reached for her morning reading material. Accident reports. These varied from day to day, week to week. Some days she studied accidents by vehicle, other days she looked at accidents by appliance—it had been no small decision to haul a minibar up to her bedroom to store cream for her morning coffee. Rachel weighed the risks, but of all 29,964 estimated refrigerator-related accidents in 1998, very few resulted in hospitalization or DOAs. Most victims were treated in Emergency and released. Some might say an accident report almost ten years old could hardly be considered accurate today, but Rachel was no fool. Recent statistics could only be more ominous.

As the publisher of a not-quite-leading parenting magazine, Rachel felt obligated to stay on top of injury statistics—unintentional injuries being the fifth leading cause of death in general and the leading cause of death in children between the ages of one and twenty-one.

The exact age group into which my children fall, she thought, nervously clicking her pen. I shouldn't say fall. Lie. Exactly where my children lie. Janie was fourteen and Dustin had just turned twelve. She stared at the blank wall across from her bed. That was nearly ten more years of worry.

Before she was three sips into her ritual, Janie thundered into the room, chasing Dustin onto the bed where she tackled him, sending him crashing onto the mattress and very nearly spiking the year's statistics.

"Guys! Cut it out," Rachel said, settling her coffee back onto the nightstand. "Someone's going to get hurt."

"It's mine, you little scab!" Janie hissed, standing up and trying to yank something out of Dustin's hands.

Lying on his back, tangled in sheets, Dustin held tight. "You think your gigantic troll toes could fit into this tiny sock?" He glanced down at her bare feet and laughed.

Janie whirled around to face Rachel, her long, nearly black hair sticking to her flushed cheeks. A tiny silver stud glinted from the side of her nose. "Did you hear that? He said I have troll feet!"

"Troll *toes*," Dustin said. "There's nothing wrong with troll feet. They're kinda cute. It's the troll toes on *human* feet that really scare the boys."

"Mom!"

"Dustin," Rachel said. "Your sister has long human toes, not troll toes."

"Mom!" Janie's mouth dropped.

"Sweetheart, long fingers and toes are quite elegant." Rachel gathered up her reports. "If you tried, you'd probably play the piano beautifully."

"With your feet!" Laughing, Dustin raised his legs in the air and wiggled his toes.

"Assface!" Janie dove on top of him and they rolled across the bed until the bedside lamp crashed to the floor.

Rachel shot up. "That's it! I'm warning you. You can get yourselves to Triage by bus!"

Both kids broke into laughter and Janie pushed Dustin off the end of the bed with her feet. "I've been touched by the toes! I'm melting . . ." Janie leaped on top of him and they both shrieked as hair was yanked and skin was pinched. In the fury of flailing body parts, Janie's knee whacked Dustin in the chin, causing him to bite his tongue.

"Ugh. I'm totally bleeding!"

Rachel inspected his tongue, which had nothing worse than a tiny scrape, and muttered, "Hm. Very superficial." She glanced at Janie, who was standing over her brother and straightening her nightie. "Janie, get to your room and get ready for school. Now."

"You're mad at me?" she squeaked. "He started it!"

"Dustin, you go get ready too. Just rinse your mouth first so you don't bleed on the carpet."

They both stood up and stomped into the hall, grumbling and elbowing each other.

"And keep your hands to yourselves—" Both doors slammed. "Or you'll both get weekend lockdown!"

"Our whole lives are in lockdown! What's another weekend?" Janie shouted from her room.

Rachel picked up her coffee and blew. They'll thank me when they live to see twenty-one, she thought. Prevention is always the way to go.

Twenty minutes later, having showered, dressed for work, and combed through her wet hair, Rachel hurried along the hallway to check on Dustin. She found him squatting on his padded window seat, still in his pajamas, pale blond hair gelled into an artful mess.

He was looking through binoculars at fourteen-year-old Tabitha Carlisle, who was getting dressed in her room next door.

"That'll be enough of that," Rachel said, fighting a smile. She took the binoculars from his hand and tossed him a shirt. "We do *not* spy on the neighbors. Get dressed. The bus will be here in fifteen." She marched out of the room. Leaning against his door, she exhaled. Dustin was right on track. Twelve years old and expressing a healthy sexual curiosity. She had written an article about this very topic for last month's issue.

With a polite knock on Janie's door, Rachel waited before entering. Parenting a teenager required equal doses of respect and intrusion. She pressed her ear closer to the door panels to hear a series of muffled thumps before Janie called out, "Come in." Rachel found her daughter standing in the middle of the room, dressed in a tank top, underwear, and army boots, her hands clasped behind her back, brimming with far too much purity for an adolescent girl. Innocence, Rachel always told her readers, should never be taken at face value during the pubescent years.

"Hey," Rachel smiled, scanning the room for clues. "What's with all the thumping and bumping?"

Janie shrugged. A chain of paperclips hung from her neck. "Just, you know, cleaning up."

Cleaning? Janie? At eye-level, with Janie's pine sleigh bed snuggled under the window, the room might make a charming photo for a B&B. But the floor was a rumpled mosaic of fabric—Janie insisted that clothing was far simpler to manage when spread out across the rug—and the ceiling was covered, plastered, every inch of it, in posters from old punk bands—the Sex Pistols, Circle Jerks, the Misfits, Siouxsie and the Banshees, Buzzcocks, the Ramones, Dead Kennedys. Some had song titles markered across them, such as "Too Drunk to F■■■," "Anarchy," and "World

Up My A■■." Janie had blacked out the worst of the obscenities, at her mother's insistence.

The absolute dearth of punk bands from the present was no mistake. Janie considered herself a purist, refusing to listen to anything but classic punk from the '70s and '80s on the grounds that the further away from the Ramones one got, the weaker one's devotion to true punk philosophy. Though, as far as Rachel could tell, Janie's anarchistic tendencies surfaced primarily in her choice of clunky black footwear and her refusal—for a three-week period last winter—to accept her allowance. Apparently, making her bed and taking out the trash for fifteen dollars a week represented a gross affront to punk ideology—a true punk would never prosper from mainstream's mindless quest for purity and order.

"If this is about Dustin's slimy tongue, he started it." Janie pushed a limp strand of hair out of her eyes.

Rachel forced a smile, noticing Janie's desk drawer wasn't fully shut. What was she hiding? A diary? A joint? E-mail from an Internet predator, God forbid? Of course . . . it could be nothing more than Janie sneaking a candy bar before breakfast. The important thing was to catch teen problems early. That's what the experts advised. Stay involved in your children's lives through constant communication.

Rachel sat on the bed. "This has nothing to do with Dustin. Just wanted to tell my girl that I love her."

Janie narrowed her eyes. "Yeah, right." Pushing her head through the neck of an oversized gray sweater, she tugged it over her heavy chest. Adolescent hormones, in the last couple of years, had transformed Janie from nimble tomboy into self-conscious woman-child bound up by a Herculean bra. The child went to bed some nights with red welts on her shoulders. Of course, with this physical change came unwanted attention—unwanted by Rachel, at least—from males, young and old. Although Janie could now outrun her mother, she'd never seemed more vulnerable.

Rachel reached out and took her daughter's hand, pulling her down onto the bed and laying an arm around her shoulders. "Is there anything you want to talk about? Because you know I'm always here for you."

"I need some new socks. Mine all have holes. It's totally embarrassing changing into gym shoes."

Socks. Not quite what Rachel was aiming for. "No, I mean life stuff. Anything bothering you?"

"I don't even have *one* pair left that isn't holey."

"We'll get you some socks, Janie. That's not what I'm—"

"You know Lizzie Walken? She has socks that match every single outfit she owns. She has toe socks, socks with ruffles, knee socks. All I have are tube socks."

"That's not true! I bought you the red pair, the pink pair . . ."

"Uh, Mom? Have you *ever* seen me wear pink?"

Rachel sighed. "I don't want to argue about socks—again." I want to make sure you're not stashing Ecstasy in your desk. That some sexed-up eleventh-grader isn't talking you into having intercourse with him. Unprotected. That some fifty-eight-year-old pervert isn't posing as a skater boy on MSN and making plans to meet you at the mall. "I just want you to know I'm here for you. If you need anything. Advice. A friend . . ."

"Oh God." Janie rolled her eyes and slumped. "The bus is coming in, like, ten minutes."

Pulling her daughter closer, Rachel squeezed her arm. "If my daughter needs me, I'll skip my morning meeting."

Picking at the palm of her hand, Janie said nothing. She looked up, her brown eyes huge, searching her mother's face. This is it, thought Rachel. She trusts me. It was their mother-daughter moment. The kind that *Perfect Parent* magazine solicits from readers, then sets in lovely type surrounded by oversized quotation marks on page 12.

Janie stood up and groaned. "Don't get all bent with your superparenting, Mom. I'm like the magician's assistant. I know your tricks. All that empathy crap is lost on me."

No page 12 today.

Janie waved toward her bare legs and widened her eyes. "A little privacy please?"

Rachel let out a long breath. It looked so easy in the magazine.

Downstairs in the kitchen, all was silent except the clinking of spoons against cereal bowls and the rattle of paper bags as Rachel scraped together lunches from a nearly bare refrigerator.

Dustin half-yawned, half-roared before saying, "My friends all get Lucky Charms for breakfast."

"Lucky for them," said Rachel.

"How come you buy this cereal anyway?" asked Janie, drowning her Apple Cinnamon Cheerios in the milk one by one.

Rachel sniffed a package of strawberries from the fridge, recoiled, and pitched it into the trash. "Good price, whole-grain oats," she said.

"This is the one Dad used to buy," said Janie. "Only not anymore, since Babe-chick Cheryl doesn't like the smell of cinnamon."

Hunched over his cereal bowl, Dustin said, "I *still* don't know why he likes her. She has all these dark bits of hair before the frizzy blond starts. It's freaky." He shivered out loud.

"Those are called roots," said Rachel. "She's just too busy managing Daddy to make it to her hair appointments, that's all. And by 'managing,' I mean 'taking care of.'" And by "taking care of," Rachel meant "fucking." She launched a moldy orange into the trash.

She hadn't been prepared for it. One morning David was stretched out in bed braiding her hair and telling her he loved her. The next morning he was scrawling his new address on the back of a bank statement and instructing Rachel to forward his mail to Cheryl's apartment. Cheryl was one of her ex-husband's inside sales reps. Now his chief operating officer at work and at home. In a wild departure from the traditional boss-leaves-wife-and-children-for-secretary scenario, David plucked Cheryl from beneath a hands-free headset. But then, he'd always been something of a maverick.

What other husband would be willing to sneak out of his own son's tonsillectomy to "solve a marketing crisis"? Or, as Rachel later found out from a neighbor, sneak the little telemarketer into his marital bed while his wife was busy choosing her father's casket?

By the time Dustin and Janie, then five and seven, came tumbling into the kitchen, David was long gone. The kids plunked themselves down at the table, still wearing their pajamas and drunk with sleep. In a daze, Rachel poured them each a bowl of cereal and herself a cup of lusty coffee. Absolute honesty had always been the keystone of her parenting beliefs, so she decided, after a few fortifying gulps, to answer Dustin's casual inquiry—"Where's Daddy?"—with the truth.

"Your father doesn't live here anymore."

Janie scrunched her nose. "Why?"

Rachel drained her cup, scalding her throat. "Because he's living with another woman, that's why."

"Why?" asked Dustin.

Be careful how you answer this, she warned herself. After all, he was and would always be their father. Rachel's grandfather, the founder of *Perfect Parent*, was constantly quoted—posthumously—

in the magazine as saying, "If it feels good coming out of your mouth, it's probably wrong."

She drew in a deep breath and looked at Dustin and Janie, both poised, motionless, over their cereal bowls, waiting for an answer. Finally she spoke. "Because her tits are the size of medicine balls. Though from what I've seen of her hips, she's got a vagina big enough to land a 747 inside."

Dustin's spoon dropped into his Bunnikins bowl with a clatter. Of course it was wrong. But, damn it, it had felt great. Besides, it was true.

Now, pulling a Magic Marker from the drawer, Rachel scrawled a J on one lunch bag and a D on the other. Janie stood up, peered inside the bag marked J, and pulled out a rotting banana. She groaned and tossed it into the trash before heading out the back door.

Dustin grabbed his own lunch bag and followed his grumbling sister. Halfway outside, he stopped, looked back at Rachel. "Mom, can I go to skate camp at The Grid this summer? The place has a snake run and a bowl with real pool coping. Cooper's parents said yes."

Cooper's mother and father wore matching leather jackets and showed up stoned to parents' night last year. Not only did they allow their twelve-year-old son to roam the neighborhood until midnight, they let him study in his bedroom with his girlfriend, door shut. Hearing they endorsed skate camp was not helping Dustin's cause. Rachel ran her fingers through his shaggy hair. "You know how I feel about skate parks, sweetie. You can skateboard on the driveway, but tricks are too dangerous. Children have *died* from it."

"I can't skate on our driveway. It's not paved!"

It was one of the things she loved most about the house she inherited from her parents—a weathered, ivy-covered Tudor perched high up on the bluffs of the Hudson River. The pea gravel–

covered driveway, overgrown trees, and peeling brown shutters gave it the faraway and bucolic feel of the English countryside. Lately, however, her home had begun slipping out from underneath her. Recent riverside development had had a destabilizing effect on the land, and the resulting erosion meant Rachel was losing nearly two inches of waterfront property each year. Her once settled world was tumbling down a deep chasm forming between the old Tudor and the house next door.

"Why don't we look into basketball camp?" she asked. "Or what about archery?"

He pulled away, stomped down the steps onto the gravel drive, his untied skate shoes kicking up dust. "My life sucks."

"We'll find a camp we're both happy with," Rachel called, following him outside. She leaned on the peeling railing of the wraparound porch and waved. "Janie, keep an eye on your brother on the way to the bus stop. I'd like you two to arrive home in one piece later."

Janie looked back at her mother and rolled her eyes. "The stop's practically next door," she said. "I think you'll see us again."

If only Rachel could be sure.

CHAPTER 3

"Dear Prudence"

—Siouxsie and the Banshees

Janie shuffled toward the bus stop, jangling the coins in her pocket. She'd be buying her lunch today. Not only did Dustin get the fresher banana, he also got the last fruit punch, which left her with the organic apple juice. And with only—she pulled out her change and counted—two dollars and eighty-three cents, she'd have just about enough money for fries. Burping and beating his chest like a baboon, Dustin was a good thirty paces behind her. That was good. Strangers driving by, she thought, do not need to know I share DNA with a primate.

Janie hated when her mother tried to pull techniques over her eyes, and had ever since her mom dragged her to her big parenting show in Manhattan. *Perfect Parent* staff members were throwing free tote bags at every slob that passed by as Janie sat in the audience listening to her mother talk about how kids needed to know "where the walls are." Her mother called it "linking" and it basically involved listening to your kid and answering like her best friend. So when darling Violet complains that Sara from ballet class said "You sweat too much," instead of calling bony little Sara a perfect example of bulimia waiting to happen, the smart parent, the informed parent, should sit down beside Violet and say something like "Well that sucks! What kind of emaciated friend would say a thing like that? You must be furious." Only Rachel would probably say to take out the "emaciated" part.

The day Janie watched her mom speak—waiting in the audience for the day to end so they could stop at a McDonald's for chocolate shakes—an angry guy with a red face sat behind her. The guy stood up and said: "I paid eighteen dollars to get into this parenting show, and twenty-one at the snack bar, all so I could hear the great Rachel Berman. Well, I've learned more about parenting from the back of a cereal box."

Janie spun to watch her mother. Rachel took a big breath and said, "That's terrible. You spent all that money and you got nothing out of the experience? I'd be upset, too."

Then the guy hiked up his pleated-pocket pants and said, "Well, it's not like I got *nothing* out of it, the part about setting limits might help with our toddler." He grinned at the audience and added, "Kid refuses to stay in bed." Rachel shot some more empathy his way and the guy practically offered to drive them home.

Anyway, Janie knew her mother's tricks. And she knew when they were being used on her, like this morning.

Three kids were already at the stop, each one moping under the budding trees, pretending the other two weren't there. It was part of the code. Bus stop kids weren't your friends. They were underdeveloped adults thrust together for the purpose of mass transportation. You were allowed a nod or a grunt as you approached the stop, but nothing more.

Janie glanced at Lizzie Walken, also known as "the Walk-in Closet." She had yet to repeat the same outfit since the year began. Lizzie had the perfect life, Janie was sure of it. No brother, beautiful parents, and beautiful grades.

Then there was Arianna Gould, Lizzie's polar opposite. Arianna wore the same black fleece sweatshirts every day. Presumably because of black's slimming properties. Someone should tell her about fleece's plumping properties. She could, however, touch her tongue to her nose, and this seemed to shut the boys up.

Then—the reason she'd been late getting dressed—Tabitha Carlisle. Gazing at Tabitha from afar, Janie stumbled over a rock. Which pretty much summed things up. About three months ago, Janie tripped over Tabitha and had yet to stand up straight.

It happened in gym class. Well, after gym class, in the locker room. Most of the girls were in the shower, but not Janie. She never showered at school. She didn't want anyone to see her naked, but Tabitha and her friends had no such bodily hang-ups. They came back from the showers barely wrapped in towels, giggling and completely oblivious to who might be trying *not* to look at them. Tabitha's clothes were in the cubby next to Janie's.

Janie had turned her back and was yanking a T-shirt over her head so no one could see the suit of armor that was her bra, when someone tapped her on the shoulder. She spun around to find Tabitha smiling and holding something out in her hand. Janie's striped headband.

"It was on the floor," Tabitha said, wearing nothing but a flimsy blue bra and panties. Powder blue. With tiny satin rosettes sprinkled across the front. Not that Janie looked. "Is it yours?"

So nervous she thought she'd throw up, Janie grunted and snatched up the headband more aggressively than intended.

"You're from the bus stop, right?" Tabitha had moved in next door a few days prior. But half her gymnastics team went to the Wilton School—the pricey alternative private school Janie and Dustin had attended since kindergarten and would continue to attend until college—so Tabitha had built-in friends. "I've learned so many names since moving, I keep forgetting."

Janie smiled. "Cool."

Tabitha smiled and motioned toward Janie's chest. "It's sweet."

"What?"

"Your headband." She reached out and touched the strip of fabric Janie still held in her hand. "I wish I had one like it." Then she turned back to her friends, leaving Janie more gnarled than the ratted nylon.

Now, Janie swallowed as she approached the bus stop. How could anyone look so good just standing there? Tabitha's long, blond hair was tucked behind her ears. Janie already knew she'd be wearing the faded khakis and three black rubber bracelets. Her binoculars were that good.

Just as Janie was preparing a witty comment—something about Tabitha's bracelets and good things coming in threes—the bus roared up and blanketed her unlaced Doc Martens in a film of dust. As the other kids hauled themselves up and into the vehicle, Janie hung back.

She had a plan.

Tabitha Carlisle was a creature of habit. Every morning, grinning at Libby Anders in the second row, she sauntered down the aisle, then flopped into the seat with the wheel well so she could prop her feet on it. Always on the left, always by the window. Janie just needed to casually slide into the empty seat beside Tabitha and dazzle her with her shining personality. Simple.

The doors yelped to a close behind Janie. Tabitha's blond hair glowed, beckoning, just where it should be—about two-thirds of the way back, on the left. By the window. For a second it looked as if Dustin, little shitface, might swing into Tabitha's seat. Janie held her breath and vowed to pound him after school, but at the last moment his revolting friend burped Dustin's name from the backseat and he continued on, clearly charmed.

Perfect.

As the bus pulled out into traffic, Janie slid into the wheel-well seat on the left. Right beside Tabitha.

Tabitha glanced up and pretend-smiled. "Saved," was all she said.

Janie jumped up, mumbled, "Sorry," and dove into the next seat back. She folded her arms across her chest and tried not to stare at Tabitha's hair the rest of the way to school.

CHAPTER 4

Rattus Rattus

As parents, we must first accept that we will make mistakes.
Many of them. If you feel you've behaved in a way you are less
than proud of, it's important to forgive yourself and move on.

—RACHEL BERMAN, *Perfect Parent* magazine

Too fast, Rachel steered the old navy Saab around a tight bend in the road. Sprawling hillside homes, architecture blurred by decades of intentionally lax clipping and pruning, peered down at the speeding commuters with disdain, while untamed forsythia bushes, bursting with yellow flowers, cheered them on.

Checking her watch, Rachel groaned. Nine forty-five. Late for her own meeting. Around the bend, traffic was at a standstill, which forced Rachel to hit the brake and idle in an irritatingly long lineup of cars. Her cell phone rang. "Rachel Berman."

"Rachel? Mindy here. Are you getting close or should I bump the meeting to later?"

"No. Josh is heading out to Houston later and I need him there. I'm . . ." Rachel craned her head out the window. Traffic wasn't moving. "I'm almost there. I won't be ten minutes."

It wasn't a total lie. At this rate, it would be at least twenty-five.

God, the car was hot. As the dirty pickup ahead of her inched forward, Rachel spotted a black Audi at the side of the road. A striking man in a crisp suit and royal blue tie, blondish, maybe in his mid- to late thirties, pulled a spare tire out of the trunk while a young girl flopped against the car in misery, whacking a naked Barbie doll against the bumper.

Poor kid. And from the way her dad was squinting at the tire jack, one thing was clear—the man had never changed a tire in his life.

Rachel averted her eyes, pretending she didn't see them. Wasn't that one of the cardinal rules of the road? If someone needed help and you weren't prepared to offer any, glance away and feign ignorance. She couldn't resist looking back. While she wasn't exactly an expert on changing tires, she knew enough to see he was setting the jack wrong side up. The girl was now tossing her Barbie in the air and darting around at the road's edge.

If Rachel weren't so late, she'd definitely have stopped.

Definitely.

Traffic sped up and Rachel tried to concentrate on her meeting. She was holding a focus group for lapsed subscribers that night, a last-ditch effort to find out why her family's magazine, once the country's primary adviser on everything from proper nutrition to temper tantrums, was slipping into obscurity.

In her rearview mirror, Rachel caught a quick glimpse of the father pulling his daughter away from the road. Traffic was now hurtling past them. Clearly, he wasn't going to be able to concentrate on both his inverted tire changing and keeping an active child away from speeding cars.

She checked her watch again. Nine fifty. How would it look if the publisher couldn't be bothered to show up to resuscitate her own magazine? She drove past a road construction crew, three or four men dressed in orange vests, the cause of the slowdown, and reached for her coffee, determined to relax and forget about the man, the child, and the tire jack. And she did relax, for about a minute. Until she remembered one small thing.

Men were easily distracted. So easily distracted that her ex-husband, long before he vanished from their lives, nearly drove to work once with Janie's infant car-seat on the trunk of his convertible, his daughter strapped firmly inside.

Rachel wrenched the steering wheel to the right, pulled off the road, and thrust the car into reverse.

"It's awfully nice of you to stop," said the blond guy. His pant legs were smeared with dirt and he had grease on his tie. "It's been a rough morning. I'm Leonard Bean. Len." He glanced toward the girl, who was trotting up and down the length of the car, shoulder pressed to metal. "This is my daughter, Olivia."

Rachel waved toward the child. "Hi, Olivia. I'm Rachel."

Olivia didn't look up, just kept cleaning the car with her sweat suit, the top of which, Rachel noticed, was on inside out. Maybe even backward. At first she couldn't make out what, exactly, the girl had on her feet, then it hit her: the gray felt liners from a pair of winter boots.

She smiled at Len. "If you could pass me that lug wrench, we'll loosen the nuts and get this tire off, slap on the spare and screw it into place. Then you'll be all set."

Len smiled. "It's that simple?"

"Believe me," Rachel said. "I was just as clueless my first time. Not . . ." she blushed, "that I think you're clueless. Or that it's your first time . . ." Oh God, that didn't come out right.

"Quite all right. I can admit it. When Triple-A said they'd be an hour and a half, I cried like a baby."

"No you didn't," said Olivia, moving toward the front of the car. "You didn't cry like a baby. You didn't even cry not like a baby." She had her sweatshirt tucked into her sweatpants, which she pulled up nearly to her armpits. Rachel couldn't imagine how that could be comfortable, but even more, how the child didn't get pulverized at school.

With one eye on his daughter, Len loosened the last nut, shimmied the tire off the axle, and dropped it onto the ground. "Don't pull your pants up so high, Olivia. The other kids wear them lower down."

"I like them high," she said. "They keep my nipples warm."

Rachel laughed. "Your daughter has an edgy sense of humor."

Len just smiled.

"Daddy, is tomorrow my birthday?"

"No. We discussed it this morning. Your birthday is in December."

"My kids were born with their birthdays scratched onto their foreheads," Rachel called out to Olivia. "That way they can start needling me for gifts months in advance."

Olivia seemed troubled by this. "Do their foreheads bleed?"

"Pardon?" Confused, Rachel looked at Len. Then she laughed. "Oh, I'm sorry, Olivia. I was pulling your leg."

The child glanced down at her legs.

Together, Len and Rachel guided the spare tire into place. Len asked, "So is this what you do all day? Rescue dads-in-distress at hectic roadside locales?"

"Oh no." She shook her head. "I'm far too busy bringing about the demise of a company my father and grandfather spent their whole lives building. How about you?"

He grinned. "Not sure I should say. I don't want you running into traffic or anything."

She thought about this, then said, "Hm. Executioner?"

"Close. I'm an attorney."

"Ahh. I've hired a few of those. Mostly to battle my ex." She paused and glanced toward the sky. "Maybe I should have hired an executioner . . ."

"Your ex?"

"Divorced. Years ago. What about you?"

"Widowed."

"Oh God. I shouldn't have asked. Sorry."

He squinted at her and grinned. "You apologize way too much for a hero."

Quickly, she looked down.

Len and Rachel took turns tightening the nuts and joked about launching their own morning-commute rescue service. Olivia danced around, telling Rachel all she really cared to know about the daily elimination habits of the Norway rat, or the *rattus norvegicus*.

"He averages thirty to a hundred and eighty droppings a day," Olivia said. "And you know you're dealing with a Norway rat and not a roof rat by the size of the droppings. Kids at school call it rat shit—"

"Olivia!" Len snapped.

Olivia sighed and continued, "—but with rodents, the poop is called droppings. That's what the researchers call it. That's how you know the researchers from regular people. The roof rat—"

"Wait," interrupted Rachel. "Are there really rat researchers?"

Olivia ignored her. "The roof rat," she said testily, "or the *rattus rattus*, has droppings more like a half inch long with no blunt ends at all. With pointy ends. So if you don't get to see the rat himself, since a rat is nocturnal and probably you'd be asleep when he comes into your kitchen, you can tell which one you got've by the droppings."

Rachel wasn't sure how to respond, so she winked at Len. "Well. I guess I'll just have to satisfy myself with the poop."

"Bet you don't know which one has a longer tail, the *rattus rattus* or the *rattus norvegicus*."

"I'll bet you're right." Rachel wiped her hands on Len's handkerchief and stood up, turning around to face the young girl. For the first time, she saw them up close. Olivia's eyes.

Rachel sucked in a sharp breath. It wasn't possible. Taking two steps backward, she bumped against the Audi. She looked away and willed herself to think about something else. Anything but the only child in the world who had a right to those eyes.

"Are you okay?" Len asked.

"I'm fine. I stood up too quickly," Rachel lied, forcing a quick smile. "Head rush."

Olivia came closer, blinking the enormous silver eyes. Her irises were as clear as frost; Rachel could almost look right through them. A dark line of gunmetal gray edged crystallized daggers that shot toward the center, where they faded into black pupils like perfectly cut holes in the January ice. Even the lashes were the same, inky black and doubly layered. Rachel felt winded.

"You don't even know?" squeaked Olivia. "How come you don't know which one has the longer tail and I *do* know and I'm only ten?"

"That's enough, Olivia," Len said, frowning.

"It's the *rattus rattus*."

Rachel looked up at Len. "I have a meeting. Better go."

"The Norway rat's tail is only, like, eight and a half inches!"

Len took a few steps forward. "Thanks for your help, Rachel. I feel I should repay you somehow . . ."

She made it to her car and yanked open the door. But before she could tumble inside and sit on her hands to stop the shaking, she heard soft footsteps running toward her. She spun around. Olivia's body wrapped around her middle, hugging her, squeezing her, burying her wolf eyes into—of all places—Rachel's womb. Olivia's lashes fluttered through the cotton of Rachel's sweater, like tiny bubbles pattering against her flesh.

Perplexed by this unprovoked display of affection, Rachel looked at Len, who seemed to find the whole thing amusing. He shook his head, smiled, and continued packing things away in his trunk, as if this was the most natural thing in the world.

Rachel needed to escape. It was too much. With her free hand, she patted Olivia's back, then stepped sideways. "Bye now, Olivia. I have to go to work."

The child didn't budge.

"Olivia, sweetie, go see your dad."

"Don't you like hugs?" she asked, blinking the eyes.

"Olivia!" Len called. "Let's get you to school. You're late."

She looked up at Rachel and shouted back to her father, "No!"

"Olivia!"

"No! No! No!"

"All right. This is your *two-minute* warning," Len said.

Two minutes? Rachel couldn't stand there, patting Olivia's back for another two minutes, pretending she wasn't dying inside. It was an eternity. She had to do something. Anything. Hating herself, she pointed back toward the Audi. "Do you think rats ever hide under black cars?"

The girl loosened her grip. "Huh?"

Rachel backed into her car and slammed the door. "If I were a rat, that's exactly where I'd go." She started the engine and watched the child tear back to her father.

Inside, Rachel sat perfectly still and focused on breathing. Reaching for her purse, she took out her wallet and opened up a tiny compartment. The photo inside was ragged and faded, but no worse than would be expected after sixteen years. Swaddled in pink flannel, the newborn's face was still clear. The thick, nearly black hair, just like Janie's. The small red mouth. The paler than pale skin. Then the eyes. Silver gray, like frost on a windshield. Fringed with the blackest lashes, doubly thick. Like Olivia's.

The only difference was the baby's eyes were slanted upward. One tiny chromosome too many.

CHAPTER 5

The Crush

Len burst out of the elevator and into the Standish, Bean and Roche lobby. The walls were cloaked in gray felt, the floor in plush charcoal carpeting; a hushed and sumptuous workshop of justice. Paul Standish's intention was that every client should feel the immediate sensation of having been welcomed home—for a mere $350–500 an hour.

Len dropped his briefcase beside his assistant's desk, nodded good morning, and marched toward the boardroom, where, with any luck, the meeting was still in high gear. His assistant, Fay, a trim woman with a judicious suit and no-fuss hair, trotted beside him. She passed him a stack of phone messages. "The first one's from Shannon."

Len groaned.

"She's changing your meeting time with Clara to four. Apparently Clara's son is home with flu and she has no child care." They rounded the corner past the lunchroom. Len's stomach grumbled.

"Hm. That I understand," Len said.

"Shannon also said she'll try to stay until you arrive."

Len slowed his step and looked at Fay. "What for?"

Fay's mouth twitched. "It's possible she has a small crush on you."

Len considered this. Shannon, his client's receptionist, *had* been casting extra attention his way. But she was practically a teenager. Len paused outside the boardroom doors. Voices boomed from inside. "Anything else?"

Fay reached over and tugged out the bottom message, setting it on top of the others. "Dr. Kate called. She wants to discuss Olivia before she leaves for a child psychology conference in Copenhagen tomorrow."

Len frowned. The doctor had left the numbers for her office *and* her cell. She'd never left her cell number before. He turned away from the boardroom and started back toward his office.

"Len, they're waiting for you!"

"I'll be a few minutes. Tell them a client dropped in unexpectedly. Say they brought a big check!"

When Olivia was diagnosed, five years prior, Len had never even heard of nonverbal learning disorders, or NLD. Neither had his wife, Virginia. According to doctors, children born with this condition rely on verbal forms of communication and not much else. Not facial expressions, not vocal intonations, not social cues. In its severest form, the disorder can prevent a child from recognizing her own mother until she hears her speak.

The human mouth, as it turned out, meant nothing and everything to Olivia. Nothing because she had no way of reading its subtle, and not so subtle, signals. Everything because this most essential channel of socialization was all she had. And, as Len's ears and nerves could attest, the girl had her own foolproof system for keeping people's mouths in full view.

Olivia was five the first time she test-marketed her bloody-murder scream, the winter before Virginia died. They'd planned a weeklong ski holiday at Virginia's parents' place in Ellicottville. Seemed like the perfect family trip, but the morning they were to leave, they awoke to a record low temperature.

"Why don't we just forget this," Len told Virginia as he peered out the icy window.

Virginia, ever the adventurer, didn't look up from the tote she was filling with gloves, scarves, goggles, and granola bars. Nasty weather wasn't going to faze her. "It's winter in the Northeast, hon," Virginia said. "What do you expect?"

They drove six hours to HoliMont Ski Area with the plan to arrange for Olivia's ski rentals and private lessons for the next day—maybe even ease some of the child's trepidation by introducing her to her instructor—then settle into Virginia's parents' chalet in the woods for a late lunch. After bundling Olivia in down jacket, scarf, gloves, and hood, they steered her to where Tristan, her instructor, was said to be waiting. Tristan was bent over, adjusting his boot, as they approached. He stood up—his face covered by a neck warmer—and reached forward to shake Olivia's hand.

No one could have anticipated the scream that followed. Nor the echo. The silencing effect of fresh snow and the muffling effect of Olivia's scarf were no match for the seven-hundred-foot amplifier that was the mountain behind them.

They could only assume she had been somehow injured. Tristan called for ski patrol, who strapped her onto the toboggan and pulled her back to the chalet by snowmobile. He stayed by Olivia's side, right through the hysteria.

As unexpectedly as Olivia began wailing, she stopped. By that time, Virginia and Len were convinced she'd cracked, ruptured, or torn something serious. At the hospital, they found no evidence of injury, not so much as a bruise or a scratch or a hair out of place. The young surgeon on staff, clearly distraught that he hadn't been able to explain Olivia's distress, turned away from the X-rays and pulled out a small flashlight to look into her eyes. "I wouldn't mind going over her one more time, just to be sure."

Virginia slid off the bed, where she'd been soothing her daughter by stroking her forehead, peered down the hall to make sure Tristan had left, and said, "You know, this might sound a little strange, but it might have had something to do with the ski instructor. Olivia started screaming the moment she met him and didn't stop until we were in the ambulance."

The doctor looked at Virginia. "What happened in the ambulance?"

"Nothing," said Virginia. "I sat up front because Tristan had medical training. One minute Olivia was screaming, the next minute, she'd stopped."

"Was the instructor doing anything, saying anything that might have calmed her?" asked the doctor.

Virginia glanced at Len and crinkled her nose. "I don't think so. He'd just taken off his gloves. His hat. His neck warmer."

The surgeon frowned and scribbled something on a notepad. "I'm referring you to a doctor close to your area, in Pomona. Dr. Kate Leopold specializes in children's anxiety."

Len squinted. "Anxiety? Olivia's five years old."

They'd had questions about their daughter's behavior in the past. But both the pediatrician and the school had said the same thing: "She'll grow out of it."

Not so with Dr. Kate.

Len and Virginia didn't despise the child psychologist herself—rather, they despised the idea of her, anyone, spending a few minutes with their daughter and knowing more about her than they did. Engaging Olivia in conversation and watching her play, sensing exactly what questions to ask her parents. Is the child picked on at school? Does she verbally fixate on certain things, unconcerned whether the people around her have heard enough? Does she have trouble following directions? Doing two things at once? Dressing herself? Does she take things too literally, even for a five-year-old?

Their answers, combined with eventual IQ testing, confirmed what Dr. Kate knew in three minutes. Olivia didn't have an anxiety disorder. She had a nonverbal learning disorder or NLD, a neurological disorder caused by a malfunction of the brain's white matter. Turned out the quirky way Olivia carried her left arm—like she was serving a tray of mimosas—had very little to do with any future career in catering and everything to do with her right brain and left brain refusing to share, like unsupervised toddlers.

Often confused with Asperger's Syndrome, NLD would forever complicate Olivia's life. Growing out of it would not be an option; the child would only learn, with repeated instruction, therapy, and role-play, to compensate. Not only that, but as she matured, she'd become more and more aware of the trap she was in. No matter how badly she wanted to escape, there was no real way out.

One of the toughest things in these cases, according to Dr. Kate, was that not everybody would understand. They would hear the term "learning disorder" and assume it was a trivial snag related to school tests and homework. After all, Olivia looked like everyone else, why shouldn't she behave like them?

Still, Virginia and Len weren't prepared for what she said next.

"What school does Olivia attend?" she asked.

"The Wilton School," Virginia answered.

"Private?"

"Yes. Why?" said Virginia.

"They'll need a note from my office to arrange things in her classroom."

"What kind of things?" asked Len.

"We'll want her on an individual learning program. And she might need an aide in the classroom."

"A teacher's aide . . . just for Olivia?" Virginia glanced at Len before asking, "Are you serious?"

The doctor closed Olivia's file, already bulging with test results, and set it on a stack of slender files—files of children whose parents walked out of Dr. Kate's office with their worlds still intact. "She'll still be in the classroom with the other kids. But she'll need her own program, her own teacher. It's standard in cases like this. A child like Olivia requires an enormous amount of attention."

Len and Virginia looked at each other as the severity of their situation sunk in. Their daughter wasn't normal. So very not normal the psychiatric community recommended a full-time educational handler. Len leaned forward in his chair. "Let me ask you something—is this teacher's aide brought in for Olivia's sake . . . or the other children's?"

"Honestly?" The doctor blinked softly and paused to soften the blow: "Both."

CHAPTER 6

$50 Bills

One of the biggest gifts you'll ever give your child is independence. Given your love and encouragement, your confidence and faith in his abilities—your child will spread tiny wings and soar.

—RACHEL BERMAN, *Perfect Parent* magazine

Watching her staff members file out of the boardroom, Rachel gathered up the list of questions they'd agreed upon. As much as she tried to concentrate on planning this evening's focus group, to listen, to breathe normally, she couldn't.

"You look like no one showed up to your party."

Rachel's assistant, Mindy Cook, was leaning against the door frame. Her petite body completely hidden behind the wall, Mindy was all spiky burgundy hair, geometric glasses, and dark lipstick.

Rachel smiled and gestured toward the pane of two-way glass stretching nearly the entire length of the boardroom, which hadn't been painted since her father, Michael Dearborn, died seven years ago. "I was just thinking. We should mount a frame around this mirror, so people aren't aware they're being watched in these groups."

Mindy tapped her chin against the clipboard she held against her chest. "Hm. And maybe a fifteen-foot fireplace under it with a really long dog lying across the hearth."

"Hilarious," Rachel said, following Mindy out of the boardroom. "So? Any news for me?"

"Well, Stan called to say our coffee shipment will be delayed again and Johnson's called. They're slicing their ad budget—" Mindy stopped. "Ooh," she said, clenching her teeth. "Did I mention your mother is here?"

Groaning, Rachel forced a smile onto her face and breezed into her late father's former office, an oak-paneled refuge lined with floor-to-ceiling bookcases overflowing with issues dating back sixty years. Her mother, Piper, stood behind the overstuffed armchair by the fireplace, rearranging the cashmere throw. In her cropped jeans, with an overgrown Rod Stewart shag, Piper more resembled a prissy rock star than the widow of a publishing magnate.

That she looked more like Rachel's older sister than her mother didn't always please Piper. To Piper—born Peggy Bates—becoming an accidental parent at nineteen and a grandmother in her late thirties forever smudged her with the mark of the lower class. At a time when her old high school friends were packed tightly into college dorm rooms, Peggy was juggling her third waitressing job, Rachel's incessant infant colic, and two parents on welfare. Without so much as one spare night a week for night school, Peggy Bates's life was headed in much the same direction as her parents'.

A rainy afternoon changed her life. One minute she was walking toward the restaurant, La Vieille Auberge, the next she was racing through a summer shower so heavy her sweater, her T-shirt, even her bra became soaked. She ran toward the double doors of the restaurant and tumbled inside, colliding with an equally sodden boy. Tousled hair clung to his cheeks and his lashes clotted together in soggy clumps. He was beautiful.

He was nothing like the boys Peggy grew up with. Not like her baby's father, a no-hoper Peggy met at a party, who headed West once he heard she was pregnant. This boy had the look of old money that Peggy only saw in her very wealthy customers. The strong bone structure, perfectly symmetrical features. The straight teeth. His brown hair—even drenched—appeared bleached out by long afternoons on a tennis court, maybe even a yacht.

He grinned, introduced himself as Michael Dearborn, and asked if she was meeting someone. Peggy froze. She had two options. Say, "I'm Peggy and I'll be your server today," don her apron, be extra attentive to the male customers, and scurry home before her parents got too sauced to listen for Rachel's cries, then do the same thing all over again the next day.

Or . . . she could become someone else.

When the dripping boy with the perfect teeth suggested they ditch their dates and warm up over takeout coffee at the bookstore down the block, she hung up her apron for good. She became Piper Bates. Soon to be Mrs. Michael Dearborn III. She would have a proper name, and, more important, her daughter would have a proper father. A proper future.

Piper's father, Bert, suffered a fatal stroke a year after she married. Her mother, Irene, lived long enough to see young Rachel win the thirteen-and-under golf tournament at the Dearborns' club. Michael's parents took Piper, Michael, and Rachel out for a celebratory dinner at La Vieille Auberge—still Piper's favorite restaurant—and returned to the bluffs to find Irene in a crumpled heap at the bottom of the stairs.

No one but Piper, and eventually Rachel, would learn that Irene's blood alcohol level had been .40. With her parents gone, all that remained from Piper's past was her daughter and the promise she made to herself: that Rachel's life would never be touched by poverty or despair, or otherwise tainted in any way. Rachel's life would not only *look* perfect, as Piper's might have come to appear to outsiders; Rachel's life would *be* perfect.

Even now, twenty-one years later, her late husband's office reflected Piper's penchant for old money and the perfect existence that appeared to come with it. Piper looked up as Rachel walked toward her. "It looks like someone's been using your father's arm-chair," she said in her smoker's voice—the only ghost from her past she could not exorcise. "I told you, this fabric's not for sitting."

"Nice to see you, too, Mom." Rachel crossed the room and dropped into her tan leather chair, perfectly broken in by her father, and his father before that, still smelling faintly of cigars. She skimmed through a stack of phone messages before kicking off her heels. "So, have you heard from Arthur?" Arthur Gold was a real estate broker Piper had met on a cruise earlier in the spring. Sixty years old with a full head of silver hair and no vices that Piper had been able to detect aboard the ship, Arthur appeared to be a great catch for Piper.

Piper stared at her daughter. "He finally called last night. Asked me to go to the theater with him."

"Perfect."

"The tickets were for tonight. Which is why I'm here. I can't find my key to your house. If I'm going to be home for Janie and Dustin after school to sit with them tonight, I'll need to borrow yours."

"So you said no?"

"I'm not going to abandon my grandchildren just so I can canoo-dle with a man I barely know."

"But—"

"But what? You asked me, I accepted. They shouldn't be alone on a school night."

"Maybe their father can take them. Let me check . . ."

"Forget it. Arthur will call again. And if he doesn't, well, I won't be the first widow to spend her final years alone." She tilted her chin upward and put on a brave smile. "At least I'll have the three of you."

Her head heavy with guilt, Rachel dug through her purse, twisted a brass key off her keychain, and laid it on her paper-strewn desk pad. "Thanks." Then she threw in: "Just remember if you give the kids grapes, slice them down the middle."

"Rachel. They're eleven and thirteen."

"Fourteen and twelve. And remember, they're not allowed to climb down the bluffs and go down to the beach."

"You used to climb up and down that slope twenty times a day as a child!"

"It's eroding now. Very slippery."

"So my grandchildren are living on that magnificent river with no access to it?"

"They have access to it. They just need to walk further down the road to the public area and use the stairs. Then walk back along the shore."

Piper looked astonished. "But it's about a mile there and back!"

Rachel shrugged. "You can drive them as far as the stairs."

With a badly disguised roll of her eyes, Piper adjusted the lamp on Rachel's desk, swung her purse onto her shoulder, and waggled her fingers good-bye. "Well, try to stay calm, dear. I promise to keep everyone whole tonight."

As soon as her mother disappeared, Rachel yanked the lamp back into place.

"Janie, the answer is no." Rachel checked her watch. Nearly seven. The boardroom would be filling up with focus group attendees by now.

"The Frisbee is only, like, ten feet down the cliff," Janie whined. "I'll hold on to a tree branch."

"No one goes near the edge of the property, do you hear me?"

"But we were playing a game with it. How about if I hold Grandma's hand? She won't let go of me."

"No. End of discussion. We'll get a new Frisbee."

Janie growled and hung up.

Ignoring her daughter's rudeness, Rachel reached for notepad and pen and hustled toward the sounds of voices gathering in the boardroom. She poked her head inside. Fifteen or twenty people, young and old, milled around the boardroom table.

From the corner of the room, Theodora Price, national sales manager, looked at Rachel and nodded toward the mirror, tapping her watch. Rachel turned around, stepping right into the path of a blond latecomer in a beautifully cut suit. His tie was flipped over his shoulder and he was eating from a carton of fries.

The distressed father from the side of the road. Len Bean.

"Oh," she managed, her cheeks burning hot. "Hi!"

He coughed, covering his mouth then rushing to swallow. "Rachel?"

"Hi." Then she rolled her eyes. "Right. I guess I just said that. Stupid . . ."

"No," he laughed. "Hi was perfect. Even better the second time."

"What are you doing—" She stopped herself. Obviously he was attending her focus group. "Stupid question. You're here for the group?"

"Yes. You too?"

"No fifty bucks for me, I'm afraid. This is my . . ." In all the years since her father died, she'd never grown quite used to saying it. "This was my dad's magazine. It's mine now." Inside the board-room, Theodora clapped her hands and announced it was time to begin. "I'd better . . ."

When Rachel motioned toward the mirror, he threw his head back and chuckled. He popped a fry into his mouth. "Ahh, we're being studied. Like lab rats."

"Please. We rat researchers prefer the term *rattus rattus*."

She looked at his eyes, clear blue with dark, tired smears under-neath. Blond lashes. He looked nothing like a lawyer. More like someone who spent sun-drenched days at the water's edge, replac-ing worn planks on docks, or buffing old boats to a loving sheen.

"Rachel!" Mindy was holding open the door to the secret room, waving her inside.

Rachel shrugged. "Better go. Sorry."

"Again with the apologies," he grinned, fishing around for some-thing in his breast pocket. He seemed disappointed, like he didn't find what he was looking for.

"Right. Sorry." She turned away, then stopped, looking back. "Some rat researcher, huh?"

How does he know where I'm sitting? Rachel wondered. Len's eyes remained glued to the exact spot where she sat, fiddling with her yellow legal pad. Could he see through the glass? And why would a guy like Len give up his Thursday night? Feeling his eyes on her body, she shifted to the left. His eyes followed.

In the stuffy room with Rachel, the accountant Linda Haas sat in the back, beside Paula Collins and Jamie Holden-Brinks from sales—their metal chairs pushed close together, confirming what Rachel had long suspected.

In the boardroom, an egg-shaped man was explaining, in a very roundabout sort of way, why he no longer subscribed. "I lost my *Perfect Parent* subscription in the divorce." He shook his head like his was the oldest story in the world. "She took all my CDs, the dogs, and the house. Of course she got full custody of the kids, so she got the magazine subscription." He rolled his eyes and huffed. The young woman beside him looked unsure of her responsibilities as his seatmate, then gingerly patted him on the back.

"I used to count the days until my next issue arrived in the mail," said a woman in a raincoat. "Had some articles laminated, so they would stay in mint condition."

Rachel felt Len's eyes on her again. She glanced toward him. Sure enough, he was staring straight at her, eyes laughing. How was it possible? X-ray contacts? She started clicking her pen.

A slender woman, in her mid-twenties at the most, held up a finger. "You might want to think about changing the title. *Perfect Parent*? It's somewhat prehistoric, don't you think?"

Linda Haas looked at Rachel and grunted. "I've been saying that for years."

"I'm well aware it isn't hip or edgy," said Rachel. "But my grandfather named the magazine. The title has history. You don't just walk away from sixty years of brand recognition. Look at Honey Nut Cheerios—everyone's heard of it, but very few people realize it contains nuts. They just know they love it. *That's* a successful brand."

Paula stared through the window. "Or an unsuccessful one."

In the boardroom, Len leaned back in his chair, clasping his hands behind his head. "I just found it offered very little to parents of special-needs children, that's all. I bought a subscription to

Parenting Now." Looking back toward the mirror, Len blushed and mouthed, "Sorry."

What was he, some kind of philanthropist? His child had the fashion sense of a toddler, but clearly Olivia was brilliant.

Paula nudged Rachel from behind, as if to say, "See?" Paula had long argued the magazine was limiting itself with its strict focus on everyday parenting. That today's children have needs the magazine was flat-out ignoring.

"I found the same thing," said another young woman. "My boys have ADD and I needed more."

"My daughter was diagnosed with Tourette's," said another. "*Perfect Parent* became useless to me. I wanted my needs addressed, at least periodically."

Jamie muttered, "Not a bad idea."

Rachel tensed. "It's not our niche. Life is crazy enough with average kids. We're strictly average parenting for average kids."

Frowning, Linda peered at Rachel over the top of her glasses. "Maybe that's why our numbers are so average."

By the time Rachel filed out of the secret room with the others, Len was gone. She headed toward her office, unable to account for the heaviness in her mood. It certainly couldn't be the results of the focus group, which, in Rachel's mind, had been a big waste of $50 bills. As she pulled on her coat, it hit her. Barring any further roadside rescues or upcoming focus groups, she had no chance of ever bumping into Len again.

Probably a good thing, considering her reaction to Olivia that morning.

She pulled her purse from her desk drawer and spotted a torn, oily piece of cardboard on her desk. Curled up on one side and reeking of fries. On it, in smudged blue ink, was scrawled, "International Summit of Rat Researchers to be held at Minnie's Bistro. Friday night. 8:00. RSVP 555-9305."

Her mouth twitching into a smile, she slipped it into her pocket and turned off the lights.

CHAPTER 7

"Anxious Boy"

—Circle Jerks

The game was called Million Trillion and it always began the same way. Locked in Janie's closet; Dustin on the right side, squatting on his sister's shoes, Janie on the left, leaning against a balled-up sleeping bag. Old ski suits, dresses, and a thick robe hung from hangers, dropping low enough to create separate rooms within the closet, preventing them from actually seeing each other. Between them, on the shoe rack, stood the plastic troll doll, the Seer of All Truths. But for a tiny thread of light cast from a penlight taped to the Seer's back, illuminating his lime-green Albert Einstein hair, the game was always played in the dark.

It started after their father left, when Dustin took a passionate dislike to Rachel's occasional night out. Particularly if said excursion was in the company of a man. His father living with Babe-chick Cheryl was revolting enough, but the idea of his mother sitting at a sushi bar, laughing at the feeble jokes of some guy whose main goal was to keep her attention *away* from her kids, where her focus belonged—she was a mother, after all—was something Dustin could only liken to familial treason.

Unwilling to interact with babysitters, the moment his mother pulled out of the driveway, Dustin usually parked himself on Janie's window seat, cocooned in his duvet—teary face pressed against the glass, exhausted—until Rachel's car's headlights lit up Janie's walls. Then he tore back to his own bed and fell asleep before his mother's key jiggled in the front door, worn out with relief.

His mother was his again.

As he grew older and became aware that huddling under a blanket until your mommy came home was the ultimate in dorkiness, Dustin learned to swallow his jealousy, and Janie, finally old enough to be left without a babysitter, devised other ways to keep him busy.

Million Trillion was born.

"I go first," Janie said now. "It's my closet."

"No fair," said Dustin. "Let's play in my closet, then."

"Are you kidding? We'd suffocate from the smell." The penlight's batteries were fading fast. "Okay. It's time," she said. "What would you rather do? Give Kirstie Lee mouth-to-mouth for a million trillion seconds, after a month at summer camp when she forgot her toothbrush again . . ."

"Ugh, sick," said Dustin, his head banging against the wall. "Big yellow fangs—"

"Or," Janie continued, kicking her brother for the interruption, "or stand up at assembly and tell the whole school you have wet dreams?"

"That wasn't a wet dream, shithead! My thermos leaked chicken soup on my bed."

"Whatever. Answer."

"Then change the dream part."

"No changes when it comes to bodily functions. You know the rules."

She couldn't see his face, but could make out his legs flopping to the side in exasperation. After a few grunts, he mumbled, "Kiss Yellow Fangs."

They both groaned in disgust.

"Now, my turn," said Dustin. "What would *you* rather do? Be walking along the river, in the dark, and find Cody Donovan sitting on a rock wearing nothing but a Timex and a smile, or be locked in a tent, starving to death, with nothing but a mad cow and a barbecue filled with a million trillion black widows? Cook the cow if you dare."

"Ugh. Donovan's *such* an asshole. Yesterday, he whipped an eraser at a substitute when she turned around to write on the board. The whole class had to stay after school."

Dustin grunted. "That's actually kind of cool."

"Is not! Give me a Cody-less question."

"*Rules.* It's Cody fighting you off or death by arachnid venom. Choose."

"You're such a jerk." Janie exhaled hard and shook her leg, which had fallen asleep. "Whatever," she said. "Cow, barbecue, spiders."

"Wait, that was too easy! I've got another one—"

"No, my turn. What would you rather do—kiss a dead body, dug up from the grave and crawling with a million trillion maggots, or tell the whole school you're scared of Mom going out?"

"I'm not scared of her going out!"

"Whatever. Mom's date nights."

"It's not Mom's date nights! I just hate the guys. But only when I'm awake. When I'm asleep, I'm fine."

Janie laughed. "Okay, in front of the Mighty Seer, I hereby qualify my challenge. Change it to a million trillion maggots or tell the whole school you hate the guys Mom dates. When you're awake. Choose."

The closet was silent.

"Dustin?"

"I'm thinking!" He thumped his knee against the wall. "How long has the body been buried?"

"Two years."

"Mine was way easier . . ."

Janie rolled her eyes. "The Seer is waiting."

"You're *so* dead."

"Answer."

"Whatever," Dustin said. "Kiss the body. After two years, how much could be left?" He shuffled around in the dark and cried out in pain. "Aww, crap! Hangers under my butt . . ."

Janie snickered.

"Okay. You ready?" he asked.

"Yup."

"What would you rather do—fall into a tank full of a million trillion jellyfish or tell the whole school the real reason you're not at the eighth-grade dance right now?"

Janie shrieked, "I'm not there because dances are like totalitarian states! I don't need a regime of zipped-up school officials telling me which moments of my life will be special."

"Methinks not," Dustin laughed. "Methinks you got pissed that no one asked you."

"How would *you* know?"

"I've heard things."

Janie restacked a pile of dented shoe boxes that had spilled over onto her feet.

One of the boxes felt prickly, rough. Janie didn't need to turn the lights on to know it was her My Little Pony art project from second grade. "What things?"

Dustin fake-yawned. "I really don't see the point in picking apart the mind-numbing facts of your day-to-day existence . . ."

"What things?"

He sat forward. "Okay. I heard that you're the clown. You're the funny girl. You can burp the teacher's math equations. And the guys in your class were saying that when a girl goofs around too much, she becomes . . ." His shrug was barely perceptible in what remained of the Seer's light.

"What? Funny?"

"Un-date-able."

As much as her every nerve was begging her to retaliate, Janie said nothing. It was true. She did play the clown at school, but not for the reason Dustin suspected.

Before junior high, Janie Berman had been the quiet one. She'd had one or two friends she didn't particularly care for—Lindy Axler, who expressed every other thought in song, typically with one eye cast on the nearest reflective surface; and Sabina Krug, who was so much smaller than Janie she never felt like a real friend, though Janie knew better than to ever admit it.

The way things changed was involuntary. With the rush of her adolescent hormones came a nervy, uninhibited persona. This new Janie could do something the old Janie could never do—make kids laugh. Like last Halloween, when all the other girls dressed as sexy black cats or brainy scientists, and Janie showed up in a child-size, drugstore Batman costume, complete with plastic face mask and a way-too-small nylon body suit. She had to wear the suit backward as the breastplate—molded plastic heroic abs and pecs—wouldn't fit over her chest. She didn't get the admiring looks the other girls got, but she never found herself pretending to do homework at an empty lunch table again. Janie never quite became one of the popular kids, but she finally had their seal of approval.

That the boys thought of her as undate-able was a gift. Now, no one would suspect the truth. The real problem lay with the girls—one girl anyway.

"I'm not playing anymore." Janie stood up, hit her head on a shelf, and tumbled out of the closet into the bright lights of her bedroom. "I don't feel like it."

"Come on," Dustin whined. "We're even."

"We're not. Yours is a personal humiliation. Mine is public."

"Same difference."

"No. You play too dirty."

Dustin squeaked in indignation. "Me? You started it." He came crashing out with a clatter of wire hangers, troll in one hand. "Fine, I'm going but I'm keeping *him* in my room until next time. *Insanie.*"

"Don't call me Insanie, *Dustbag*!" She gave him a tiny shove.

"Hey!" His hands flew up to his head. "A little respect for the hair, please?"

"Just go!"

After Dustin left, Janie stared into her mirrored closet doors, motionless. Slowly, she pulled off her zippered sweatshirt, and turned sideways. She sucked in her stomach, checking out her reflection. If she didn't breathe, she looked okay in her tank top and yoga pants. It was her lungs that got in the way.

She exhaled and watched her body slump back into position. Whatever. Maybe later she'd do some sit-ups. Maybe not. Last week she'd tried sticking her finger down her throat after dinner—it seemed to be the perfect answer—but it didn't work. It only left her with a scratchy throat and a bad headache.

Wrapping herself in an old shirt of her father's, she flopped down on her bed and flipped open the latest issue of *Seventeen* magazine. Photo after depressing photo of gorgeous girls. She stopped to read about applying lip gloss over lipstick, and noticed an article titled "How to Snare the Guy Next Door." Janie rolled her eyes. Why couldn't there ever be articles about liking girls? Where was the Idiot's Guide to Fourteen-Year-Old Female Outcasts Flirting with Goddesses Next Door?

Her eyes drifted back to the article. She smiled. If this advice worked on boys, why shouldn't it work on girls? She reached a black marker and crossed out the word "Guy," replacing it with "Goddess." Then she went through the article doing the same all the way through, starting with "Be an expert listener" and ending with "Leave ~~him~~ *her* wanting more."

With great care, inch by inch, she ripped out the article so the tear wouldn't obliterate any precious words—if she stood any chance at all of snaring this particular goddess next door, she'd need every single one of them.

CHAPTER 8

Digesting Magenta Crayons

Communicate. It's vital that you speak to your child with the same respect you'd give to your coworker. Children need to feel their needs, wants, and opinions are heard. Valued. Cherished.

—RACHEL BERMAN, *Perfect Parent magazine*

With great flourish, the waiter set a white plate in front of Rachel, then Len. He bowed and vanished. Lit only by flickering votives, Minnie's Bistro smoldered with intimacy—its walls, painted black, wrapped Len and Rachel in velvety shadows.

Agreeing to see Len again had not been an easy decision. With this very appealing male came a girl whose gaze, for Rachel, was thick with memories. She'd reasoned with herself that if she saw more of this man, she'd eventually grow accustomed to looking at his daughter. What did they call it? Desensitization.

Rachel flashed a smile before looking down at her plate and wondering where the rest of her meal might be. Five open mussels lay artfully arranged in a wine and garlic broth, which smelled heavenly, but wasn't going to do much to satisfy her hunger.

Len looked equally disappointed. Four squares of ravioli on a painterly puddle of mushroom sauce. He shook his head. "You'd better keep all appendages away from me. I'll gnaw off your hand to survive if it comes down to it."

"Hm, cannibalism. I've had worse first dates." She pulled a strand of flesh from a yawning black shell. "I haven't had a smaller meal, though. Trade you a mussel for a ravioli square?"

"I don't do mussels. Or any type of shellfish."

"Religious?"

"Just intelligent. Shellfish are the bottom feeders of the ocean, the filters." He pointed toward her plate. "What you're eating there is the oceanic equivalent to the strainer in your kitchen sink." He winked. "Enjoy."

A wave of horror washed over her. How could this knowledge have escaped her? She'd researched all the popular food-borne gastrointestinal microorganisms, hadn't she? *Clostridium botulinum*, salmonella, E. coli, even the dreaded entamoeba parasite. Clearly, she'd overlooked an entire genus of underwater pathogens.

She pushed her plate away.

Forcing a smile, she watched him eat. His white shirtsleeves were rolled up to the elbow, exposing forearms that looked deceivingly like they'd jacked up more than a few cars, in spite of all evidence to the contrary. When he leaned his elbow on the table, she noticed a smear of blue paint on his wrist.

"Were you painting today?" she asked.

He nodded, swallowing. "Dinosaur tails. My daughter's art project."

"Just the tails—no bodies, heads, necks, ears?"

Len smiled. "It was a study of tails. Though Olivia lost interest after about two or three, so I conceptualized the last thirty or forty tails on my own."

Her ex-husband wouldn't have been caught dead smeared with his children's paint. He didn't paint. David preened, David signed checks, David entertained clients. And in between, he diddled telemarketers. There was something inherently sexy about a man as unstudied as Len. It might have been the polarity between he and David, but then again, it might have been the way he looked in faded jeans.

"Very impressive. Especially for a lawyer. Would I be correct in assuming, with your burgeoning passion for disconnected body parts, that you're a criminal lawyer?"

"I do family law," he said. "You know, divorce, separation agreements, wills . . ."

"Prenups?"

"Yes."

"Mm. Where were you fifteen years ago?"

He smiled. The waiter drifted closer and tried to remove the bread basket. Len motioned for him to leave it. "That's the bulk of what I handle," Len said. "Most days I'm trying to negotiate which party keeps the theater seats, but on occasion I handle custody cases. And adoption."

Rachel choked a bit and reached for her water glass. "What sort of adoption cases?"

"Mainly representing adoptive families against birth mothers, that sort of thing. It's a small part of what I do."

Rachel said nothing. With her fork, she pushed a mussel shell around her plate.

"I think that's enough about me—what about you? Who's watching your kids tonight?"

She looked up quickly and forced a smile. "Janie. She's fourteen, old enough to sit, but Dustin tends to get anxious when I'm out. So sometimes I'll call my mother in—if I think I'll be late."

"So tonight was meant to be an early night." He winced and sat back in his chair. "Ouch."

"No." She laughed. "My mom had a date."

"Hmm." Len didn't take his eyes off her, just chewed on his lower lip and stared.

"Hmm, yourself. What about Olivia?"

"A new sitter. Wendy. We haven't had the best luck with baby-sitters."

"My neighborhood had a surprising scarcity of teenagers when my kids were small. It always made me suspicious they were hiding themselves."

"I think teenagers today have actual lives." He popped a piece of bread in his mouth and shook his head. "It's a terrible thing."

"Mm-hmm. You know, I've been sitting here trying to decide how you got that fabulous tan."

"And what did you come up with?"

"That you either have a tanning booth in your basement or you slathered yourself with tinted moisturizer."

"And what if I did?"

"I'm heading back to that bus stop."

He laughed. "Well, you can save your bus fare. I just got back from a long weekend in Myrtle Beach. Annual golf trip with the boys from college."

She smiled. "So, three days of beer, burping, and Doritos. Real cultural stuff?"

"Not as bad as that. Although, I must admit we have one ritual we can't seem to break." He looked at her, his cheeks flushed pink. "But I haven't known you long enough to spill it . . ."

"Oh, come on. I can take it."

He considered this. "Okay. But remember, we go way back, the boys and I." He swallowed the remains of his wine and studied her face. "We urinate over the side of the hotel balcony. All four of us, in unison. He who lasts longest gets free breakfast the next day."

She smothered her smile in her napkin. "Doesn't the hotel have a problem with that?"

"Oh, we never go back to the same place twice. That would be insanity."

Her cell phone rang from inside her purse. She glanced at the display screen. "It's Janie," she explained. "I'll just be a second." Into the phone, she said, "Hi, honey."

"Mom, I'm trying out for this elite summer hockey camp! Tryouts are in two weeks so you *have* to drive me to practice tomorrow or my entire life is over. Everyone is going, even the new kid next door, Tabitha, I think her name is. Oh yeah, and Dustin's out of control. Is biting considered assault? Because I had no other choice."

Rachel smiled at Len and said into the phone. "Yes, I'm having a lovely time, Janie. Thank you for asking." Len made an approving face.

"Mom! What about hockey practice?"

Silently vowing to ground her daughter once she got home, Rachel said, "I love you, Janie. Sleep well."

As she slipped the phone into her purse, Len's phone rang. He held up one finger to Rachel and picked up. "Yes?" He nodded, looked at Rachel, and smiled. "Olivia," he mouthed to her. His entire conversation consisted of grunts, "Mm-hmm," "Really?" and "Absolutely." She watched the look on Len's face as he spoke, unaware he was being studied. His eyes softened as he spoke to his daughter. His mouth curled up at the sides, barely susceptibly, with either amusement or adoration. Or both.

God, he must be a great father.

Len told his daughter to get washed, that he loved her, and not to fall asleep under her bed again.

Sipping from his coffee, Len laughed to himself, then said, "Olivia wanted me to ask if you were aware that mice gnawing from a magenta crayon will have magenta droppings."

Rachel ran her finger along the edge of her cup. "Actually, I'm curious . . . during the focus group the other night, why did you ask for articles about kids with special needs? Olivia could probably write for our magazine." She dipped a finger into her coffee and licked it. "In fact, maybe she should. Magenta mouse facts might help us win back readers."

"She might be gifted in some areas. But she has a nonverbal learning disorder, NLD, sort of like autism without the desire to isolate. She isn't great at expressing them, but has normal emotions. Makes her inability to 'fit in' that much more painful—for both of us."

"I had no idea." Or I wouldn't have come, she thought. Rachel felt sick. "Is this something you knew right away?"

"Well, Virginia and I noticed she didn't respond to facial cues, didn't smile when we smiled, laugh when we laughed. That sort of thing. But babies are such mysterious creatures . . ." He shrugged.

"So how did you find out?" Rachel asked.

"She was five. It was the winter before Virginia died, actually." He signaled to the waiter. "Would you like to head over to Chaz Madison's to hear a little jazz?"

Yes. No. "Excuse me," she said, standing up too fast.

"Don't flee right away," he joked. "Think it over for a moment."

She attempted to smile, but waved her hand and mumbled something about looking for the ladies' room.

Inside the restroom, she leaned over the sink and focused on breathing. It was too much. Too close. She'd never be able to look at him without guilt so thick she could taste it.

Rachel had been nearly eighteen when her baby was born. Josh was seventeen. The pregnancy was a reckless slipup that never should have happened. Two teenagers parked on a scenic winding road, aptly named "Skyline," fumbling around in the backseat. It wasn't their first time, they should have known better. Things got heated up and when Rachel opened the condom wrapper with her teeth, the latex caught on a sharp edge of the foil. But . . . it looked fine. A month and a half later, behind a locked stall in the girls' restroom, pregnancy test dipstick in hand, Rachel discovered it hadn't been.

Josh insisted she abort. And part of her wanted to. Other people did it, right? That way she wouldn't have to face her parents. But she stopped at the bookstore on her way home from school one day and wandered into the pregnancy section, picked up a book, and flipped to the page on fetal development. She saw the photo. The one that showed the nine-week-old fetus with already formed arms and legs. Her baby was the size of a grape. It was already moving, already had fingerprints. But what struck Rachel's core was learning that if you placed an object in the baby's palm, the baby would try to grasp it.

Impossibly tiny webbed fingers wrapping themselves around . . . what? What could possibly be small enough to fit in those hands? The head of a pin? A blade of grass? A strand of Rachel's own hair?

From that moment on, she was certain she could feel movement. Faint, carbonated bubbles tickling her insides. She told her mother and father that night over roast beef and cold asparagus. There would be no abortion. Not even an army of medical personnel would be able to hold her still long enough. She'd made her choice.

The decision to give the baby up for adoption was Piper's. Not coincidentally, it came on the day they received results from the prenatal testing, completed in Rachel's seventeenth week of pregnancy. In spite of Rachel's young age, all tests pointed toward the child having Down's syndrome. Rachel prayed the results were wrong. If, by some miracle, the baby was born with the perfect number of chromosomes, she hoped, she prayed, her mother would change her mind.

When Rachel finally pushed the baby into the world—in a cold, white room filled with overhead lights, beeping machinery, and too many masked and gloved medical personnel to count—she knew the truth before anyone spoke a word. It was in the eyes of the doctors, nurses. In the hushed voices, the purposeful movements. They swept the baby away from Rachel and onto a scale, where they measured, weighed, and wiped the cheesy white coating, the vernix, from the infant's delicate skin. As one nurse swaddled the child in drab green flannel, another came to Rachel's side and took her hand.

Before whisking Rachel's baby out of the room, the nurse said, "You had a girl."

Had.

Now, in the ladies' room, Rachel held her hands under the icy water. How could she entangle herself in the life of someone else's special-needs child if she had opted out of her own daughter's life, however unwillingly?

The guilt would crush her.

She'd say no to the jazz club. No to any future dates. She'd bumbled along reasonably well before Len, she'd bumble along just fine without him. She took a deep breath, patted her hands dry, and marched toward the table, prepared to tell Len she had to get home. She had a busy day tomorrow.

As she got closer, she noticed him spitting on his linen napkin and rubbing the paint off his wrist. Then, realizing what he'd done to the napkin, he glanced around and slipped it under the leaves of the fern behind his chair. He looked up as she approached, his face still flushed from embarrassment.

Say it, she commanded herself. You need to get home.

"Does this jazz club serve dinner?" she asked, her hands shaking. "Because I'm still starved."

CHAPTER 9

If You Give a Mouse an Oreo

Len opened the front door to find the babysitter asleep on the couch. Olivia's favorite movie, *The Incredibles*, played on the TV. Tonight's babysitter had been a real find. Wendy was every parent's dream. Too responsible to have a boyfriend hiding in the bushes waiting until the coast was clear, and too industrious to leave the child alone during *Sex and the City* reruns. The girl stirred.

"Hey Wendy," Len called. "How did it go?"

She jumped up and reached for her sweater, her hair molded into a peaked rooftop. She did not look happy. "Thank God, you're back."

He didn't need to ask. No matter how much junk food he stuffed into the kitchen, no matter how much he upped their hourly rates, they rarely came back. He watched as Wendy headed straight for the front door. When she reached for the doorknob, Len stopped her. "Don't tell me you're going home without being paid . . ." He laughed, pulling out his wallet. "I'm sure you earned every bit of this."

She pushed her hair behind her ears and nodded, bugging her eyes. "Uh, *yeah*?" she said—like a question. After ramming the bills into her bag, she tossed him a smile full of pity and slipped outside.

Ah, well. Another one down.

There was a time when Len's parents would have offered their assistance. Back when Olivia was younger, after Virginia died, they were determined to help Len raise his daughter.

Glancing around the living room, on the day after Olivia's sixth birthday, Len's parents had made a good-hearted show of hiding their horror. Life without Virginia in the eight months since her death, without any sort of dependable child care, meant menial tasks went undone. Maybe that wasn't quite accurate. The laundry got put into the machine, washed, and transferred into the dryer. It just never quite made it back into the dresser drawers. The basket progressed as far as the living room before some sort of Olivia-related catastrophe drove Len to drop everything to soothe, bandage, discipline, feed, or water his daughter.

The dishes were slightly less troublesome; they washed, rinsed, and dried themselves within the very same appliance. No transfer required. The clean dishwasher became its own cupboard. The dirty dishes, however, were left to fester in unbalanced stacks in the kitchen sink until the dishwasher was, mercifully, empty once again. If Len had known his parents were coming, he'd have made some effort to clean up. At the very least, he'd have swept the floor and hidden the dirty plates.

Grace and Henry Bean had sat side by side, perched on the edge of the sofa. Grace's ankles were daintily pressed together. Everyone remained silent as Henry pinched a wad of tobacco and, carefully holding his pipe over the tiny bag, filled the pipe's bowl. After packing the moistened tobacco firmly, but not too firmly, Henry took three unlit puffs and sat back, satisfied.

"Our gift wasn't much of a hit, was it?" Grace asked of no one in particular. "The fellow at the toy store said it was the most popular puzzle they had. It's three-dimensional, you know."

Len nodded. "Olivia loves it. Thank you." It was a total lie. Len couldn't imagine a worse gift for his daughter, who had trouble pushing a button through a hole.

"Loves it? I believe her exact words were, 'Ech. I hate puzzles,'" laughed Henry.

Len reached for a pair of his daughter's mittens on the floor. "She's just cranky." When his mother appeared concerned, Len added, "Nightmares last night."

"Poor thing. I chose it because it was in the shape of a princess castle. She does still love castles, doesn't she?"

Again, Len lied. "Absolutely. It's the perfect gift."

"Maybe she'll give it a try after we leave?" asked Grace.

"I'm sure she will," said Len.

"When you were her age, you loved puzzles," said Henry.

Grace's eyes had drifted back to the overflowing laundry basket. "It's too much for you."

"What?" asked Len.

She waved toward the jumble of shoes in the hall, the stack of newspapers scattered in front of the fireplace, the pizza box leaning behind a chair. "All of this. Olivia. Without Virginia."

"We're doing okay."

"Leave him alone, Grace," said Henry. "A little mess never hurt anyone."

"No," she said. "It's more than that. I'm going to send Marta over here once a week to clean—"

"Forget it, Mom," Len said. "I can hire someone myself."

"I'm not forgetting it. Marta's looking for someone to replace her Tuesday client. Bob Rennert." She glanced at Henry, whose brows had shot up. "Prostate cancer," she explained. "It was very fast."

Henry shook his head and went back to his pipe. Just then, Olivia came stumbling into the room, hair curtained across her face, using Len's tennis racket as a scoot-along-the-rug snowshoe.

Henry perked up. "You like tennis, Olivia?"

The child didn't answer, just continued scooting.

"Olivia," said Grace. "Your grandfather asked if you enjoy playing tennis."

Again, Olivia ignored the question.

"Why don't you come over to Grandma and sit on her lap," said Grace, holding her arms out toward her granddaughter, waggling her fingers to sweeten the offer. "Maybe we can braid your hair, get it out of your eyes."

Olivia pushed a thicket of hair off her forehead only to have it fall across her face again. From where she stood at the window, sunlight flooded her delicate features, illuminating her untarnished skin, electrifying that untamable russet hair. Her one exposed eye glowed as if lit from within, the gray of her iris blanched into an iridescent near-white. For the first time, Len noticed her bushy eyelashes weren't black at all. They were impossibly dark auburn.

Grace gasped, looked at Len, and whispered, "My goodness, she's a beautiful child."

He nodded almost imperceptibly, so lost was he in the very fact of his daughter.

Henry glanced up from his pipe for a moment and shook his head, sighing. "Going to have to fight off the boys one day."

Len stiffened. Henry meant it as a casual remark. A compliment. The father of another girl would be flattered. He might chuckle, ruffle his daughter's hair, and make a lame joke. Something like "I'll be waiting for them with my shotgun." Or "I don't know how I'll survive the teen years."

Not Len. What boys, or, God forbid, men, might think about his daughter one day, when her body began to burgeon, made Len's mouth go dry with panic.

Parents of children with nonverbal learning disabilities had layers of worry, like a tightly budded rose. But parents of *girls* with NLD faced another, more terrifying layer. Learning-disabled females were typically overly trusting, gentle, and desperate for social acceptance. A dangerous formula when devoid of a healthy level of prudence, observation, and skepticism.

A father's instinct to protect his little girl was natural. Len's instinct to protect Olivia was near savage.

He changed the subject. "I hear we're in for snow tonight."

Henry sucked on his pipe, closed his eyes, and smiled. He'd always loved a good storm.

"I see Virginia in her," said Grace, watching Olivia drop to the floor and drive the tennis racket across the carpet with her hands. As the handle banged repeatedly against Grace's chair leg, she eyed her son. Len knew his mother thought Olivia's on-again, off-again communication skills were no different than the empty Chips Ahoy! package sitting on the coffee table. The natural consequence of family torn apart by tragedy. And, like the mess, simple to resolve.

"Let her be, Mom. She's playing quietly."

His mother looked at his father. Clearly, this was a problem they'd discussed before. Grace touched Len's arm. "We're not blaming you, Leonard. But sometimes if you just put your foot down . . ."

Len struggled to remain calm.

"Do you know that Zucker rats can never ever feel full?" Olivia had stopped skating and stared at her grandmother, licking her lips. "They eat and eat and eat."

"What about puppies, love?" asked Grace, who had never understood how a girl could birth a rodent obsession in the first place, let alone nurse it for three years.

"They eat until they almost explode," said Olivia.

Grace told her granddaughter she was fascinating, and turned to Len. "She's obviously a very intelligent girl. Don't shortchange her because of what some doctor says." She blinked several times. "Your father and I think it's time we got involved."

So it was settled. Every Sunday morning, Grace and Henry would pick up Olivia and take her to their golf club for indoor tennis lessons and a quiet lunch overlooking the snow-covered eighteenth hole. Len would get a few hours to himself, and they'd get a crack at bettering Olivia's meager social skills.

His parents showed a remarkable degree of determination. They arrived at the door at ten o'clock sharp to find Olivia sitting in the front hall wearing pajamas and her father's winter boots. Grace managed to wrestle her into tennis whites, but the child refused to even look at the gleaming Nikes with pink pompoms on the toes. Nor would she contemplate wearing her own boots.

Grace gave Len a look that said, "Watch this and learn." Smiling at Olivia, she set down the rules, "You can wear your dad's boots into the car, but you'll change into your Nikes as soon as we get into the club or else Grandma won't allow you dessert."

What did Olivia care about an ice cream parfait three hours in the future? She heard she could keep the boots, pulled a jacket over her tennis outfit, and hopped into the backseat.

As they backed out of the driveway, Henry opened his window and called back, "We'll have her back by three." Len waved and looked at his watch.

It was barely eleven thirty when they pulled back into the driveway.

Not only had Olivia lost her dessert by snubbing the regulation footwear, but during practice, she refused to hit balloons to her partner, thumping them against the ground with her racket until they popped. The cost of the balloons was absorbed by the club. The cost of the club's racket was charged to Henry's account. Then Olivia spun in circles with her eyes shut, striking her partner—the eight-year-old grandson of the golf club president—in the cheekbone.

Len's mother had walked Olivia to the front door, pushed the hair off her granddaughter's forehead, and kissed her good-bye, then, without meeting Len's gaze, she said, "Don't forget Marta on Tuesday. She prefers Pledge to Endust," and headed back to the car.

She never mentioned Sunday morning tennis again.

Now, before padding down the hall to check on his daughter, Len stopped to pick up the phone in the kitchen and listen to his voice mail.

"You have two messages," his phone informed him. He heard a woman's voice. "This message is for Leonard Bean. It's Marlene from Dr. Tanzer's office. I'm calling to remind you about your physical Monday morning at ten. Just remember you'll be fasting—nothing to eat or drink after dinner the night before except water." He deleted the message. He'd forgotten all about his appointment.

The next message was from his client's infamously flirtatious receptionist, Shannon. How on God's earth did she get his home number? "Hi Leonard. I just wanted to tell you I've pulled all the files you needed." There was a short pause, followed by the sound of her drinking something. "I, um, just wondered if you wanted anything else included in the package. If you think of anything . . . anything at all, my home number is 902-555-1171. Just in case."

So Fay was right.

His head throbbed. He reached up and rubbed his eyes, thinking he'd like nothing better than to crawl into bed, alone. Well, maybe he'd have preferred a certain apologetic magazine publisher to crawl in with him, but, barring that, he'd love to squeeze in a few hours of sleep before Olivia woke up in the morning.

As he got closer to his daughter's room, he heard thumping sounds coming from behind the closed door, and his heart sank. Olivia was still up. Sure enough, when Len peeked inside, he found her bouncing on her bed in her long flannel nightgown, milk bottle full of clattering pebbles in her hands, atop a tangle of blankets and a squashed package of Oreos. "Sticks and Stones" by Olivia's favorite band, Aly & AJ, played in the background.

Len turned off the CD player. "Olivia. It's after midnight. Get into bed."

She squealed and giggled, backing against the wall. Birthday Wishes Barbie's alarmed face poked out from beneath Olivia's bare feet. "I'm already into bed!"

Sighing, Len took the bottle of stones—which seemed to be heavier than the last time he'd held it—from her hands and pulled from the bookshelf her favorite book, *If You Give a Mouse a Cookie*. The child was far too old for the story, but still demanded it night after night. Len could recite the entire text in his sleep. "Okay, settle down. It's story time."

Olivia stopped jumping long enough to chirp, "That being said, I don't want to read a book. I actually want to bounce all night!" Then she leaped up again.

"Olivia!" A sharp pain shot across Len's left temple. He didn't have the energy to correct the child's use of way-too-adult terms. "Daddy is not in the mood for this."

She stopped again. She'd never been able to coordinate the mechanics of simultaneous walking—or bouncing—and talking. "Actually, I *am* in the mood for this!"

Len took a deep breath and noticed the smell of dead animal still hadn't left the room. Now, what had Dr. Kate said about getting Olivia to behave? Try to echo her feelings. Get into her shoes. Len looked at his daughter. "Bouncing is fun, isn't it? Actually?"

She bounced higher.

Clearly, that didn't work. Len tried again, rubbing the pain in his head. "And why *would* you want to stop jumping? You're having too much fun."

She stopped and nearly lost her balance. "Yeah." Then bounced.

"It must suck when your mean old grump of a dad tells you to stop having fun." Len watched Olivia's hair flap up and down against her face. He thought the pain in his head was now throbbing in time with the thumping bed.

Olivia dropped to her knees. "I don't have a mean old grump for a dad. I have a man for a dad." Just as Len smiled and leaned forward to kiss his daughter, Olivia grabbed the book from his hands and accidentally whacked him in the chin, drawing blood. Completely oblivious, she thumbed through the book, humming.

The child had no buffer zone, no spatial sense of where her body ended and someone else's might begin. Olivia had once explained that if you cut off a rat's whiskers and set him loose in a dark room, he'd bump into tables, walls, and cupboards. In a way, it summed up her own bodily awareness—Olivia was simply born without whiskers.

The upside was that the child still watched TV sprawled across her father's lap, allowing Len to revel in the delicious un-self-consciousness of childhood a little longer than other parents. The downside, of course, was constantly running out of Band-Aids.

"So, what happened with Wendy tonight?" Len asked, holding a tissue to his chin. "She seemed to be upset about—"

"She told me to make a treasure box. For all my treasures." Olivia sprung across Len's lap, jabbing her elbow into her father's thigh, and ran to her desk. There, she picked up a small, glitter-covered cardboard box and held it up for Len to see.

"Lovely. What's in it?"

"A tooth I lost that time the tooth fairy forgot to actually come is in it," she said. "And a picture of Mommy so if she ever comes back I'll recognize her."

Len said nothing.

Olivia walked across the room, carrying the box. "Wendy said I should put in things I love most. So that's what I did."

"Show me."

She ripped off the lid. "Oh yeah, Georgie Boy!"

The room filled with a stink far worse than the four-day-old stink. From the mud-encrusted, partially decomposed gerbil, now some twelve days dead and exhumed from the mossy earth, emanated a stench so bad Len choked back vomit. He grabbed the box and rushed toward the back door. "Where was Wendy when you were digging him up?"

"In the bathroom. And she went right back in after she saw him."

By the time both Georgie Boy and Olivia were settled back in their respective beds, Len lay beside his daughter, reeling from a heady mix of exhaustion, alcohol, and damp night air.

"Daddy?"

"Mm?"

"Did you find a home for any little kids today at work?"

Len shifted closer to Olivia's warm body so as not to fall off the side of the twin bed. "As a matter of fact, yes. I did up papers for a new couple who own a furniture store. They're adopting a boy, a twelve-year-old."

She yawned. "Is tomorrow my birthday? Are any kids coming?"

"Tomorrow is not your birthday. But we're going to have a great day. I'll make you pancakes for brunch, then—"

"Jeremy Knight got Brian and Trevor and Dakota Goodman in trouble today for stealing my pencils."

Len lifted his head from the pillow and glanced at his daughter, impossibly fragile-looking as she stared up at the ceiling and blinked. "I should hope so. Did he send them to the office?"

Olivia nodded. "You're my special person at home and he's my special person at school. So that's pretty good."

"I'd say you're very well covered."

"I used to have three."

"Three?"

"Three heroes."

He kissed the top of her head. "Yes, you did."

Olivia held her fingers over her head and stared up at them. "What's her name?"

"Who?"

"The lady you went on a date with tonight."

"Rachel."

"Is she nice?"

Len thought about the way Rachel always apologized. Then apologized for apologizing. "She's very nice."

"Does she have kids?"

"She has two. A boy and a girl."

The child's eyelids drifted shut, then flew open again. "Daddy?" she whispered.

"Yes?" Len's headache hadn't subsided, in spite of the two extra-strength Tylenols he'd popped. He tightened his hold on Olivia and closed his eyes.

"Do you think Rachel wishes she had three kids? Like another girl who knows lots of stuff and doesn't actually have a mother?"

It was a question his daughter asked each time a new woman came into their lives—anyone from nannies to teachers to those rarest of creatures, Len's dates. Mothers, in Olivia's young eyes, were the most special people of all. "I don't know, princess." Len smiled sadly, pulled the covers up and over her shoulder, and tucked them under her chin. "But I don't see how she couldn't."

Monday morning, Doctor Tanzer pulled his glasses from the top of his head and scribbled something in Len's file. "And if you can't escape the stress of being a single father, you'll just have to find other ways to unwind. Buy yourself a yoga DVD and do it before your daughter wakes up in the morning. Or go on a news fast." The doctor looked across the examining room at Len, who was standing directly beneath an air vent and trying to keep his paper gown from blowing open.

The tiny room was positively glacial. The air gusting down from the ceiling onto his bare back had to be fifty degrees. "May I get dressed now?" Len asked.

"Go ahead. I'm going to order a few tests." Dr. Tanzer perched himself on a wheelie stool. "These are all routine for a man your age." He slid his glasses further down his nose and peered at Len over the top. "How are those headaches of yours?"

Len looked up from pulling on his socks. "I still get them. Actually had one so bad the other day, I had to lie down."

"Have you felt any sluggishness? Changes in energy level?"

"Of course. But I hear three hours of sleep a night will do that to you."

"Nausea?"

Len had one foot in his trousers. "Once. Maybe twice."

Dr. Tanzer stood up. "Hop back up on the table, Len. I'd like to have another look."

Len hobbled to the table while pulling up his pants and jumped up without buttoning. Dr. Tanzer peered into Len's right eye, then his left. "Your eyes look fine, but I'd like to add a couple more tests to your list. Nothing to concern yourself with. Strictly precautionary."

CHAPTER 10

"Green Fingers"

—SIOUXSIE AND THE BANSHEES

Wearing a Siouxsie and the Banshees T-shirt over torn jeans, Janie slid her tray along the steel rails to the shortest lunch lady, who scooped massive helpings of lasagna, Thursday's special, onto her plate from beneath the glass sneeze guard. Out of the corner of her eye, Janie caught sight of Olivia Bean walking by, holding one arm in the air and shaking it like she was jangling a wristful of bracelets. Which she wasn't. Janie wondered for the zillionth time why Olivia's father didn't take a brush to all that rusty hair. Better yet, a pair of hedge clippers.

Beatrice Stein pulled up a tray behind her. "Whoa, you're brave," said Beatrice, staring at the enormous pile of pasta on Janie's plate. "That would go straight to my ass."

Janie shrugged. "On me, it'll just go to my boobs."

Beatrice chanced a quick look at Janie's chest. Her eyes widened and she laughed. As she walked away, Janie called out, "I'm planning to leave my body to science. Just to confuse future generations!" But Beatrice was out of earshot. Then Janie felt Tabitha Carlisle's golden presence behind her. She quickly pushed her tray further along the rails.

"Caesar salad," said Tabitha. "Oh, and no dressing. Please and thank you."

Janie slid her green canvas bag onto her tray, blocking Tabitha's view of her gluttony. She bent down and pretended to tie her boot, forcing Tabitha to move around her.

Janie's appetite was gone. She checked that no one was looking, then abandoned her tray, pulling an apple out of a glass-fronted fridge and sidling up behind Dustin, who hadn't noticed her.

"Is there any milk in that mushroom soup?" he asked the staff.

Janie bit into her apple. "Are you kidding? You, the guy who ate a hot dog right out of the garbage can, are suddenly concerned about dairy consumption?"

"We're recording the food groups for *health*, Insanie. Writing down everything we eat." He tapped his head with an index finger. "Always working. Twenty-four hours a day."

"That would explain the grunting and groaning sounds coming out of your bedroom every night." Janie slipped past him, grabbed a bottle of orange juice from the cooler, and stopped when she saw Tabitha in line for fries. Janie smiled. No dressing on the salad, a bottle of water, and potatoes swimming in grease. It wasn't feast or famine for this goddess, it was feast *and* famine. Janie could respect that.

She lined up behind Tabitha. The two girls stepped up to the french fry station just as the hair-netted lunch lady pulled a fresh vat out of the oil. After peering more closely into the basket, the woman fished out something long and brown and knobby, and hurled it into a garbage can.

Janie looked at Tabitha. Tabitha stared back, lifting her eyebrows. They walked away together, abandoning their meals. "I'm so gonna heave," Tabitha laughed. "That *had* to be human."

Janie almost sank to the floor, laughing. "No. It looked like E.T.'s finger. It was otherworldly. I practically saw it flip us off."

Tabitha crinkled her nose in disgust. "Well, I'm never eating anything in this place, ever again."

"Me neither."

"I saw you at hockey practice," said Tabitha, after a group of girls passed by. "Was that your first time playing?"

So Tabitha had noticed her shitty skating. "No. But my ankle was sort of sprained, so, you know, I sucked. Plus my skates were too tight."

"Drag."

"My data promised me new skates next time I see him."

"Cool. Are your parents split?" asked Tabitha.

Janie held her breath as Inside Out Girl made her way toward a nearby trash can with a banana in her hands. Olivia stopped, finished peeling, and stared at Janie as she bit into it. Ugh, Janie thought. Go be weird somewhere else. The kid chewed for a moment, then turned around, and followed a bunch of fifth-graders out of the caf.

"Are your parents divorced?" repeated Tabitha.

Janie looked up. "Oh, sorry. Yup."

"Me too. My dad just moved out for the second, and probably final, time. It sucks for the kid—the whole going-back-and-forth thing."

"Yup." Lame answer—*Yup*. Tabitha looked around the room in an obvious quest for friends. She was losing interest. Janie tried to think of something to say. Nice weather? No. Too middle-aged. How do you like your new house? Too neighbor-lady-spying-through-the-curtains.

The Goddess-snaring article was full of come-hither advice she'd kill for right now. A lot of good it did, folded up and hidden in the side pocket of her army bag. Faced with Tabitha's sunburned nose and throaty giggle, Janie couldn't remember a thing it said.

Tabitha took a step backward, clearly trying to disentangle herself from what had rapidly become a dull conversation. Without the horror of a dismembered and overcooked finger to amuse them, Janie Berman and Tabitha Carlisle had very little in common.

Think fast, Janie thought. Her mind raced, searching the nooks and crannies of her life for something captivating to say. She had nothing.

Although . . .

If her mother's voodoo worked on kids, got them to listen and stop despising their parents, wouldn't it be possible for it to work on other people, too? Especially the "get onside with your child" theory. "We kids are just pawns," Janie blurted out.

Tabitha, who was waving at her friend Charlotte, looked back, confused. "What?"

"Pawns of divorce. We're forced to live our lives here or there, depending on what some asshole judge says."

Tabitha nodded. "I know! Forget having your own plans on a Saturday night. If it's 'Daddy's weekend,' you miss every awesome party, every sleepover. It totally sucks."

Not exactly Janie's experience. What awesome parties? The parenting voodoo, however, was working like magic. Just stay on Tabitha's side. "I hate that," Janie said. "I miss everything, too!"

"Like that party at Nadia's two weeks ago—the one where Avril Lavigne was supposed to show up . . ."

"Avril Lavigne was supposed to show up?" Avril was beyond hot. She was scorching. Blistering. Third degree.

"Yeah, didn't you hear? Avril is Nadia's third cousin or something. Or maybe Nadia's stepsister is Avril's second cousin. It said on the invitation, remember?"

Janie was so many tiers down from the school's A-list she'd never even heard about the party. "Yeah, I kind of remember seeing it. Did everyone hang out with her?"

"No. Avril didn't show."

There was one piece of advice from the Goddess article Janie did remember: Leave her wanting more. And it would take everything Janie had to follow it. She stood up and swung her purse over her shoulder, her stomach rumbling with hunger. "Typical," she said, like a jaded Hollywood warhorse. "Gotta go. People are waiting for me." And, exactly like the magazine article said, she sashayed out the door without so much as a backward glance.

CHAPTER 11

He's Come Undone

"S orry I'm late," breathed Rachel as she rushed across the lobby of the York Street Cinema. She reached up to kiss Len on the cheek. Dressed in dark jeans, boots, and a sleeveless beige turtleneck with a gold chain strung around her waist, mahogany hair streaming down her shoulders, she didn't look much older than the herd of Friday night teenagers pouring through the doors to see the latest slasher flick, *Bloodbath*. The only real giveaway was the laugh lines around her eyes.

"Normally, I'd have been stressed about getting a lousy seat," said Len, handing their tickets to an usher, then guiding Rachel into the darkened theater. The dim glow of the movie, which had already begun, allowed them to see three things. Random bits of popcorn were sailing through the air; the theater was undulating with fidgety young bodies; and the only empty seats that weren't singles were in the very last row. "But this time I won't mind sitting at the back."

She grinned. "Hoping to get lucky in the dark?"

"If it will distract me from the movie, yes."

They picked their way along the row, littered with flip-flops, cast-off purses, and candy wrappers, and dropped into their seats. She leaned closer to him and whispered, "Sorry."

"That's two apologies in as many minutes. Not that I'm keeping track."

"About the movie, I mean. I can personally guarantee it will be the worst thing you watch this year. I promise to refund your money."

He pulled a package of smuggled licorice from his jacket pocket, opened it, and offered her a piece. "Remind me why we're here again . . ."

"Dustin is *dying* to see this movie." Rachel moved even closer, which Len didn't mind at all, and cupped her hand over his ear, whispering, "I've heard that somebody goes crazy and murders a mother and her two daughters, leaving the teenage boy to raise himself. I want to be sure the murderer isn't the mother's new boyfriend."

Len laughed, the smell of her lemon shampoo making him giddy. He stretched his arm around the back of her seat and rested his hand on her bare shoulder. Her skin felt cool, firm. He waited for any sign of her shrinking from his touch. None came. "Well, just as long as he isn't a lawyer."

She poked him in the ribs, taking his breath away.

They watched in silence as the mother introduced her benign-looking poet boyfriend to her three kids over tuna casserole and green salad. He ruffled the bobbed hair of the younger daughter and announced the traffic had been terrible. Rachel yawned, letting her head lean back onto Len's shoulder. She left it there.

Her lips weren't three inches from his.

"Why exactly do we care how this particular family is murdered?" Len asked.

"We're only concerned with the 'who.' Dustin's biggest fear in life is me dating. If *Pentameter Boy* here is the killer and Dustin watches this, I'll be sitting home alone every Saturday night until my son heads to college. We're talking six years, fifty-two Saturday nights in a year. That's . . ." Rachel chewed her lower lip as she calculated. "Well, that's a lot of Saturday nights."

Len studied her. "We can't have that."

The poet excused himself from the table and slipped into the kitchen. He should have headed straight for the sink to top up his water glass, the one he claimed, not ten seconds prior, needed filling, but as he approached the enormous wooden chopping block, he paused and stared at the mother's new carving knife.

Rachel pulled her purse onto her lap. "Okay. That's all I needed to know. Want to grab a beer?"

"God, yes." Len followed her through the row of teenagers, one of whom mumbled, "Make up your fucking mind," and back out into the brightly lit lobby. "Poor Dustin," said Len. "Undone by the knife used to chop the romaine." He held open the outside door for Rachel. "Does he know you're here?"

She nodded. "He was worried one of his friends would see me. In addition to being terrified I was going out with you again."

"Mm. Might have been better not to admit to the film."

"It's the one promise I made to my kids when they were young—I give them the truth. No matter how painful."

"Well, the truth about that movie is, I've never seen anything quite as painful."

"I won't argue that."

Rachel stretched her arms over her head as they walked out into the warm night air. It seemed everyone had the same idea. The sidewalk was overflowing with couples sampling an early taste of summer, strolling hand in hand or sitting over drinks in awning-covered patios. Reluctant to take Rachel's hand—rubbing her arm in the shadowy theater was one thing, reaching for her hand in front of martini-swilling strangers on the sidewalk was far too presumptuous at this stage—Len began walking in the general direction of his car.

As they approached Roosters, a chic little bistro with a rustic yet modern edge—clean-lined benches made of barn beams, stainless steel walls—Rachel stopped. "What about this place? I've been dying to try it . . ."

"I was thinking we could hop in the car, drive down to Merryston. There's a great little restaurant overlooking the river—"

"Merryston's forty minutes away."

"It's a nice night. We can put the top down. You'll get chilled. I'll warm you up. I have it all worked out, as you can see."

"Yes, you do . . ."

"Or we could bribe our babysitters and check into a little motel." He looked at her quickly and winked. "Just for a quick contest over the side of the balcony. Loser buys mimosas the next morning."

"Mm. This is all *very* tempting. It's not every day a girl gets invited to take a part in a pee contest . . ."

"Don't say 'pee,'" he said. "It'll mark you as an amateur."

"We can't have that."

He motioned toward his car. "So . . . Merryston?"

She shook her head. "I can't be out too late tonight. I have to get the kids to the pediatrician for their checkups in the morning, and if I'm out late, Dusty won't sleep. Then he won't get out of bed and we'll miss the Saturday morning appointments we've had booked for two months, and Dr. Grenier's secretary will think I'm an uncaring mother."

He laughed. "Oh, I don't think there's any danger of that."

Pausing to glance at the menu affixed to the restaurant's hostess podium, Len sensed Rachel was no longer with him. He spun around to see her standing a few paces back, knitting her eyebrows together and biting her lip. Brown curls danced around her face in the evening breeze as couples passed her by. Had he offended her? Had she been expecting him to more ardently defend her caring-mother status?

"Three hundred and twelve," Rachel said.

"What?"

"It would have been three hundred and twelve Saturday nights on my own if Dustin had seen the movie. Give or take."

Len smiled to himself. To hell with hand-holding. Right there in front of the patrons of Roosters, he took Rachel by the shoulders and kissed her.

When Dr. Tanzer mentioned he'd ordered a few extra tests, he'd neglected to prepare Len for just what to expect. Len had never experienced claustrophobia before, but being inside the MRI unit the next week was like suffering his own burial.

The tunnel was too cramped. Too close. Who thought to make this machine all white? It was like being in a colorless coffin. The machine hummed and clicked a bit louder, sending a fresh surge of sweat down the back of his neck.

He closed his eyes and tried to imagine a sandy beach. Children jumping over undulating waves. Women in flowered bathing suits—no, *Rachel* in a flowered bathing suit, her freckled arms making the floral pattern overly busy, overly delectable.

The MRI's softer clicking sounds switched to loud banging, ripping his thoughts away from the beach and thrusting them back inside the pipe. He regretted having pulled out the earplugs they'd offered him. Not being able to hear, at first, had worsened the claustrophobia, but now he was left with the sounds of shovels slamming against his casket.

The banging stopped. The technologist's voice boomed, "That's all, Mr. Bean." The table clicked, then began to move, pulling him out feet-first. Breathing normally once again, Len sat up, thrilled to have survived. "My God, that's some piece of technology. You'd think someone would have dreamed up a way to get a small TV in there. Even some graffiti would have been nice."

The technician helped Len off the table without so much as a smile. "Graffiti would interfere with our images." The technician blinked. "I'll have to ask you not to leave just yet, Mr. Bean. There's something I'd like the radiologist to have a quick look at before you go."

CHAPTER 12

A Girl Like That

*After a divorce, there will come a time when you are ready to
reenter the dating world. Alleviate the fears of your children
by listening to their concerns and assuring them that their
lives will not be negatively affected in any way.*

—RACHEL BERMAN, *Perfect Parent* magazine

Pulling the Saab onto her gravel driveway, Rachel cut the corner too close again, wincing as a thorny hedge scraped along her car door. Piper looked up from the flower bed at the base of the wraparound porch and pulled back her pink glove to check her watch. As if Rachel should have known her mother would be trolling through her tulips at ten o'clock on a Saturday morning.

"Those tryouts were fixed," Janie grumbled in the backseat, tugging at her hockey jersey, borrowed from her brother. "You should complain."

"Your grandmother's here. Try to put on a smile for her."

"How can I smile when my life's just been ruined?" Janie jumped out of the car and stomped past her grandmother, leaving Piper to eye Rachel, bewildered.

"What have you done to Janie?" Piper asked, holding an unplanted orange petunia.

Rachel slammed her car door. "I haven't done anything. My daughter apparently doesn't agree that hockey players need to know how to skate."

"That doesn't sound like my granddaughter," Piper said, lowering herself onto a green vinyl cushion and tucking the flower into the ground.

For the first time, Rachel noticed her tulips had been hacked down and were lying, cast off, on the flagstone path. "What are you doing?"

"I'm fixing your garden. Whoever planted your tulip bulbs didn't plant them deep enough."

"*I* planted them. Plenty deep."

"Three inches. You must dig your hole *seven* inches deep or they won't make it. Why the white tulips, anyway? When this was my house, I planted orange petunias every year."

"But my front door is red."

Piper looked up at the door, shielding her eyes from the sun. "I've been thinking about that. What do you think about black?"

Rachel sighed.

"Arthur and I went into the city last night. We went to the Frick, then out for pasta. He thinks you should sell the house."

"What?"

"He volunteers with the conservation authority on erosion control. He says underground water runoff and vibrations from local construction are only going to exacerbate the problem. And it won't be long before it becomes a huge issue." She snipped another tulip and tossed it into a heap. "Your land will become impossible to sell. If you have any left, that is."

"Tell Arthur thanks, but I've done my research. It'll be two hundred years before I lose my backyard."

A loud bang came from the back of the house. Janie and Dustin thundered across the porch in stocking feet, both clutching the phone. "It's Dad," Dustin said, sweeping his hair to one side. "He wants to take us glow-in-the-dark bowling tonight!"

Janie whispered, "Babe-chick is out of town."

"Please, Mom. Please!" Dustin jumped up and down. "I've never been glow-in-the-dark bowling. Or glow-in-the-dark anything!"

David had the kids last weekend. He always did this. Called with a casual but irresistible invitation on Rachel's Saturday nights. And, despite what her lawyer advised, Rachel could never say no to Janie and Dustin's pleading faces. "Sorry guys. Not tonight. Tell your father you have very big plans with your mother tonight."

The kids looked shocked. "We do?" asked Janie.

"We're having company. My friend Len is bringing his daughter over to meet you."

"Which friend is this?" asked Piper.

Janie's face fell. "I better not be getting a sister."

"Len's just a good friend of mine and we thought it might be fun if they came over for dinner and a game of Monopoly. Or maybe Twister." It had seemed like a good idea last week as she and Len shared a narrow booth and a few liqueurs over candle-lit white chocolate cake at Roosters. And when Len's hand accidentally brushed against Rachel's thigh, the idea seemed even better. And later, leaning against Rachel's front door, when they said good-night and Len leaned down to kiss her and she forgot how to breathe, the idea sounded best of all.

Janie and Dustin groaned. "How old is his kid?" Janie asked.

"Where did you meet this man?" asked Piper. "And when?"

"I think she's ten. She's, she's . . ." She's scaring me to death, Rachel didn't say. "She's a lovely girl, I've met her. She's sweet and very smart. Her name is Olivia. Olivia Bean."

The collective shriek startled Piper into snapping one of her tiny flower heads with her thumb. Disgusted, she threw the plant onto the tulip pile.

"Olivia Bean?" screeched Janie. "*Inside Out Girl* is coming? Are you kidding me?"

"What?" asked Rachel. "You know her?"

Dustin scoffed. "She's only, like, the biggest dork in school! The kid goes to rodent camp! And her clothes are always on wrong."

"She runs around school trying to hug everyone," said Janie. "She's freaky."

"Janie!" snapped Rachel. "I didn't raise you to speak that way about people. Olivia just processes things differently, that's all."

"How long have you known this man?" asked Dustin.

"Come on, you guys," said Rachel. "It's just a simple dinner."

Janie spun around and marched toward the back of the house. "You better not marry him. Because I'm not going to be *Janie Bean*!"

For a few moments after the kids disappeared, Piper said nothing. Finally, she looked at Rachel. "It's the first I've heard of this man."

"We've only been out twice."

"And you're introducing him to Janie and Dustin? Isn't that a bit impulsive? A bit out of character for you?"

Rachel fidgeted with her purse. Of course it was impulsive. Irresponsible. Risky. It went completely against her usual paranoia-driven instincts. Then again, so had stopping to change a stranger's flat tire. "Not at all. It's two families eating steak. Besides, I've already met his daughter."

"And what if it doesn't work out? Won't it be awfully confusing for a girl like that?"

Rachel narrowed her eyes. "A girl like what?"

Piper scowled, shaking her head and gathering her tools. "Don't play games with me, Rachel." She lowered her voice to a whisper: "A girl who is obviously far from normal."

Rachel said nothing.

With a small broom, Piper began sweeping the walkway with short, brisk strokes, much like the excruciating way she once brushed Rachel's thick hair. "It's your life, darling," she said eventually. "I'm not going to start interfering now."

Rachel was never supposed to have seen her baby's face. The delivery nurse, Margaret, who held Rachel's hand, had scooped up her baby and skated quickly through the swinging door to where the adoptive parents were waiting. Piper had given specific instructions that no family member, including Rachel, was to look into the baby's eyes, believing it would hurt less that way.

Rachel and her baby remained in the hospital for a few days, separately, until a battery of tests were completed. No one at the hospital would answer her questions, other than to assure her that the infant was doing well. But on the third night, Margaret came back on duty.

She tiptoed into Rachel's shared room and placed a box of chocolates on the table beside Rachel's bed. "I stole this from the staff room. Thought it might cheer you up."

Rachel—who'd woken up that morning with aching breasts, swollen and firm—nodded and sat up. Managing the first smile since the birth, Rachel reached for a chocolate and said, "I've been thinking about her." What else would she possibly have done over the last few days but think about her daughter? "I'd like to name her Hannah. From my favorite Woody Allen movie."

Margaret's eyes were moist. "Ah, sweetheart. You can't name her. That's the job of her new parents."

"But they haven't taken her yet. What do you call her?"

"Baby Girl Dearborn."

Dearborn. Rachel had never considered the irony until that

moment. She stuffed a chocolate cherry into her mouth and chewed it without tasting.

As Margaret started to leave the room, she paused and turned around. She whispered, "Would you like to see her? Just once?"

Rachel swallowed. "Really?"

Margaret nodded, patting Rachel's hand.

"Oh, please."

Margaret was back a few minutes later, pushing a glass bassinet. She reached inside and pulled out the baby, turning around and nodding to Rachel to sit up. With her free hand, Margaret pushed a pillow beneath Rachel's left elbow.

The baby was bundled in pink, swaddled so snugly only her face and two tiny fists showed. Thin black curls framed her beautiful face. Her eyes slanted upward slightly at the corners. Her rosebud mouth was perfect, with what looked like a small blister in the center of the top lip. From sucking, Rachel thought.

Hannah's head lay in the crook of Rachel's arm, her tiny face close to Rachel's breast. "Something just happened," Rachel said, feeling a rush in her breasts and liquid flowing down her torso. She glanced down at her nightgown to see wet stains spreading across her chest.

"Letdown," Margaret said. "Your body knows who's in your arms, it knows what it's meant to do now."

Rachel looked up. "You mean I should . . . ?"

The nurse closed the curtain around Rachel's bed. "It'll be our little secret."

At that moment, Hannah's eyes opened. She turned her head against her mother's breast and opened her small mouth, her tongue rooting for nourishment. Quickly, Rachel dropped the nightgown from her shoulder and tucked it behind Hannah's head.

"That's right," said Margaret. "She smells her mother. Now bring yourself closer, close enough for her to taste it."

Rachel looked up, blinking back tears and laughing. "Like this?" She leaned forward, accidentally knocking Hannah's cheek with her engorged breast. The infant's mouth lunged toward it, missing the nipple entirely and latching onto Rachel's flesh. "Oops." Rachel pulled her skin away and Hannah squawked in frustration. This time, Rachel lifted her breast and guided her nipple into Hannah's open mouth. The baby latched on wider, was still for a moment, probably surprised, and then began to suck. A smooth, rhythmical motion with sounds Rachel had never heard before. The wet swish of sucking, then a tiny swallow wrapped in a contented sigh.

"She's drinking," Rachel whispered, laughing. Tears streamed down her face now. "She's drinking from me."

"Shh!" said Margaret. "Yes, Hannah's drinking from you."

Rachel glanced at Margaret, who was watching like a proud grandmother. "Will you get in trouble?"

"Maybe. Maybe not."

Rachel grinned and wiped a tear from her cheek. "Thank you."

Hannah's eyes were bright in the faint glow from the hallway. She looked up hungrily at Rachel as she continued to feed, her almond-shaped wolf eyes frosted silver, like ice. With her free hand, Rachel touched Hannah's nose, cheek, forehead.

The child was so beautiful it hurt.

Rachel looked up. "Will she ever know?"

"Know what, love?"

"That she was once mine?"

"She'll be told."

"But will she understand?"

Margaret shrugged, smiling. "Most children born with Down's syndrome have a mild to moderate mental disability. Some have almost none. There's no telling this early, love. No telling at all."

CHAPTER 13

"Gimme Gimme Shock Treatment"

—THE RAMONES

Tabitha hadn't moved in almost eight minutes. Lying on her bed later that afternoon, flipping through the May issue of *Seventeen*, she had stopped at an article apparently so engrossing that the only body part still capable of movement was her feet, which waved from side to side, in perfect unison, like a pair of windshield wipers.

Exhilarated and terrified at the same time. That's how Janie felt about spying. Exhilarated because, at any moment, Tabitha might decide to try on her faded mini and dance all sexy in front of the mirror. Terrified because it put Janie right there in Tabitha's room, though it was nearly impossible for her to be caught from behind her bedroom curtains next door. Tabitha would have to be looking back into Janie's room with her own pair of binoculars, which she didn't possess. Or if she did—here was a depressing thought—she didn't think there was anything worth examining on the other side of the window.

Janie watched as Tabitha set down the magazine and stretched, before climbing off her bed and kicking off her sweatpants. Just then,

Rachel pushed open the door and sauntered into Janie's room. She looked around like she was expecting to be met at the doorway by a waiter with a plate full of canapés. "Hi, hon," Rachel said.

Janie flung the binoculars down. "Hi."

Noticing the binoculars, Rachel came closer and peered out the window. "What were you looking at?"

Bird-watching wasn't going to fly, so to speak. "Me and Tabitha have the same issue." She held up the *Seventeen* magazine. "We were looking through it together."

"Why don't you just go over there and look at your magazines in person?"

Janie shrugged and flipped through the pages. "Too much work." She froze as her mother reached for the binoculars, turning them over in her hands.

"They're heavy," said Rachel. "I never realized they were so heavy."

"Yeah," Janie whispered, willing something to happen to stop the train wreck that would surely come next.

"You got these from Grandma, didn't you, for your birthday? Which one was it—your eleventh? Or maybe your twelfth?"

Janie said nothing, just prayed Rachel wouldn't get a glimpse of Tabitha's attire next door. Or lack of it.

"Janie? Was it your eleventh or twelfth birthday?"

Rachel looked toward Tabitha's window. Janie held her breath but, by some miracle, her mother set the spy glasses down on the seat cushion and smiled. "Come on downstairs, sweetie. I could use some help with dinner."

Janie didn't budge.

"We're having guests, remember?"

"They're your guests, Mom. This dinner has nothing to do with me."

"Anyone who walks through that front door is *our* guest. I expect you to treat Olivia no differently than you'd treat anyone else," Rachel warned. "Or there will be severe consequences."

Dustin burst into the room. "Mom, can I go over to Cooper's? He just got this new mini bike and he said his parents will drive us out to Northridge Flats to—"

"Does anybody listen to a word I say?" Rachel said. "We have dinner guests coming!"

Dustin flopped backward onto Janie's bed. "Aww, crap. I totally forgot."

"Watch the mouth, mister," said Rachel. "And go get showered before Olivia and Len arrive."

Dustin kicked his sneakered feet against the bed frame. "I SO don't want to meet them. Or *shower* for them."

"Ugh, you're stinking up my bed!" said Janie.

Ignoring his sister, Dustin said, "Believe me, Mom, Inside Out Girl will not be getting dressed up for us. And since when do I have to start meeting your boyfriends?"

"Len's not a boyfriend, honey. We're just two families getting together for a nice meal—"

Dustin's eyes lit up. "If I stay home tonight, can I go to skate camp this summer?"

"Can you people go fight somewhere else?" asked Janie.

Rachel marched Dustin out of the room, saying, "No skate camp. But you can help me clean up the front hall so Olivia doesn't trip over your skateboards, your backpack, your basketball . . ." She closed the door behind them.

Finally. Grabbing the binoculars, Janie jumped onto her knees for one more peek, but Tabitha and her bare legs were gone.

CHAPTER 14

Cupcake Therapy

I don't think we should actually go to Rachel's house," said Olivia from the backseat. "Let's just go home."

"I'll be with you the whole time," Len said.

The sun hung just low enough in the sky to make the drive a perilous endeavor. Len suffered the glare with sunglasses, and glanced in the rearview mirror to see his daughter's face bobbing up and down from behind the bakery box lid. For the occasion, Olivia had pulled on a pink winter hat she'd worn when she was about seven. It didn't quite fit around her head and had slid upward, creating a gigantic woolen teat on top of her unbrushed hair. Her ears, pushed down and out by the cap, smoldered red in the early evening sunlight.

The girl looked like an unwashed pixie.

"Don't touch those cupcakes, Olivia. People don't like dirty fingers in their food."

"I'm not touching. I'm smelling."

"It looks like you're licking." Len spun around and held out his hand. "Give those to me."

Olivia mashed the box close to her body. "No! You said I could hold it all the way until there so I'm holding it. All the way until there."

Len turned the car onto Rivermoor Boulevard, hoping like hell the glare of the sun didn't trigger another headache.

"Do her kids call her Mom or Mommy?"

"Not sure." When Len thought about Rachel, Mommy wasn't quite what came to mind.

"Am I sleeping over with Janie?" she asked.

"No."

"Am I sleeping over with Dustin?"

"No! You do *not* sleep over with boys!"

"Why?"

"Because it's just not done. Ever." Len looked into the backseat and reached around to push the box closed again. "You've got blue icing on your chin. You *are* licking those cupcakes."

The car went silent except for the thumping of Olivia's head against her seat. Then, "I feel like throwing up."

"You're going to have a great time, you'll see."

"Okay. I'll try," Olivia said, scrunching up her face and looking out the window.

"That's the spirit."

"I'm going to throw up!" Olivia unbuckled her seat belt and unrolled the window, hanging her head and shoulders outside as Len dodged traffic to pull off the road. He jumped out to help her away from the car and into the bushes.

They waited a few moments. She stood hunched over at the waist, leaning onto her knees, while Len knelt beside her. Close enough to be the supportive parent; far enough to keep his jeans unsullied for Rachel. Olivia burped twice and let out a long groan.

Nothing happened.

"Do you still feel sick?"

She nodded, her face contorted. "Here it comes, it's coming!" she said, clutching her stomach.

"It's okay, let it all out." Len rubbed his daughter's back.

Still, nothing happened.

"Sometimes it takes a few minutes," Len said.

A tiny thread of blue drool appeared in the center of Olivia's lower lip. Slowly, it stretched downward, swaying in the breeze as it dangled below her knees. When the strand finally touched the ground, she wiped her mouth and stood up straight. "Whoa." She smiled. "All done now."

"That's it?"

"Yeah." She scampered back to the car, buckling herself in and settling the cupcake box on her lap. "We better get there before I eat any more."

CHAPTER 15

That's How a Kid Knows

The informed parent knows not to take a child's words or behavior personally. Remember, you are the adult, and react with the cool detachment that comes with maturity and understanding.

—RACHEL BERMAN, *Perfect Parent* magazine

Dustin, Janie, come down now!" Rachel called from the bottom of the stairs. "They'll be here any minute. And Janie? No Buzzcocks T-shirts, please."

She hated being so nervous. The way her fingertips tingled. She'd just walked into the living room, picked up a pillow to begin fluffing it a third time, when the doorbell rang.

"They're here!" Pulling a tube of lipstick from a drawer in the hall, she swiped it on and batted her lips together before opening the door. Len stood on the mat, wearing what must be his uniform, battered jeans and a white top—this time a creamy turtleneck.

"Hey," he said, leaning inside to kiss Rachel on the cheek. "We come bearing cupcakes. *If* any survived the journey, that is."

Olivia darted out from behind her father's legs and thrust a crumpled bakery box into Rachel's hands. She wore a Snoopy

T-shirt, turned right way around, a corduroy miniskirt, green tights, and winter hat and boots. Her chin was covered in blue icing.

The child danced from one foot to the other, pausing every few seconds to glance quickly at Rachel, then stare down at the ground. Len chuckled. "I'm afraid we've been stressing somewhat," he said.

"I'm afraid we've been *barfing* somewhat," said Olivia without a trace of a smile.

Rachel's instincts kicked in. She stepped onto the porch to do what she did with her own kids at the first mention of illness— touch their foreheads with the back of her hand—but stopped herself short. From a three-foot distance, she assessed the color of Oliva's cheeks, the glassiness of her eyes. It was how Piper had taken her temperature as a child—from afar, safely out of range of her aura of contagion. Her mother never got the most accurate reading, but then again, she never missed a golf game.

Rachel's reasons, though, were far different. "You're not feeling well, Olivia? You don't look like you have a fever."

Moving his daughter toward the front door, Len said, "Nothing more than a bit of nerves. And triple-thick blue frosting. She'll be fine, won't you, princess?"

Olivia ran behind Len and hid herself from Rachel, relieving Rachel of having to do the same.

"Janie and Dustin are upstairs," she said. "Maybe you can go up and tell them you're here." It'll give me time to adjust, she didn't say.

The child shook her head and clutched Len's legs harder. Len smiled, shrugging. "I think she might be more comfortable around her dad for the first little bit," said Len, pulling off his daughter's hat. Olivia snatched it back.

In the kitchen, Rachel parked herself at the island and reached for the bottle of red wine she'd opened up earlier, as Len made himself comfortable on a barstool. As comfortable as he could be, Rachel thought, without surgically extracting his daughter from his right leg.

"Olivia, there are some carrots on the table by the fireplace. Why don't you go help yourself?" Turning to Len, Rachel added, "Don't worry, I always quarter them lengthwise."

"Why?"

"So the kids don't choke. Doesn't everyone?"

Len laughed. "Sure, for toddlers. You've been chewing up your own carrots for how long now, Olivia?"

She buried her face into Len's sweater and said nothing. Something slipped out from under her T-shirt and clattered onto the floor.

"Whoops." Len leaned down to pick it up, then handed it back to her. "She brought along some of her favorite music to show Janie and Dustin." He winked at Rachel. "Something to bond over, you know."

Rachel smiled at Olivia. "That's a great idea. What band is it?"

The child stuffed the CD back into her shirt and hid her face.

"Well, I'm going to have a little wine," Rachel said, turning to Len. "Unless you'd rather have champagne?"

"I don't drink champagne."

"No," she said with a sly smile. "People who pee off balconies generally don't."

"I'll have you know we only relieve ourselves from the very finest establishments."

She nodded and took a huge gulp of wine before slicing two tomatoes with an enormous knife. "How very swish."

"We like to think so," said Len.

Olivia, inching out from behind her father, stuck a finger in her mouth and mumbled, "Does your corn-on-the-cob have handles?

Because I hate it when there's no handles and I get burned-up fingers."

Rachel bent down to her level. "You'll be happy to know we do have handles. And you can have first pick." She stood up again, turned to her chopping block and resumed slicing the tomatoes.

"I don't like the wooden handles. They fall out when I'm eating. So that's why I only like the plastic handles."

"Olivia," warned Len.

"You're in luck," said Rachel, scooping tomato cubes into a ceramic bowl full of lettuce. "We only have plastic handles. And with no broken metal thingies."

"Are they yellow? Do they look like little plastic corn-on-the-cobs?"

"I think they might."

"I think you're the most beautiful lady in the whole world."

Rachel smiled at Len and picked up a cucumber. "That's so sweet. You're pretty beautiful yourself."

"You look like Mommy."

She froze.

Len laughed and rubbed his daughter's back. His cheeks were flushed with pink. "Well, they do both have brown hair and are both very beautiful, but that's about it. Why don't we go see what's on television—"

"No. They both have noses and ears and chins and arms and stomachs and—"

"*Olivia*," said Len.

The child ignored her dad and moved closer to Rachel. Too close. She blinked up at her. "You look just like her picture. Exactly." Olivia patted her Snoopy-covered chest with her finger-tips, scrunching up her face like she was in pain.

"That's enough, now. We're embarrassing Rachel."

Rachel's heart thumped. Unsure how to respond, she went with her first instinct—cowardice—and shrugged. "Oh, people are always telling me I look like someone or other."

Olivia continued to stare at her as she chopped the cucumber into cubes. Eventually, she said, to Rachel's relief, "Emmie at school has a Ferrari."

"A kid at school has a Ferrari? That has to be wrong," said Rachel.

"Her dad has a Ferrari," said Olivia. "It's yellow and has a little horse on the front."

Len turned to stare at what was left of the fire in the next room. He grabbed the newspaper from the kitchen counter. "Your fire is dying. May I?"

Rachel nodded, and he crossed the room and settled himself in front of the fireplace.

"Do you want some cucumber?" Rachel asked Olivia. She scooped up a small handful of cucumber chunks and dumped them on the island in front of the girl.

"I love cucumber. Emmie gets a lot of good stuff, like a cell phone and swear movies that Dad won't let me see. Emmie's going to come to my birthday party. She got adopted when she was a baby. That's because her actual real mother didn't want her too much."

Rachel froze, her knife in midair. Her fingertips, her ears, her chest throbbed with a rush of blood. Settle down, she told herself. She's a ten-year-old girl who doesn't know the first thing about real life. As calmly as she could, Rachel said, "That's not necessarily what happened. All mothers love their children. But some mothers give up their babies so the baby can have a better life."

"Emmie does have a better life. Now she has a Ferrari," said Olivia, slipping a cucumber cube into her mouth and chewing. "Anyway, that's how a kid knows."

Rachel waited. When Olivia didn't elaborate, she asked, "Knows what?"

"That's how a kid knows if her mother loves her. If her mom isn't there, she doesn't love her."

Rachel felt her stomach drop. She glanced across the room to see Len still preoccupied with the fire.

Olivia looked at her, oblivious to the flaming daggers she'd just thrown Rachel's way. She was so unperturbed, in fact, that her eyelids drooped at half-mast. The child was completely neutral while Rachel had wound herself into choking, suffocating knots. She dropped the knife with a clatter and snatched up what was left of Olivia's cucumber pieces, hurling them into the trash.

Olivia stared at the spot where her unfinished snack had been. She blinked fast and furious.

Shit, shit, shit. "I'm sorry, Olivia. I didn't mean . . ."

Olivia ran from the kitchen and threw herself onto the sofa, burrowing under a folded quilt, while Rachel smiled at Len and tried to pretend nothing had happened.

Having no luck soothing his daughter, Len returned to the kitchen and picked up his wineglass. "She's not herself tonight. I think when I told her she'd recognize Dustin and Janie from school, it completely unglued her." He lowered himself onto a stool.

Rachel picked up a red pepper and turned it over in her hands, which were still shaking. "Sounds like she misses her mother."

"She doesn't remember much. Virginia died when she was five."

"How did Virginia die?"

He let out a slow breath. "Very suddenly. Even though it was raining, Virginia rode her bike to the school, pulling Olivia in her little bike trailer. By the time they got there, Olivia was cold, damp. Miserable. She gave Virginia a hard time in the foyer, the teacher said. She wouldn't take off her wet raincoat and refused to go into the class. What made it worse was Virginia had forgotten Olivia's Birthday Wishes Barbie, which she never went anywhere without. So there was Olivia, kicking and thrashing in a pile of kids' boots and jackets. Virginia promised she'd go back and get the doll, if only Olivia would go inside. Olivia finally agreed to sit quietly in the boot pile with the teacher until Virginia returned. The whole trip should have taken twenty minutes.

"The police said it happened instantly. On Virginia's way back with the doll, a car clipped the bike trailer as she crossed an inter- . section, and the force threw her bike into the path of an oncoming van. The rain was nearly blinding and the first driver swore he never saw her.

"Olivia waited on the floor, buried under the coats, crying, until I got there an hour and a half later." Len massaged his brow, then let his hand fall into his lap, staring intently at nothing in particular. "It was horrible."

God, what a thing for a young father to go through, Rachel thought. She sank down onto the stool next to him. She put her hand over his. "How did Olivia take it?"

Len twirled his glass, then stopped, seeming to lose himself in the spinning liquid. He looked up, his face taut. "She still doesn't fully understand it. Still thinks she'll see her mother again. Thinks Virginia just didn't want to come home."

Rachel looked into the great room where Len's daughter leaned on the edge of the sofa, wrapped tightly in the blanket, with only her face and one small foot showing. The child gazed, motionless, into the fire. *That's how a kid knows if her mother loves her. If her mom isn't there, she doesn't love her.* Olivia had been waiting five years for Virginia to return, all the while thinking her mother just didn't care. The child was talking about herself. And Rachel had snatched up her snack like a bully.

"Olivia," Rachel called softly. "Do you want to see those corn holders? You can get them out of the drawer for me, if you want."

The girl didn't answer. In the tiniest movement, she shook her head side to side.

Just then, what sounded like a team of horses thundered down the stairs. Janie skidded across the slippery floor in the front hall, herding her brother into the kitchen by poking him in the back. One final nudge landed him beside the stove. Rachel noticed he wore the same grass-stained khakis she'd told him to change out of, and Janie was lost inside an orange sweatshirt, size XXL, that made her look like a pumpkin squashed on the road the day after Halloween.

"Hey," they both grunted. Janie glanced at Len, then down at her feet. Dustin looked around the kitchen as if seeing it for the first time and determined to commit every detail to memory.

Len stood up and reached for their hands to shake them. Dustin and Janie barely knew what to do, blushing profusely. "Mr. Dustin and Miss Janie," Len said. "I've heard all sorts of things about you. And don't worry, none of them good."

Janie giggled nervously. Dustin ran his finger along the counter's edge and checked for dust.

Len waved a finger toward Janie. "You know, I think I recognize you from the school. Olivia will recognize you for sure." He turned around. "Sweetheart, come and meet Rachel's kids."

The girl didn't budge, so Len went to get her, leading her by the hand back into the kitchen. She looked petrified, her eyes wide as doughnuts. "Olivia, Janie and Dustin. Dustin and Janie, Olivia."

Rachel's kids mumbled a hello at the same moment Rachel, slicing broccoli now, noticed a dark stain spreading down the legs of Olivia's green tights. The child was wetting herself. Before Janie or Dustin noticed—without stopping to think about excessive bleeding, unsterilized metal blades, statistics for death by staph infection—Rachel held her breath, maneuvered her thumb directly under the knife, closed her eyes, and pushed down hard.

It worked perfectly.

She shrieked in pain—very real pain—and Dustin and Janie, as well as Len, rushed immediately to the island, ushering her to the sink where they busied themselves running her hand under the tap.

Olivia ran straight to the bathroom, her nervous slip-up completely undetected.

As Rachel wrapped her thumb in paper towel, Janie and Len debated whether or not the laceration needed medical attention. But Rachel wasn't listening. *That's how a kid knows.* How could she have missed this? Hannah wasn't out there in the world wondering if her birth mother loved her. With no evidence to the contrary, Hannah *knew* she didn't.

CHAPTER 16

"No Feelings"

—SEX PISTOLS

When Len had suggested the kids go "play" upstairs after dinner while the adults enjoy a liqueur by the fire, Janie glared at her mother, who smiled and said nothing. Turned out the glare cost Janie precious seconds, as it gave Dustin just enough time to slip out the back door with his skateboard. Which meant she was stuck entertaining Olivia Bean.

Alone.

Upstairs, Olivia ran straight for Janie's window seat and dove headlong into the cushions, her dirty boots thumping against the glass panes. Sitting up, she reached for Janie's binoculars and, holding them backward, tried to peer through the window toward Tabitha's house. "These things don't work very good," she said, turning them over and over before giving them a try upside down.

The sun was nearly down, blackening the tree branches and rooftops that grazed the edge of the fading sky. Lights had been turned on next door, illuminating the interior rooms like small stages and making it all too easy to see Tabitha Carlisle watching TV with her best friend, Charlotte.

Which meant one thing. Janie Berman's guest was equally visible.

"Yeah, those binoculars are busted," Janie lied, stretching behind the girl to tug the curtains shut.

"Who's your favorite band?" asked Olivia.

Janie looked in the mirror and sucked in her stomach. Damn. She should never have eaten that second blue cupcake.

"Mine's Aly and AJ," said Olivia, oblivious to Janie's lack of interest. "They're *so* cool." She pulled a CD out from under her shirt and held it up for Janie to see.

"Who?" Janie took it from her hand. Two pouty teenage girls with long blond hair stared back at her. The CD was called *Into the Rush*. What a couple of sellouts, thought Janie. They both looked like Britney Spears and the title was beyond lame. One thing was certain: Olivia needed to be introduced to some real music.

"My favorite song's called 'Sticks and Stones,'" said Olivia, pulling her pink cap down until it nearly covered her eyes. "It goes . . ."

Janie burped softly into her hand. "Forget that. Popstar bimbos are for losers." She tossed the CD onto the window seat and waded through the rumpled clothing on the floor to the other side of the room. "I'll play some *real* music for you." She leaned down, thumbed through her collection, and pulled out a CD. "Ever heard of the Sex Pistols? This song's called 'No Feelings.'" Janie pushed a few buttons and looked back at Olivia, who sat on her hands and bounced up and down in anticipation.

The song began with a few thumps, a couple of scratches, and a bar of frantic electric guitar. Janie blasted the volume and grinned. She shouted, "You like it?"

All bouncing stopped. Olivia wrinkled her nose. "Sure."

Janie turned the volume up higher. "The singer's name is Johnny Rotten."

"What?"

"JOHNNY ROTTEN!"

"I can't understand what he's saying!" Olivia called back.

"That's the whole point," Janie said with a nod.

The song worked itself into a frenzied conclusion and Janie shut it off. "I love that band," she said. "They're *so* real. No mainstream bullshit. You want me to burn you a copy?"

Olivia nodded. As Janie inserted a blank disc, the girl came over to watch and dropped down onto a cast-off denim jacket on the floor, her knees snaked out on either side as if she had no bones. "Can I take it home with me?"

"Mm-hm." Janie fiddled with the stereo, which seemed to have jammed. "This thing's a piece of shit. I totally need a new one."

Olivia scooted closer, her knee pressing into Janie's shin. Janie couldn't be sure, but she thought the child smelled like pee. Olivia said, "Janie?"

"Hm?"

"Who's your, um, you know . . . your special person?"

Janie looked up fast. "What?" She glanced toward the window to be sure the curtains were still squeezed shut. "That's kind of personal. I don't share that kind of info with . . . well, with anyone."

Olivia frowned. "I'm not anyone."

"Sorry."

"Can you tell me someday?"

"Maybe someday."

"Janie?"

"Hm?"

"Is it someday yet?"

"No."

"What about now?"

Blowing her hair out of her eyes, Janie looked at her watch. Nine seventeen. It was going to be a long evening.

Without any sort of warning, Olivia squealed and flung herself into the unloved clothes. She rolled around, wrapping herself in various items—black-and-white striped tights, army pants, a fraying tank—and beamed through the strap of a bra Janie had outgrown months ago. "No mainstream bullshit, right?"

"Mm."

"I'm going to tell everyone at school you're my *best* friend."

Janie froze. Her life just got a whole lot more complicated.

CHAPTER 17

Danger Pay

*Be careful when introducing your children to the new partner
in your life. The risk you run with little ones is that they will
form an immediate attachment.*

—RACHEL BERMAN, *Perfect Parent* magazine

Sitting on the sofa, directly across from Len, Rachel readjusted
the cushion behind her back. The only sounds in the room
were the snapping and hissing of the damp fire logs. She tucked
her hair behind her ears. Crossed her legs. The conversation had
trickled into oblivion after the kids thundered upstairs, and the
strained silence in the room threatened to pronounce Len and
Rachel incompatible. Or worse, Rachel worried, pronounce her to
be wholly dreary.

She sprung forward to pour more wine, fully aware she was
already over her absolute limit of three glasses but willing to suf-
fer tomorrow's crushing headache if it bought her a moment of
busyness now. "So, did you ever think of having more kids? I mean,
before . . . ?"

"We'd talked about it. Two kids wouldn't have been easy, not
with Olivia, but we figured we could bring on a team of nannies."

Rachel smiled.

Len picked up his glass and shook his head. "Virginia wanted a son next. Wanted to call him Redmond. The crazy thing is, we'd just started trying that week."

"Oh God," said Rachel. "I'm sorry for asking."

He said nothing, just stared into his glass.

Rachel looked away from him, cursing her question. She stood up quickly and looked out the back window, where she saw Dustin alone in the garage practicing a skate trick without much success.

Over and over, he set his board straight, perched carefully on top, centered his weight above the balls of his feet, and leaped up while simultaneously attempting to flip the board with enough force that he could land atop again. Over and over, the board shot out from underneath him. Over and over, Dustin landed on the cold, hard cement floor. After a few particularly nasty falls, Dustin rolled onto his stomach and pounded the concrete with his fist.

Len, who had followed her gaze, started toward the back door. "I'll go give him a hand. I used to skate back in the day."

"No!" Rachel rushed to stop him. Being peeled off the pavement would not soothe the boy's spirit. Not when the rescuer was his mother's new boyfriend. Rachel trotted after Len into the cool night air. "We'll just call him in for dessert, pull out the Twister . . ."

It was too late. Len was already jogging into the garage and lifting Dustin off the floor. As Len brushed off Dustin's clothes, the boy flashed his mother a wounded look. She would be hearing about the injustice for days.

"It's okay," Dustin said, backing way from Len and rearranging his rumpled hair. "I'm fine."

"Kick flips are tough to learn. Let me give you a few pointers . . ."

Len couldn't have known his next move would be considered the Ultimate Sin. He picked up Dustin's board, the boy's paramour, and after admiring the patchwork of stickers adorning the underside, set it down and climbed atop. The board groaned its objection as Len sprung up and down to test the tightness of the trucks, the feel of the deck. Dustin, probably not breathing, began to circle.

"Watch this," said Len, repositioning his left shoe. "You want to make sure your foot is angled in and your heel hangs off the side of the board. Your toes are just below the bolts . . ."

"Dustin," said Rachel. "Pay attention."

The boy rolled his eyes. "Can I just get my board back, please? I want to go inside."

"Don't you want to learn how to do it?" asked Rachel.

"It's the same motion as when you ollie, only with the kick flip, you kick your foot *away* from the board . . ."

"I can figure it out later. Seriously."

"Len, maybe we should let him go." She slapped at a mosquito, moving back toward the house. "It's getting buggy out here."

Thankfully, Len stepped off the board and surrendered it to Dustin, who leaped up on it, settled his front foot on top of the bolts, his heel nowhere near the edge of the board, and jumped up. He lost his balance and the board shot out from under him, straight into Len's shin. It had to hurt like hell, but Len's only reaction was a quick tightening in his jaw.

Dustin scooped up the skateboard, mumbled a quick "Sorry," and tore into the house.

Rachel rushed into the garage. "Are you okay?"

"I'm fine." Len walked with her across the driveway. "He'll get it. Kid's got seriously good balance."

He slowed as he approached the porch steps. Rachel, already at the top, turned to see he was limping, his blond hair flopped over one eye as he climbed. Before he reached the top, she stopped him and kissed his cheek, prickly with a long day's growth.

"What's that for?" he asked, his grin lopsided.

She led him toward the porch swing. "Danger pay."

CHAPTER 18

The Doll's Hand

It was pouring when Len dropped Olivia at school Monday morning, pouring harder when he'd gone home to a message from the neurologist's office saying they needed to see him, and pouring harder still when he pulled into the parking lot at the medical arts building.

God, he hated the weather.

Virginia died in April. One of the most weather-laden months of the year. Ironic that a woman who braved the rudest of conditions, whose most beloved pastime was taking a leisurely hike in the rain, who chided those who lived their lives skirting around puddles—was killed by what worried her least.

The aerosphere had chosen drizzle for the morning of Virginia's funeral. A cruel and uninspired choice, considering it was a carbon copy of the morning Virginia died. Len had stared straight ahead, through the limousine windshield on the way to the burial site, numb, watching misty rain dribble down the glass. As quickly as the wipers cleared the view of the hearse in front of him, streams of water blurred it.

An atmospheric apology perhaps, though far too little, far too late.

A sea of black umbrellas burst into somber bloom as funeral attendees stepped out of cars, shivering while they waited for pallbearers to lead the way. The driver of the hearse opened the back door, exposing the hand-polished hardwood casket Len had chosen two days prior.

Olivia trotted beside her father, sheltered by his umbrella, winding her arms in the hem of her new dress. It was one size too small but the navy fabric matched the sweatpants Olivia insisted upon wearing underneath. Besides, it had been the easiest thing to pull off the rack at Neiman Marcus.

"Where's Mommy?" asked Olivia as they approached Len's parents, Henry and Grace, who were standing next to the hearse. Virginia's family had yet to emerge from their hired town car.

Len had explained it too many times to count. He reached down to pick up his daughter, pressing her against his body. "Mommy's in heaven, sweetheart. Like I told you."

"When she gets back is she bringing my Barbie?"

The pallbearers carried the coffin across the grass to the grave site, as the rain gathered strength and the minister struggled to keep his notes dry. Olivia sat in a little pile at Len's feet, sucking her thumb. The child had to be exhausted. She'd barely had ten hours sleep in seventy-two hours, thanks to the still-missing Birthday Wishes Barbie.

The minister pulled his collar closed and began to speak. "It is with profound regret that we gather here to mourn the loss of . . ."

Grace nudged Len and gestured down the row of mourners to where Virginia's cousin Jeremy was holding up a brown paper bag. Jeremy was almost smiling as he passed it through the crowd toward Len. One by one, guests took the bag, looked at Len, and passed it on, whispering something to the next person. Sort of a macabre version of broken telephone. When it reached Grace, right next to Len, she listened, nodded, and passed it along to her son, whispering in his ear, "Jeremy got it from the police. From the scene." The bag was so drenched it split open as Len took it in his hands. Just as the minister began to speak, Len pulled the paper apart to see what was inside.

Birthday Wishes Barbie.

Len's body went limp with relief. He could never give Olivia the ultimate prize—her mother—but he could offer this one small comfort. He handed his umbrella to Grace and knelt down in the grass. In an instant, the child grabbed Barbie, mashed the naked doll against her chest and leaned back against her father, her eyes shut tight. She rocked back and forth, patting her doll's head and murmuring, "She *did* bring Barbie." With the minister's voice droning in the background, Olivia looked at her dad and smiled. "Is Mommy here?"

One of the doll's arms stuck out across Olivia's shoulder, the delicate palm of her hand pointing up to the sky. For the first time, Len noticed it. A tiny streak of dried blood smeared across the fingers.

"No, baby," Len whispered. "Mommy's not here."

Now, shifting in his chair, Len waited for Dr. Foxman, the neurologist recommended by Dr. Tanzer, to speak.

"We've gotten all your results back," the doctor said, pulling the glasses off his nose and closing the file. Leaning back in his chair, he pushed his fingertips together and sighed. "I wish I could say the news was better."

Len stopped fidgeting and waited.

"There *is* a tumor. It's not in a place we can easily reach to perform a craniotomy, or a biopsy. What's usually done in these hard-to-reach masses is we perform a closed biopsy, or a needle biopsy, whereby we drill a tiny hole into the skull, through which we insert a long needle into the tumor to collect a sample of cells."

Masses.

"However," Dr. Foxman crossed his arms and leaned forward on the desk, "in your case, we'd rather not. You see, Mr. Bean, I'm afraid it's too late. It's already spread. I'm terribly sorry to have to tell you this, but what we've found in your lymph nodes confirms . . ."

Fear. It should have been Len's first thought. Complete and utter terror that his time on earth was coming to an end and he was to go on to the very least understood place known—or unknown—to humankind.

But he didn't feel fear.

Sadness, even, might have made more sense. He should have wept perhaps, about the unfairness of receiving a death sentence barely a third of the way into what he'd always believed would amount to a rather lengthy sojourn.

But there was no sadness. Not right away.

The feeling that permeated his being was unmistakable out-rage, he thought, as puddle water seeped through his leather shoes. The savagery of the day's weather now made sense. It may not have played a hand in orchestrating the . . . masses inside Len's head but it flaunted its derision by saturating him in what suddenly appeared to be a vicious, utterly unbecoming, daylong neener-neener.

". . . not entirely sure why such things happen to otherwise healthy individuals . . ."

A quiet roar rushed through Len's head. The neurologist and his file folder suddenly seemed far away as Len's chair hurtled backward. Slivers of his life flew past him—the framed map across from his office desk, the sandwich he'd eaten in the car on the way over, his mother's favorite tea towel, Rachel's laugh lines.

Olivia.

". . . we've found that while many patients choose to fight it as long as they're able, in your case we'd completely understand if you chose to live out the next year or two as best you can . . ."

Oh God. Olivia.

PART II

CHAPTER 19

Closed

Nothing, anywhere, will bring you more joy or more anguish.

—RACHEL BERMAN, *Perfect Parent* magazine

Rachel laid her head in her hands, hunched over the kitchen table. She'd barely slept. For the first time in years, she had the dream again—the one where she was holding Hannah as a newborn and put her down in the grocery cart while she reached for her wallet. When she looked back, Hannah was gone. Rachel tried to run, tried to scream, but no sound came out. Eventually, a woman holding Hannah walked toward Rachel, smiling. She said, "Look at my baby. Isn't she beautiful? I gave birth to her." It should have been easy for Rachel to lunge forward and grab her daughter, but she was never able to move her arms or legs, never able to make a sound.

She looked at the clock on the stove. 8:20. She despised school holidays. Surely to God someone had realized by now that nearly every parent in the country had a job to go to and didn't have the luxury of staying home every time the teachers' union elected to hold a meeting during school hours.

Technically, Janie and Dustin could be left on their own, Janie being fourteen. But the truth was, Rachel wouldn't get a lick of work done worrying what sort of trouble they'd get themselves into over a nine-hour stretch. Leaving them at bedtime was far simpler—no meals were involved and they weren't nearly as fresh and rested.

The front door thumped shut and footsteps headed toward the kitchen.

"Mother?" called Rachel.

Piper breezed into the room in white yoga pants and a hot yellow T-shirt with her shaggy-on-purpose hair pulled up into a perky ponytail. She reeked of summer breezes and vitality. A good night's sleep. Rachel glanced down at her own gray suit and wondered if she might have time at lunch to zip out and pick out a few summery outfits, then remembered she'd scheduled a midday managerial meeting to discuss layoffs. She pushed her hair off her face and gulped down her coffee.

"Hello, sweetheart," sang Piper.

"Want some coffee?"

"God, no. I don't touch it anymore. It makes me jittery."

Jittery sounded pretty good compared to what Rachel was feeling, which was more like paste. Lead. Mud. Maybe all three. "Did you see Arthur last night?"

Piper tried to hide her grin. "I did."

"And . . . ?"

"And nothing. We had Chinese for dinner, popcorn at the movie . . ." She set a few bags on the counter, her back to Rachel. "Poached eggs for breakfast."

"He stayed over?"

"I've brought some cold cuts for lunch." Piper pulled containers out of a paper bag. "Does Dustin like coleslaw?"

"Mom!"

"*I* stayed over. What on earth am I waiting for? We're both adults. Besides we're completely compatible. The man finishes my sentences." She looked at Rachel. "He has a buyer for your house."

Rachel laughed. "Oh, he does, does he?"

"An elderly couple from the Midwest. They're not concerned about erosion at all. Not at their age, being childless."

"No."

"They're very wealthy . . ."

"Forget it." Rachel scooped up her purse and placed her empty mug in the sink. "Remember, don't leave it out too long."

Piper stopped. "Leave what out?"

"The potato salad. It's going to be humid today and the air-conditioning is acting up. Just keep it in the fridge until the last minute. Is the coleslaw creamy?"

"I have absolutely no idea."

"Read the label. It'll say if there's mayonnaise in the ingredients."

Piper placed the containers in the fridge. "If there's a little mayo, we'll probably survive it."

"Don't go making me out to sound crazy. I'm just saying if it's creamy, treat it the same as the potato salad—refrigerate until the last minute. It's common sense. Salmonella is no joke."

"Just get yourself to work. I can guarantee we'll be in one piece when you return." Piper raised her eyebrows. "Salmonella-free."

Rachel peered into a canvas bag and reached inside, pulling out two DVDs, *Robin Williams Live on Broadway* and *The Shining.* "What's this?"

"Entertainment, obviously. It's supposed to rain later. You didn't think *I* was going to tell them jokes all day? Robin Williams will do a far better job."

"Mom. Dustin is twelve. He's not watching either one of these. Look, *The Shining* is rated R. And Robin Williams is rated . . ." Rachel turned the DVD over and scanned the back.

"Do you honestly think they haven't heard all this from their friends?"

Rachel put them back in the bag. "That's not the point. *The Shining* will terrify him and he'll use every bit of foul language from the other one at school. We have plenty of suitable DVDs in the drawers beneath the TV. They can choose from those."

Piper hoisted herself up onto the kitchen island and crossed her bare feet under her legs. She smiled glibly. "Hurry home, dear. We'll miss you."

The morning after her night with Hannah, Rachel had slept late. She woke up in her hospital room and looked around, blinking in the bright daylight, unable to organize her thoughts after such a deep rest. She hadn't slept well in the months of her pregnancy, even worse after Hannah was born. It was as if one of her limbs had been hacked off and was alive and well and living at the end of the corridor.

Having had a taste of her baby, or her baby having had a taste of her, Rachel wanted more. If she could see Hannah one more time, just for a moment, she'd be okay. No. That was a lie. She'd never be okay. She just wanted more. Wrapping herself in her robe, she left her room, keeping her head lowered as she passed the nurses' station. The nursery must have a window.

No one could stop a girl from looking through a window, could they?

She continued along the hall, past the private rooms filled with mothers feeding, changing, mothering their babies. Just before the end was the nursery. Sucking in her breath, she tiptoed close and saw two rows of glass bassinets offering up pink and blue bundles like éclairs in a bakeshop window. Frantically, she scanned the faces wrapped in pink. There were only five, none of them Hannah.

Her breath turned ragged. She tugged on the arm of a passing nurse. "Please. Where's Hann— Where's the baby girl with the black hair and the rosy mouth and the eyes, the silver eyes . . ."

"The one that was being adopted?"

"Yes!"

"She went home with her new parents early this morning. Left in a car seat, surrounded by toys, balloons. She's one lucky little girl."

Rachel couldn't breathe. She nearly dropped to the floor.

She'd missed her last chance. Slept right through it.

Late afternoon sunlight settled across Rachel's desk, intense enough to illuminate the VISA statement warning Rachel that her company credit card was dangerously close to exceeding its limit. Beside that was a stack of paychecks, all patiently vying for Rachel's signature. Next to the checks lay a resplendent sheet of creamy letterhead from the law offices of Kaufman, Keller and Zane, informing Rachel that her client, Irish & Lamb infant wear, one of *Perfect Parent*'s largest accounts, was breaking its advertising contract. Irish & Lamb had held the coveted inside front cover position since the days when her grandfather ran the magazine.

She dropped her head into her hands and closed her eyes. It took a special kind of person to fuck up a successful business to such an extent. She slid the papers to one side of the desk and felt a bit better. Somehow the less space her troubles occupied, the smaller they seemed.

Reaching across the desk to flick off her lamp, Rachel spotted her address book and stopped, her hand poised in midair. Forget it, she told herself. Just finish destroying your family's business and go home to Janie and Dustin.

She opened the book and flipped to the page lettered L. Leaside Adoption Agency. Staring at the number, she took a deep breath, then picked up the phone. She dialed, then hung up, asking herself, as she did the last time and the time before that, whether she could handle the news, good or bad. She dialed again. Maybe no news was the whole problem. Maybe if she got any news at all, she'd be able to move on.

The line rang once. Twice. Just as she started to hang up, a woman answered.

"Leaside Adoption, may I help you?"

Rachel tried to speak but nothing came out.

"Hello?" the voice said.

She cleared her throat. "Yes, hi. My name is . . ."

"Yes?"

"My name is Rachel Berman. Or it is now, anyway. It used to be Dearborn. Rachel Dearborn. Oh God. I'm sorry, I shouldn't have called."

"It's not always an easy call to make, dear. Is there something I can help you with?"

"Um, yes," Rachel said, sucking in a deep breath. "I just have a question, actually. Do mothers—birth mothers—ever get to, well, do they ever get to see the . . ." the unspoken words "little ones" brought tears to Rachel's eyes. She whispered, "the children they've given up?"

"Well, it depends on your arrangement. How long ago did—"

"Sixteen years. Her name was," Rachel paused, swallowed, "Baby Girl Dearborn. I was told it was a closed adoption, but I was allowed to send a letter once."

"You sent a letter?" the woman's voice perked up. "Maybe you have extra privileges. Did you check in to see if your child responded?"

"Well, no." Rachel leaned forward on her desk. "I was going to check in. But then I just, I don't know, I was afraid . . ."

"Of course. But sometimes, if both parties agree, you can communicate through the agency, which might be the case for you. Let's just see. Your child's birth date, please?"

Rachel gave her the information and listened to classical music while on hold. She forced herself to breathe.

The woman was back. "Miss Dearborn?"

"Yes?"

"I've got your file here . . ." Rachel could hear papers shuffling around. "Oh," she said, before pausing too long. "Oh dear. I'm sorry. The letter you wrote is still in the file. Which means the parents refused to accept it. Many parents won't take a thing from the birth mother."

"But, all I said in it was that I loved her. I'm no kind of threat, believe me. All I wanted was for her to know it wasn't an easy decision for me. An adopted child needs to know that."

"I know, dear. She can see it when she's eighteen, if she chooses. That's not too far off."

"No," Rachel said. "She's, she's mentally disabled. I don't know how badly, but no matter what the law says, she'd probably need her parents' help to find me."

"I see. And they don't want contact. I wish I could be more helpful, but there's nothing I can do. The best thing for you, love, is to just move on." The woman pushed out a heavy sigh. "I don't suppose one ever fully recovers from such a thing."

"No," Rachel said, her voice splintered. "I don't suppose one does."

CHAPTER 20

"Holidays in the Sun"

—Sex Pistols

Janie set the ancient hedge clippers to snip a long branch, but the rusted blades were too dull to penetrate. Instead of snapping cleanly and dropping to the grass, the branch splintered and flattened into a mushy center where the blades became wedged in the pulpy wood. Sweat rolled into her eyes. She dropped the clippers to the ground and used her shirt to wipe her face. It had to be ninety degrees in the mid-June sun. Janie looked over at her mother, cool and comfortable in the shade, snipping around deep purple lilac blooms. "Mom, do you want to switch places yet?"

Rachel looked up at the lineup of shaggy dogwood bushes stretching all the way to the bluffs and shook her head. "Let's wait until we get halfway along, then we'll switch."

Great. Janie picked up her shears and hacked uselessly at the next branch.

"There's a phone message for you in the kitchen," said Rachel. "Did you see it?"

"From who?"

Rachel laughed, wiping her face on her sleeve. "It was kind of cute, actually. She asked if you could come for a sleepover."

"Who?"

"Len's daughter. Olivia."

"Holy shit." Janie dropped the clippers under the bush. "I'm nice to her for half an hour and she thinks we're best friends."

"First of all, watch your mouth or you'll be grounded. And second, lighten up on Olivia. She hasn't had an easy life. Len says she gets picked on at school."

"Who doesn't?" As she reached for her clippers, Janie spotted someone next door, dipping her toe into the pool. But not just any someone. Tabitha. And not just any Tabitha. Tabitha in a bikini.

"Hey Tab," Janie called through the bushes, waving her cutters. "Over here!"

Tabitha looked up, smiled. She made her way toward the bush and parted the leaves. "Hey!"

"Going swimming?"

She shrugged. "Nothing else to do on a Sunday."

"Yeah. Unless your mother's using you as cheap labor. *Free* labor."

Tabitha poked her head through the bush and looked around. "Whoa."

Janie nodded.

"Brutal."

"Yeah." Janie motioned toward some men digging in the garden, by the deep end of the pool. "What's going on?"

"My mom's getting some garden work done. A new patio and a rock waterfall that'll pour into the pool."

"Wow," was all Janie could think of to say.

"See you." Tabitha let go of the branches and walked away. She looked back over her shoulder. "If you get done soon, come over and swim."

The clippers dropped to the ground again. Swimming with

Tabitha Carlisle? Could there be any better offer on earth? "Mom! Mom!" Janie tore over to where Rachel was working. "Tabitha just invited me swimming! I *have* to go!"

Rachel stepped back to assess Janie's progress. She crinkled her nose. "You haven't made much of an improvement with that dog-wood . . ."

"Please Mom! I'm *so* hot. I'll help you after, I promise."

"Are there any boys over there?"

"No."

"Are any boys on their way over?"

"No!"

Rachel twisted her mouth to one side. "Okay. Go. Your bathing suit is in the antique trunk on the upstairs landing. But no diving. These backyard pools aren't deep enough."

The door slammed behind her as Janie tore up the stairs and yanked open the battered trunk. She dug through last year's clothes, tossing T-shirts, shorts, and sundresses all over the hallway. Her bikini was *not* in the trunk! The only suit Janie could find was a ratty old one-piece Speedo.

Damn!

She raced into her room and looked out the window. Tabitha was making her way down the pool steps into the water. Janie yanked open her bottom dresser drawer and ferreted through the jumble until her fingers brushed against cool Lycra. Her bikini. But the whole thing was puckered and shredded at the edges. She shrieked. The bikini looked like it had been clawed apart by wild animals.

She threw open her window. "Mom," she called. "What the f— What happened to my bikini?"

Rachel shaded her eyes from the sun and squinted up at Janie. "Did you just swear again?"

"No! What happened to my bikini?"

"I don't know . . . oh yes! I'm sorry, honey. It went through the dryer with Dustin's running shoes. But don't worry, I'll take you shopping for a new one soon."

Janie slammed down the window. Shit!

Tabitha giggled from the shallow end while Janie pulled off her shorts and T-shirt. "What are you? Some kind of lifeguard?" Tabitha asked, looking at the enormous red Speedo.

"My mother destroyed my bikini in the wash." Janie rolled her eyes. "Typical."

Tabitha said nothing, just let her head drop behind her, drenching her long hair. Tabitha didn't have to say anything. Janie knew what she was thinking. She was thanking God she had a way cooler mother. The kind of mother who probably buys her daughter *three* bikinis at a time. The kind of mother who says, "Fuck the eroding shoreline" and builds a pool in her backyard. Then, Janie thought, glancing at the crew of sweaty guys digging in the garden and sneaking peeks at Tabitha, hires a team to build you a waterfall. Janie could put up with any amount of leering for her very own waterfall.

And Tabitha *had* to be thanking every god, from the ancient Greeks forward, that she had a mother with such killer genes that she could buy skimpy little bras from hot lingerie boutiques, instead of reinforced chest girdles from Sears.

Tiptoeing down the cement steps, Janie shivered. The water was freezing. Quickly, she ducked in up to her shoulders, hating the icy cold but loving being camouflaged from the neck down.

"My mom doesn't turn on the heater until the last day of school," Tabitha said, tossing Janie a purple noodle while she floated toward the deep end. "Two more weeks. I don't mind. I love the cold."

Janie dunked her head, then followed, teeth chattering. "Me too." She became aware of one of the diggers, an older balding guy with a dark tan and a scraggly beard. He eyed Tabitha as she propelled herself forward with a smoothly executed dolphin kick.

"I love swimming," Janie heard herself say.

"Are you going to Veronica's pool party tonight? *Everyone* will be there."

Veronica Hamilton was having a party and hadn't invited her? "Nah," said Janie. "I'm so over pool parties."

"Yeah, well, I'm not going either. It's my dad's weekend. He says he wants me to be there to bond with Kristina's little mucus-makers at some indoor amusement park. But what he really wants is free babysitting so he and his, his . . ."

"Babe-chick?" Janie suggested.

Tabitha disappeared under the water, then resurfaced, grinning. "Yeah. He and his *babe-chick* can walk around holding hands and creating everlasting memories."

"Whoa," said Janie, waving her hands beneath the surface. What she said next was important. Tabitha was in a vulnerable state. She needed a friend. Someone to turn to in times of pawn-of-divorce stress. The Goddess article wouldn't help. The one and only time Janie had followed it's advice she'd been led *away* from Tabitha, the opposite of where she'd like to be.

Of course, her mother's parenting advice had worked like a charm. Janie thought back to what Rachel always said about separating battling siblings. She looked at Tabitha and squinted. "You're not going to your dad's on the same weekends he has Kristina's kids, are you?"

Tabitha nodded.

Janie threw her head back and groaned. Then, without success, attempted to shift her noodle to flatten her chest. She made a nasal buzzing noise. "Ehhh. Bad answer. Think about it. If they have all the kids on the same weekend, who do they have the next weekend?"

"No one?"

"Right. You need to divide and conquer. Do you really want your dad having forty-eight hours of uninterrupted time with the woman who trashed your family?"

"I never thought of it that way before."

"What about your mother? Does she have a hot new man?"

"Yup. Sean. But he's all right. He's in charge of our backyard remodel."

"Does he have kids too?"

"Nope."

"Lucky," said Janie. "You won't believe who my mom's dating. You know that girl who runs around school in her boot liners?"

Tabitha shrieked. "Your mom's dating Olivia Bean's dad? Oh my God!" She flopped backward and floated on her back, clutching a pink noodle and laughing. "That's so BAD!"

Okay. So maybe it wasn't the smartest thing to share. "You can't tell anyone, promise?"

"Maybe she'll become your sister and you can get matching footwear!"

That wasn't funny. Not remotely.

"At least you can find out where she gets those SpongeBob sweatpants!" Tabitha rolled over and faced Janie now, her giggles causing her to choke on water, the top edge of her bikini top being stroked by waves. "Are you messing around with me?"

Janie couldn't answer right away. She found it nearly impossible to stop the subliminal images her brain kept flashing before her eyes, especially the one where she tossed aside her Styrofoam noodle and grabbed hold of Tabitha, tickling her and getting tangled in her wet hair. "No. It's true. But you can't tell anyone."

Tabitha giggled one last time, then said. "I won't. I swear."

Okay. As Rachel would say, there was a wrong time and a right time to implement your own agenda. While a child was calm and open to negotiation was the right time. Janie yawned. "So, uh, what about next weekend, if you're around, and as bored as me, do you want to go see that slasher movie?"

"I can't," said Tabitha, gliding toward the deep end. "That's the weekend my dad's free. I need to trash it for him."

Damn it.

Under the diving board, Tabitha stopped, turned around, and looked back at Janie. The white of the board's underside made the water's turquoise glow flicker across her face. She reached up and gripped the board, her blond hair fanning out on the water's surface. Like a mermaid.

It was impossible for anyone to be that gorgeous.

Janie felt like an ogre, squinting back at Tabitha in the glaring sun, her colossal mammaries floating up to the surface, bobbing around like buoys, threatening to smother her. It would be her luck—to be suffocated by her own breasts.

Tabitha sighed. "This is boring. I should go do my geometry."

"No!" Janie treaded her way to the edge. "Let's play a game."

"All right. Truth or Dare?"

There was no way Janie was going to accept any dares in her bathing suit. "I've got a better one. Million Trillion."

"Huh?"

Janie explained the rules, which took very little time, since the only rules in existence were that you had to offer two choices and one of them had to involve a million trillion of something. At least one choice had to be horrific, the other had to be embarrassing. "It's best played in the dark," said Janie. "Locked in a closet."

Tabitha looked skeptical.

"It needs to be that dark. I play it with my brother. But we usually bring in one small penlight. We tape it to a stupid troll doll so it points straight upward. I guess that part's kind of lame."

"I used to have a troll. With green hair."

"Ours is green, too!" said Janie, encouraged by the coincidence. "We call him the Seer of All Truths. He keeps you honest."

"Sounds weird."

"It's way cooler than Truth or Dare."

Tabitha scrunched up her face like she'd smelled something rotten, then shrugged. "Whatever, okay."

Janie floated closer and whispered, "Cool. What would you rather do—open your locker right before the morning bell and have a million trillion tampons fall out, or give Ethan Beechers a blow job?" There. That was a good one.

"Eww!" Tabitha shrieked. "I have to choose one?"

Janie nodded.

"Is everyone in the hallway?"

Janie nodded again.

Water lapped against Tabitha's throat as she thought about it. "I'll have to go with Ethan. If it's as small as they say, it wouldn't take long."

Not the response Janie had been hoping for.

"My turn," said Tabitha. "What would you rather do—walk in on your own father doing it with his babe-chick or pull on a boot filled with a million trillion scorpions?"

The scorpions in the boot were a little lame, but she was still learning. "Easy. Boot. My turn." This time, no attaching Tabitha's lips to any male body parts, large or small. Janie thought for a moment. "What would you rather do—be tied to a beach chair, naked and soaked with honey, with a million trillion fire ants crawling all over you, or . . . um . . . kiss another girl?"

"Gross!" Tabitha squawked.

It seemed pretty straightforward to Janie. "Answer. And remember, the Seer of All Truths might not be here with us physically, but spiritually, he's right on the end of that diving board."

Tabitha shrugged. "Okay. Fire ants sting real bad. My cousin got bitten in Florida."

"It would probably hurt even more if they were inside your nose."

"Yeah. I guess."

Janie floated away, pretending for all the world that she didn't care. Kiss another girl. Kiss another girl. Say it!

Tabitha sighed. "Well . . . I have a big phobia about bugs, so, kiss another girl, I guess." She floated closer, squeezing her lips into a knotted smile. "Who knows? Could be kinda fun."

Beaming inside, Janie let go of the purple noodle and let herself sink down under the water. Then, when she was deep enough that she was absolutely sure she couldn't be heard, Janie Berman screamed.

CHAPTER 21

Matzo Ball Soup
at Milton Street Deli

Milton Street Deli was famous for two things. First, the tattoo on its husky owner, Saul—a near life-size pastrami on rye, complete with festive toothpick and pickle. Second, the matzo ball soup. Languishing in a broth loaded with strips of chicken, diced onions, carrots, celery, leeks, and Saul's mystery ingredient, were two matzo balls so light not only were they said to "walk on water" on top of the broth, but they dissolved the moment they touched the tongue.

It had been his parents' idea to take Len out for lunch before Olivia finished school for the summer. They'd seen him twice since . . . the verdict, both times with their granddaughter flitting in and out of the room. Not that it was a bad thing. With Olivia around, Grace and Henry had been forced to hold their emotions tight— Len didn't think he could have taken anything beyond the looks of horror on their faces.

It was what had stopped him, many times over, from telling Rachel. He loved the way she looked at him—sly, sexy, loving, admiring—did he really want that to change? For her to look at him with pity? Or, worse, continue *seeing* him out of pity? The thought of it made him sick.

He couldn't remember exactly how he'd broken it to his parents. On the way over to their condo, he'd analyzed a slew of possibilities—start by saying he'd had a wonderful life? Or begin with the headaches and launch right into test results, using dispassionate medical terminology? Lay out the prognosis as a simple fact? In the end it just came out, quite unremarkably.

One minute he was sitting in a chair asking if it was okay that Olivia watch TV in their bedroom. The next minute he'd said it. His mother clutched her throat. His father set down his pipe. "No," Grace said, her face drained of blood.

"Are they sure?" asked Henry.

Before Len could answer, Olivia raced into the room, holding *People* magazine over her head. She parked herself on the floor nearby and flipped through the pages.

Grace muttered, "How long?"

"One to two years," Len said.

Henry dropped his head into his hands. "I'm canceling the cruise."

"No," said Len. "Don't cancel. You'll be back in a few weeks—"

"What's a cruise?" asked Olivia.

Henry and Grace didn't speak. Len said, "A cruise is a big ship. It's going to take Grandma and Grandpa around Europe soon. Portugal, Italy . . ."

"We're staying," said Grace.

"We're staying," said Henry.

"Italy?" Olivia shrieked. "There's rats there. Rats climbed onto a ship from Italy in 1347 and they were infested with diseases."

Grace said, "Maybe we should go into the other room . . . ?"

"Maybe you'll get to have rats right on your ship. They can get into your room through a hole," chirped Olivia. Then, without warning, she scampered out of the room and into the kitchen. They heard the sound of her rooting through the fridge.

"How long have you known?" asked Henry.

"Not long. A couple of weeks."

"But there has to be some kind of treatment. What are they going to do for you?" asked Grace.

"It's gone too far."

"I don't believe it," she said. She looked at Henry. "We'll get a second opinion. We have some very renowned doctors at the club."

"This isn't the kind of thing you take lying down," Henry said. "You can fight this, Len. We'll fight it with you."

"Roof rats climb into really high up buildings," Olivia announced as she came back into the room with a mouthful of apple. She wandered to the window and looked down. "Just like this one. So if you don't find any on the boat, you'll probably get one at your apartment anyway. And *rattus rattus* can fall twenty-five feet without dying or exploding. But you have to remember to access to water him every single solitary day . . ."

Grace put her arms around Len, her hands caressing the back of his head. He could feel her thin body heave with sobs.

"And he has about thirty-five to a hundred and eighty droppings in one day . . . what's Grandma doing?"

Henry stood up fast. He blew his nose and tucked the tissue into his pocket. "What about mice, Olivia? Think you can identify their droppings?"

Olivia looked as if she'd been handed a ticket to Disneyland. "Sure!"

"Come back into the kitchen," Henry said, holding out his hand. "I need your rat researcher opinion about something I found under the sink."

Olivia scrambled off the couch and followed her grandfather. "When the droppings are real fresh, they're all shiny, but old droppings . . ." They disappeared into the kitchen.

Grace pulled back from Len and glanced after them, "Does she know?"

Len shook his head.

Grace smiled through her tears. "She's such a good girl." Cupping his face with her hand, she added, "And you're a good boy."

Milton Street Deli was unusually quiet for a weekday lunch hour. Saul himself was out from behind the deli counter. "Ahh, the Bean family," he said as he approached, pulling a pencil from behind his ear and a notepad from his shirt pocket. "My favorite legume."

No one at the table spoke. Eventually, Henry said, "Just soup for us, Saul. And coffee."

Shaking his head, Saul muttered, "Oy. At this rate, I'll never retire." He parked his pencil and disappeared.

"So?" said Henry. "What did Doctor Peterson say?" Dr. Keith Peterson, a well-respected neurologist, was a close relation of Marshall Peterson, the golf club treasurer. He'd agreed to offer Len a second opinion.

"He agreed with Dr. Foxman."

Grace and Henry were quiet for a moment, absorbing the dissolution of their last hope. "He's absolutely sure?" asked Henry.

Len fiddled with his dirty silverware and nodded, forcing himself not to rub the side of his head, where the pain was pulsating in time with Rod Stewart's "Do You Think I'm Sexy?" which was pumping through the air at the deli. He was careful never to touch his head in front of his mother, not even to scratch. It sent her into a pointless panic.

"Your father and I have been thinking, talking," said Grace. "We want you to know that Olivia will be just fine. We'll raise her the very same way we raised you. She'll never want for anything. She'll never feel unloved. You need to know that."

Len turned his attention to the ketchup bottle now, tearing at the label. They hadn't discussed Olivia until this moment. He'd been hoping they were just avoiding it. They couldn't handle their granddaughter for half a day. Imagine what a lifetime would do to them. Worse, what it would do to Olivia. "Mom, I know you love her—"

"We were thinking you should probably move her in early—and you, too, of course—so that way you'll . . . so there'll be a smooth transition. It might be less disruptive than"—Grace paused, unfolded her paper napkin, and spread it over her lap—"than waiting."

"I don't know," Len said. "I still haven't worked anything out—"

"What's there to work out?" asked Henry. "Virginia's parents, may they rest in peace, aren't an option."

Grace shook her head. "Terrible thing, that. I'll never fly in a private plane again. Never."

Henry tapped his pipe on the table, then looked at Len. "You have someone else in mind?"

"No. But—"

"I've already cleared out my sewing room," said Grace. "It will be her room completely. We'll have it painted in her favorite color."

"Mom, I love you for offering. But that would mean switching schools. Not good for a child like Olivia. She can stay at Wilton until . . ." He'd been about to say "college."

Henry said, "That's what we wanted to discuss."

Grace jumped forward in her seat, the table seeming to cut her in half. "We've found a lovely school for her. It's called the Beacon Institute and it's less than an hour away."

Len pushed the ketchup aside. "I know all about Beacon. It's not right for Olivia."

Henry said, "It's perfect for her. It's a special-needs school. We drove out there last week and spoke to the headmaster. She's waiting for you to call—"

"Olivia's not going to Beacon."

"It's one of the finest special-needs schools in the country, Len," Grace assured him. "They really prepare these kids for independent living."

Len rolled his eyes. "I checked it out years ago. The program runs seven days a week, from nine in the morning until evening, with a fifty-minute bus ride tacked on both ends . . ."

"We weren't going to send our granddaughter on the bus," said Henry. "We'd drive her ourselves. Hell, we'd move closer to the institute if it would make things easier."

"I'm sorry. I know you mean well, but Olivia's not going to attend an institute. It's the very opposite of what she needs."

"Darling," said Grace, laying her hand on Len's, "this just might be the most perfect solution we're going to find."

CHAPTER 22

"Behind the Door"

—Circle Jerks

On Monday morning, the last week of school, wearing the school's mandatory gray Wilton sweatshirt, Janie guarded her position of dead last in a line of sweaty eighth-grade girls jogging through the woods. If Monica Larson slowed down, Janie slowed down more. If the depressed chick—the one who sewed her own clothes with her eyes closed—in front of Monica stopped to retie her shoe, Janie stopped to retie both.

At the very back of the line, you could see which skinny girl had the worst cellulite. You could take extra walk breaks without the girl behind you rolling her eyes and passing you by in an athletic huff. And, best of all, if you fell really far back, you could wait to pass the pile of mossy logs, cut to the right, and bypass the whole gaggle of them. You could slash your woodland climb in half, coming out on the soccer field at the place where everyone breaks apart and sprints to the gym doors anyway. So no one notices you totally cheated.

Janie burst into the gym in fourth place and low-fived Ms. Dawes, the gym teacher, who said, "Nice work, Berman. See what happens when you put forth a little effort?"

Janie despised long-distance running almost as much as short-distance running. Running was for lean, competitive types. Ms. Dawes barked at the girls to grab a mat and cool down. As Janie dragged her mat as far away from the gym teacher as possible, she noticed Dustin and his friends hovering around a group of younger girls by the gigantic, folded-up accordion divider that halved the gym during team sports. She turned around and let her mat slap down onto the varnished floor before climbing down onto her knees and flopping on top of it. While she lay on her stomach, she tried not to look at Tabitha, all the way at the other end of the room, reaching forward to touch her toes.

Out of the corner of her eye, she saw a blond girl push a pony-tailed girl from the herd of Dustin-infested middle-graders. The blond waved the other girl to keep walking. As the kid ambled down the center of the gym, Janie looked again. Shit. It was Olivia, and she was headed straight for Janie's mat. Janie scrambled into position and stretched down over her legs, letting her hair mask her face.

Please turn around, Olivia, she pleaded silently. Please!

With her nose practically touching her knees—a gymnastic undertaking she'd never have been able to achieve without the looming threat of humiliation—Janie listened as the girl's footsteps passed right by. Thank God, she thought. She collapsed sideways onto her mat to see Olivia heading past the eighth-grade girls and straight across the gym floor to where the eighth-grade boys were doing sit-ups. She stopped in front of Cody Donovan—Tabitha's best friend's ex-boyfriend.

Positioned directly in front of him, Olivia looked like she was about to burst. Her mouth broke into a big, toothy grin and she said, "Yes."

Cody sneered and glanced around, to show any and all persons who might think otherwise that he was in no way condoning this unauthorized approach. "Yes what?"

Olivia began stepping from one foot to the other, tugging a clump of hair out of her ponytail. "They . . ." she pointed back toward the kids in the doorway—all of whom were purple with laughter. "They said you wanted me to be your friend. They gave me your note." She pulled a balled-up paper from her pocket and stretched it open as a ripple of giggles billowed across the girls' side of the gym.

"What's going on over there?" called Ms. Dawes, climbing off her mat and marching toward Cody.

Olivia looked up. "I'm just talking to my friend."

The gym roared. Laughter bounced off the painted cinder-block walls and the wooden benches. It thumped off the floors, hit the ceiling, and rushed back down like a tornado, wrapping itself around Olivia's little body. She began to whirl, one hand yanking at her hair, the other hand clutching the note to her chest, blinking back tears.

Cody snatched up the paper and examined it. "It's not from me." He crumpled it up and threw it toward the younger girls. "Sorry, sweet stuff. I'm not your friend. Come back in a few years and we'll talk. More than talk."

Just before Ms. Dawes reached her, Olivia—face twisted and red—spun around and tore out of the gym, pushing through the crowd of kids, who only laughed harder when they realized the child had gone into the boys' locker room.

Little shits, thought Janie.

She jumped off her mat and raced after Olivia. With her fore-arms held high, she barreled through the fifth- and sixth-grade nothings, knocking Dustin to the ground. "Why can't you little ass-holes leave her alone?"

She burst through the still-swinging door to the nearly empty boys' locker room and found Olivia in a rumpled heap on a stack of discarded towels, sobbing and rocking herself back and forth. She touched the child's shoulder. Olivia startled, spinning around, then smiled wretchedly when she saw Janie. She pulled herself to her feet, exposing a large wet spot down one leg of her sweatpants, and leaped forward. She locked her damp little body onto Janie's.

Janie held her. A group of seventh-grade boys came in, needling her for trespassing, but that Janie could take. She refused, however, to let them see Olivia's tears. Standing between Olivia and the boys, she peeled off her sweatshirt and tugged it over the girl's head, pulling it low to hide her pants until Janie could get her to the office. Then, with only her strapping bra and damp white undershirt to hide behind, Janie took the girl's small hand and marched out of the locker room.

Leaving Olivia in the office secretaries' maternal hands, Janie swung into the hallway and came face-to-face with a group of boys leaning against the wall.

"Nice superhero-ing, Berman," said Ritchie, a ninth-grader who hit six feet in seventh grade and had yet to show any signs of leveling off. "Too bad your cape got piss all over it."

Cody Donovan pushed himself off the wall and looked her over with a predatory grin. "Undershirts are better anyway. Especially on you." His friends milled around him, snickering.

Janie spotted Tabitha and Charlotte heading toward the office. Not good. She definitely did not want Tabitha to see her being victimized. Quickly, she ducked into the girls' bathroom and locked herself in the last stall. She listened while the door swung open again and, of all people, Tabitha and Charlotte came in behind her.

"God, that Ritchie's hot!" said Charlotte, making purse-clicking sounds over by the sink.

"You think?" asked Tabitha. "He's too tall for me. How would you make out with him? Standing on Cody's shoulders?"

Charlotte laughed. "Cody's got to be good for something."

"I want someone shorter. Closer to my height."

Holding her breath, Janie stared at the inside of the stall door, covered in graffiti: Jessie B. sucks toes, Sierra Hertzman was going to marry her boyfriend Brad (who'd been cheating with Emily Waldron for a week now), Dean Reiser's cell phone was "filming you now."

"Ugh, you're *so* predictable," said Charlotte. "Knowing you, you'll probably marry the boy next door."

"I seriously doubt it. The boy next door to me is about twelve. I'd be better off marrying his sister." They walked out giggling.

A grin spread across Janie's face. She threw her arms above her head and cheered in silence, then reached for a pen lying on the floor beside the toilet and hunted for blank space on the stall door. She scrawled "JB + TC" and wrapped it in a heart. Stepping back from her handiwork, she frowned. The letters came out great, but the heart twisted like a jagged coat hanger at the bottom.

CHAPTER 23

What to Do with Bedlam
and Delight

*Release yourself from guilt. Every parenting decision you've
made has been born of best intentions.*

—RACHEL BERMAN, *Perfect Parent* magazine

Rachel rang the doorbell for the third time. Still no answer.
Strange, since Len's Audi was in the driveway and she could
hear the Doors playing from inside the house. She pressed her face
to the window and stared in at the empty living room.

"No one's here," said Dustin. "Let's go home."

"No way, pal. You're not getting off that easily." Rachel had
received a phone call from the school the night prior, informing
her of Dustin's satellite participation in a prank involving Olivia.
"They're probably out back."

With Dustin dragging his feet behind her, she led the way
toward the backyard along a stony path canopied with birch trees.
What was once probably a lovingly cared-for shade garden, complete with glorious hostas and ferns, now ran riotous with weeds,

some of which were tall enough to be saplings. Broken branches lay strewn across the path. Still, the overall effect was a dreamlike combination of bedlam and delight.

In the equally shady, equally charming, and equally unkempt backyard, Rachel found Len sitting on a weathered Adirondack chair, staring into space. Behind him, the sun was dipping down below the line of fir trees along the western edge of his property.

"Hey there," she called out.

Len smiled, sort of, and stood up, greeting her with a discreet kiss on the cheek.

Rachel waved Dustin over. "I've got someone here who has something to say to a certain someone else," she said, nodding toward Olivia, who, she'd just noticed, was tramping through a bed of wildflowers, wearing plaid shorts and what could only be her father's winter boots. Her arms and legs were covered in mud. "Is it all right that Olivia does that?" she asked. "Stomp through your flowers like that?"

Len glanced at his daughter and sniffed. "Oh. Yeah. We don't care much about those."

"Olivia," Rachel called. "Come on over and see Dustin. He has something to say to you."

Olivia turned and her face lit up. She came bounding, crashing through a patch of red poppies, sending delicate crimson petals fluttering through the garden. Stampling across the lawn, she came to stand, a mud-and-broken-flower-encrusted swamp creature, facing Dustin. She was barely able to contain her joy.

"Hi Dustin."

Rachel nudged her son from behind. In monotone, he said, "Olivia-I'm-sorry-I-made-fun-of-you-in-gym-class. It-was-wrong-and-I'm-shamed—"

"*Ashamed*," Rachel corrected.

Dustin slumped his shoulders. "*Ashamed*. Can you . . ." He shot Rachel a pained look, "find it in yourself to forgive me?"

Rachel nudged Dustin again. He held out his hand for Olivia to shake.

"Okay," she chirped, ignoring the hand. She took Dustin's entire body—arms and all—and squeezed him madly, her beautiful, filthy face mashed against Dustin's white shirt, her eyes shut tight, face dreamy.

Dustin looked down at his muddy arms and groaned, "*Mom.*"

It was the hug that kept on hugging. Unsure how to stop it, Rachel glanced at Len, who watched the whole thing with a miserable smile. Finally, Rachel said, "Olivia, do you have any rodent books in your room to show Dustin?"

Olivia released her soiled hostage and trotted toward the house, babbling something about the next day hopefully being her birthday.

"I'll go with her if you agree to skate camp," said Dustin.

"That's bribery," said Rachel.

Len looked up. "Extortion, actually."

"Extortion." Rachel spun Dustin around to face the house and nudged him. "Now go!"

Dustin grumbled something Rachel was glad she couldn't hear as he trudged toward the back door, flicking mud from his arms.

After a longer kiss, Rachel trotted into Len's kitchen to dig up some wine. She pulled two cloudy glasses from a cupboard and leaned across the paper- and file-strewn kitchen table for a bottle of pinot noir. Something fluttered off the table, so she set the bottle down and picked up a small photograph from the floor. It was a black-and-white picture, a young Len dressed as some sort of a monster for Halloween. "Cute," she said out loud.

The title of a document poking out of a blue file caught her eye. "This is the Last Will and Testament of Leonard Kendrick Bean." She crumpled her brow and nudged it aside with her fingernail. Beneath it was a legal-size envelope labeled "Power of Attorney."

Her pulse quickened as she noticed a memo clipped to the file. It was a note from Len to his assistant asking her to "draw these up right away."

Right away?

Certainly when Olivia was born Len and Virginia must have drawn up wills—as every other parent does, however reluctantly. And certainly he'd feel the need to update things from time to time. But not with urgency.

Her head began to swim with absurd conclusions. Could Len be dying—or, worse—planning to die? People like Len don't get sick. The guy refused mussels, for God's sake.

Here I go again, she thought. The man does a little filing, a little planning, and I'm imploding with panic. Smart people, especially smart parents without an ex-spouse around, made wills. Smart lawyers probably made wills quickly. Len was an intelligent man, and instead of planning his eulogy, she should get the hell outside and pour the guy a glass of wine.

By the time Rachel stepped back into the yard, the sky had faded to a deep indigo above the now inked-over tree line. Tiny lights in the garden, set to timers, flicked on, dotting the bushes and weeds like motionless fireflies. She sank into a wooden chair as Len reached for the corkscrew and set to work opening the bottle.

"I'm so sorry about what happened yesterday. I don't know what got into him."

The cork came out with a pop. "Well . . . kids."

"If they just stand by and watch, they're just as guilty. Dustin *knows* that."

"It's not your fault, Rachel. Forget about it. Olivia has her own way of dealing with this sort of thing . . ." As he filled the glasses, his cell phone rang from the ground by his feet. He passed Rachel her glass, sipped from his own, and checked the caller ID. He silenced the phone and tossed it back onto the grass.

"What was that?" Rachel asked.

"Nothing. The receptionist of one of my clients seems to enjoy tracking me down after hours. It's ridiculous."

"She's calling you after work? About what?"

Len waved the question away. "Nothing. Everything. Shannon calls to say a package might be late. Or a package might be early." Len chuckled into his glass. "Last week she offered to pick me up and drive me to the Audi dealer after work when my car was in for service."

"Did you let her?"

"Of course not! I had a doctor's appointment after."

"That's what stopped you?"

"No." He looked at Rachel. "I was tempted, though. She said she had a box of chocolate *ruggelah* in the backseat."

"And that's all it would take to lure you away from me? One box of melted *ruggelah*?"

"Only the chocolate kind." Reaching out to touch her arm, he trailed one finger down to her hand and picked it up. He smiled sadly. "I'd never leave you for cinnamon."

"That's comforting," said Rachel.

It wasn't all that surprising, a woman throwing herself at Len. He was a good-looking lawyer. Single. Not only that, but he was nice. Nice was getting harder and harder to find in the world. Maybe Rachel shouldn't be taking this so lightly. Especially since Len seemed . . . subdued tonight.

"You're sure you're okay with the Olivia-and-Dustin thing?" she asked.

"Cross my heart."

"So, uh, how does she get away with all this flirting—this Shannon person?" Rachel asked. "Where does she work?"

"Just over on Charleston. At an adoption agency I work with."

Rachel froze. Her hand shook so hard her wine lapped against the side of her glass. She set it down so Len wouldn't notice. Clearing her throat, she asked, "Which one?"

Len jumped forward and slapped at his arm. "Mosquito!" His eyes searched the air above his arm, as he waited for his attacker to land again.

"Which adoption agency?" she repeated.

"One of the local ones. It's called Leaside." With his palm, he smacked his arm again. "Gotcha."

Rachel could only squeeze her eyes shut and look away.

CHAPTER 24

Promiscuity Barbie

Len picked his way across the puzzle-strewn floor and informed Dr. Kate's secretary that they were somewhat early for Olivia's appointment. He found two seats next to the stately and oversized dollhouse—Olivia's favorite play area—and settled himself while his daughter dropped onto the red carpet and thrust Birthday Wishes Barbie sideways into the townhouse kitchen, a perilous environment for Barbie's exposed assets.

It seemed Barbie wasn't long for the kitchen. Olivia pulled her away from the stove and, holding the doll upright, tried to ram her into the upstairs powder room, a room cursed with an extraordinarily low ceiling, even for a dollhouse. Every week Barbie was forced to endure the same thing—being simultaneously slammed into floor and roof in Olivia's effort to squeeze the doll inside the stunted rooms.

The man next to Len chuckled. "Nonverbal LD?"

"How'd you guess?" said Len.

"I've been bringing my daughter here for eleven years. Did the same thing with her Barbies every week for six of those years. She never used to have much spatial awareness."

"Did it improve—her spatial awareness?"

The man nodded. "Sure. Or maybe she just stopped playing

with the Barbies, I can't remember." He laughed at his joke and checked his watch. "This isn't our usual day here. If she doesn't come out soon, I'll be late getting her to music class."

"She's musical, your daughter?"

"It's helped with . . . well, Dr. Kate recommended music therapy in addition to this." He lowered his voice. "Kendra had a problem with a boy in the neighborhood last year. It left her, and us, traumatized. Music helps her forget."

Len watched Olivia pull another Barbie from the bin and begin to undress her. Knowing full well it was intrusive, impertinent, he asked, "Did, uh, may I ask what happened to Kendra?"

The man frowned and tucked his magazine under his arm. "She was thirteen. He was eighteen. She had no friends her age. So when he asked her into his basement to look at his aquarium, she was thrilled." He sighed heavily. "He forced himself on her."

Len looked from the distraught father to Olivia and back again. "Is she . . . was she okay?"

"Physically."

Len's chest heaved with horror. It was his biggest fear.

A pretty teenage girl emerged from Dr. Kate's inner office. Hiding behind a curtain of brown hair and a binder covered in musical notes, she nodded to her father and hurried toward the door. Her father stood up, then turned back to Len. "You'll want to watch your little girl carefully. She's going to turn a lot of heads in a few years. They won't all belong to good people."

Len stared at Olivia, watching her rip the clothes off Dr. Kate's Barbies one by one, tossing the tiny outfits behind her on the floor. Finding the perfect guardian wasn't going to be enough. As a teenager, she'd surely walk to and from the store by herself. There would be moments, for the rest of her life, during which she'd be entirely alone. Entirely vulnerable.

He needed to protect her from the inside out.

"Olivia, sweetheart. Do we have to strip the clothing off every single doll?"

"We don't, but I do."

"You know, Daddy has a little game we might play. Is there a boy Barbie in that bin?"

Olivia reached into the box and pulled out a male doll. "He's called Ken, Dad."

"Right, Ken. I'm going to be Ken and you're going to be Barbie." He took Ken from her hands only to have her snatch him back again and set about removing his blazer.

She tugged it off one arm. "Wait till I get his clothes off. Then we'll play . . ."

"No!" Len took Ken from her busy hands and worked the jacket back on. "Ken's clothes are NOT coming off. Not now. Not ever. And while we're at it, put some clothes on Birthday Wishes Barbie."

"I like her naked."

"She will *not* be naked. She's meeting Ken!" Len dug through the bin and pulled out a doll-size shirt, a skirt, and a pair of brown boots—none of which went on easily. After nearly fracturing Barbie's arms and legs in his attempt to clothe her, he said, "There. That's better. Now she looks . . ." Actually, in her Velcro halter top, miniskirt, and thigh-high boots, she looked sluttier than she did naked, if it were possible.

Olivia grabbed Barbie by the hair and stood her on the floor, facing Ken.

"Now," Len said. "Here's the scenario. Barbie and Ken have never met. Which makes them strangers. Barbie is walking home from high school and this new boy, Ken, stops her."

"Does he go to her school? Because then he's not a stranger."

"No. Ken is Catholic. He goes to a special school on the other side of town." Len leaned closer and widened his eyes. "Or so he tells her."

"What's his favorite band?"

"Britney Spears."

Olivia made a face. "Who's his special friend?"

"Let's just start at the beginning. Barbie is walking along . . ." He nodded toward her hand for her to begin.

She pushed Barbie up close to Ken. "Hi."

Len pulled Ken away. "No! Barbie does not run up to boys like that! She's a lady."

"Then how do they meet?"

"Barbie is minding her own business like her father always taught her. Ken walks up and says hi first." He bounced Ken up and down. "Hi, I'm Ken!"

"I'm Barbie." Barbie waggled side to side.

"Hey, we live on the same street," said Ken. "That means we're neighbors."

Barbie fell over onto the carpet, then got picked up and set straight again. "That's pretty good."

Ken sidled closer, then pointed toward the dollhouse with his head. "I live right here. Do you want to come inside? I've got some Halloween candy left over. I keep it in my room."

Barbie stared straight ahead for a moment. "I can't eat Halloween candy unless my dad checks it for razor blades first."

Len slid off his chair and onto the floor. "Good, Olivia! You remembered our candy rule. This is very good!"

"*Dad.* You're supposed to be Ken! Not my dad."

"Right. Sorry." Ken touched Barbie's arm. "We don't have to eat candy. We can just listen to music and talk."

Barbie stayed perfectly still. "Your music is mainstream bullshit."

Len's mouth dropped open. As shocked as he was, he faced a dilemma. Should he scold his daughter for her filthy mouth, so she'd learn this sort of talk was unacceptable in polite society? Or commend her for refusing to allow Barbie to be hoodwinked into Ken's squalid lair? "Perfect, Olivia!" he said, pulling Ken away in his triumph. "You're not giving in to him. Good girl."

"You're supposed to be Ken!"

"Right. Let me think . . ." Len repositioned Ken in front of the house. "Barbie, do you want to come inside and see my aquarium full of fish?"

"Sure!" Barbie rocketed into the air with excitement, losing her Velcroed top in the process. Olivia bundled Ken into her Barbie-holding hand and shoved the two dolls, bare-breast-to-face, into the attic bedroom without a moment of spatial interference to slow them down.

Dr. Kate's secretary leaned across her desk. "Olivia, honey. The doctor will see you now."

Len gaped as his daughter sprung to her feet, stripped off Barbie's remaining clothes, and raced toward the inner office, swinging the imperiled doll by the hair. Ken lay perfectly still on the attic floor. Like Len, he was at a loss for words.

Olivia didn't need one guardian. She needed a whole army.

CHAPTER 25

"Moral Majority"

—DEAD KENNEDYS

Janie pulled her geometry book from her locker Friday morning, the last day of school, and caught sight of herself in the mirror she'd superglued to the inside of her locker door. She pulled out a black kohl pencil and swiped it across her lash lines, upper and lower, then smudged the lines until she looked like a rock star who'd been up all night dodging paparazzi and trashing hotel rooms.

Satisfied that her mother would freak, she slammed her locker door shut.

Olivia was on the other side.

"Hi Janie!" She wore what appeared to be inside-out Lisa Simpson pajama bottoms. Behind her stood two snickering fifth-graders. One was the blonde who set her up for humiliation in the gym.

"Olivia, you should get back to class . . ." Janie began.

"I told Callie Corbin and Samantha you're my special person and they didn't believe me," Olivia said. "They said prove it so I'm prove-itting. Proving it."

Tabitha's friend Charlotte walked by, sneering. With a stack of books clutched to her chest, she slowed down and looked, incredulous, from Janie to Olivia and back to Janie. She snorted. "Please tell me this isn't happening," she said. *"Again."* With a nauseated roll of her eyes, she walked away.

"I have to go," Janie said to Olivia.

Either Callie or Samantha, Janie had no idea which was which, broke out laughing. "I knew Janie Berman wasn't your friend, Bean!"

Janie leaned down over the blonde and hissed, "Shut the fuck up you little—"

"Tell them how we're going to have a sleepover this summer," said Olivia. "Tell them how you're just like my sister, Janie!"

The door to the girls' bathroom swung open. Tabitha Carlisle strode out into the hall, hair and hips swinging. She smiled at Janie and waved, heading straight for her.

"Olivia, you have to go. Right now," whispered Janie.

Tabitha raised her eyebrows as she surveyed the scene. She shook her head, clucking her tongue. "I don't know, Janie Berman. You're going to get a reputation if you keep this up."

"They were just leaving," Janie said.

"You toddlers are swarming my Janie," Tabitha said. "It's rude."

My Janie.

"Get lost, kiddies," Tabitha said, linking arms with Janie. "We need to talk big-girl talk."

Janie covered her chest with her books and allowed herself to be led away. With a quick glance back, she saw Callie and Samantha disappear into the stairwell. Olivia stood, motionless, for another moment, before dragging her feet toward the stairwell at the other end of the hall.

"You do realize hanging with that kid will strip you of your social life. People have barely stopped talking about the other day in the gym."

"Hanging with her?" Janie's laugh rang too shrill in the empty corridor. "I'd rather hang her."

"Mm. Anyway, your advice earlier was perfect. I totally wrecked my dad's weekend."

Olivia Bean was forgotten. For now. "Cool. I hope you messed up their alone time. All of it."

"I did. As soon as I got there, I pulled Kristina into my room and told her I—just that moment—got my first period. She spent, like, no time with my dad, other than running to the store three separate times to pick me up different sizes of pads. I kept saying I needed bigger ones. The last package they brought home was for women who'd just given birth! I told her I needed my Red Tent experience. You know, from the book? I never read it, but my mom said it's where these women with their periods meet up every month. In a tent. I told Kristina I wanted *us* to bond in a small room where we could share our hopes and dreams. Share the wonder of menses." Tabitha snickered. "You should have seen the expression on her face. She looked like she wanted to cry from happiness and throw up all at the same time."

Janie didn't know whether she was going to cry from *un*happiness or throw up. The thought of two days locked in a small room with Tabitha was almost more than she could bear. Janie forced a smile. "Perfect."

Nothing could have prepared Janie for what came next. Tabitha said, "Let's go find seats," and motioned for Janie to follow. Until then, Janie's social value to the A-listers, school royalty, had only been as the jester. She was meant to entertain the popular kids, to reinforce their own superiority—as long as Janie was around to laugh at, they'd never, ever have to laugh at themselves. And today, she was going to walk into class alongside the monarch herself, Her Royal Highness, Tabitha Carlisle.

Barely daring to breathe, Janie tiptoed inside and slipped into a seat next to Tabitha and Charlotte, and directly behind Cody Donovan.

Cody spun around just as Tabitha announced, "Janie's been teaching me the coolest things . . ." and proceeded to explain Janie's version of her mother's lame parenting advice.

When she was finished, Cody grinned his approval, looking Janie up and down. "That's some sweet stuff, Berman," he said. "Too bad school's almost over. I might need you to discipline me one day. Nothing major, you know, a little spank here and there."

Charlotte said, "I don't think we need to hear that so early in the morning, Donovan."

Janie looked down at her pencil, still feeling the heat of Cody's stare.

"Not a problem," he said lazily. "I've got all summer to expose myself to Janie."

Revolting, Janie thought. Still, it felt so fucking good to be worthy of more than a laugh. Feeling her cheeks burn, she opened her binder and decided maybe, just maybe, things were looking up.

"What's with you and Inside Out Girl, anyway?" asked Charlotte.

Janie laughed. "*Absolutely* nothing."

"Good," Tabitha said before spinning around and picking up her pencil.

CHAPTER 26

Inexplicable

The Peytons didn't look nearly old enough to be parents. Both of them wore sneakers. Hers were fresh-from-the-box white, perhaps in an attempt to create the impression that she was fully capable of making a wholesome home for nine-year-old Liam, the child they'd been waiting months to adopt. Her husband's sneakers spoke less of his hopes and dreams and more of the work he did—contracting—covered as they were with paint splatters and grease. The couple might not have had an abundance of money, but Len had sensed when they walked into his office nine months ago that they would be ideal parents.

Tammy had been adopted at nine herself, and made it her lifelong goal to do the same for another child the moment she was able. She and Philip were waiting to hear that Liam's adoption was final.

Len's words were going to crush them.

"We've got the whole evening planned," said Philip, bouncing his palms against the arms of the chair. Through the glass window behind Philip, Len could see coworkers charging past in a blur of conservative suits and tidy blouses—a bustling highway of finely cut dark wool and crisp cotton that stood in sharp contrast to Philip's faded but carefully ironed Old Navy T-shirt. "First we'll take

Liam home," Philip continued, "let him see his room and unpack his things, then we'll take him to Roxborough Station for burgers. Then—"

"I'm afraid we have a problem," Len said.

The light in their faces blew out. Tammy's eyes grew wide. She sat perfectly still. "What kind of problem?"

"The biological father has stepped in." Len softened his voice. "He wants custody of Liam."

Tammy reached for Philip's hand. She looked as if an eighteen-wheeler had just crashed through the shelving behind Len's desk. Philip leaned forward. His right hand curled in and out of a fist. "But everything's in place. His room is ready, we've talked to the school . . ."

"It's not that simple," Len said. "His father has parental rights. There would be a long court battle, with enormous expenses—this thing could drag out for months. And Liam wouldn't be living with you during this process. He'd be with his father."

"I don't care," said Tammy, her eyes shimmering with unshed tears. "I want to fight for him."

"I don't recommend it," said Len.

"I'm with Tammy," said Philip. "We want what's best for Liam. And that's us."

Len leaned forward on his desk. He rubbed the side of his head, where he felt the pinprick starting. "I'm so sorry to have to tell you this. But Liam wants to live with his natural father."

With Olivia finally in bed for the night and his head throbbing, Len wandered into the living room and, without turning on the lights, lowered himself onto the couch. Rain was bucketing down from the sky, creating a misty halo around the glow of the streetlamps.

He felt like shit. The Peytons had been inconsolable, not at all interested in the files of the other children Len had researched before their meeting.

Outside, something moved in the dark. Len leaned forward. A woman wandered in front of his house—no umbrella, no rain hat—just ambled along, looking down at her shoes, as if the cold rain wasn't troublesome in the slightest.

He set down his drink and crossed the room to the window. The woman spun around in front of his driveway and stood perfectly still. For the first time, he could see her face.

Rachel.

He rushed to the front door and pulled it open to find her stepping onto his straw mat, water dribbling down her cheeks. She was shivering. Without a word, he pulled her inside and shut the door.

Ten minutes later, Rachel was sitting cross-legged in Len's living room with a dry towel wrapped around her shoulders. He handed her a glass of red wine and she sipped hungrily. Despite Len's questions, she still hadn't spoken.

Len dropped down onto the carpet and turned to Rachel. She scrubbed her hair with the towel, then sipped again.

Rachel looked up. "I think she'd do anything for you."

"Who?"

"Shannon." Rachel wrapped her hands around her glass and watched the liquid swirl. "From the adoption agency."

"All this," he gestured toward her wet head, the rain outside, "is about Shannon? Surely you can't be jealous of—"

"There's something I haven't told you," she said. She hugged her knees to her chest and told him about Hannah. Over the first glass of cabernet, she told him about the torn condom, about the pregnancy, about the hospital tests and Piper's insistence that Rachel keep her life sparkling and shiny by giving up Hannah for adoption through an agency called Leaside. Over the second, she told him about the night with Hannah and Margaret and the reason she'd never been able to sleep late, ever again.

Len listened to the whole story in near-silence. He reached out and set his hand on her forearm. "And you've lived with this for sixteen years?"

Rachel nodded.

"God, you're strong."

"Strong? I handed my baby to the nurse like I was handing her a stack of folded linens. Where's the strength in that?"

"In getting out of bed each morning," he said, "raising those two beautiful children of yours. I don't think I could have done it."

"But you're raising Olivia all by yourself. You're doing the right thing. The *only* thing. You can live the rest of your life content. Proud."

He smiled sadly. The rest of his life was not something he was content with. "Have you contacted Hannah?"

"I've tried. It's a closed adoption."

"Ah."

"But now there's this Shannon. It's perfect. You can ask her to look something up. She'll give you Hannah's last name and her address. She'd do it for you in a heartbeat! All you have to do is ask."

"But, Rachel, I can't. I can't do that. It would be unethical. I could get in serious trouble . . ."

"It's a tiny name. How would anyone find out?"

"Rachel . . ."

"She'd never even question it. She's the receptionist, she looks up names for people all day long. No one would get hurt. I'm not going to bother Hannah's family, or, or make off with her in the night. I just want to know where she is. I need to know she's okay."

"I'm sorry," he said. "I'd do anything I could for you, but not this. I've never abused my client relationships, ever. It's just not something I could do. Please understand."

She pulled away and stared into the blackened fireplace. Then turned to him, eyes cold. "I'd do it for you without question."

"You're not a lawyer . . ."

She laughed angrily. "*That's* not a good argument!"

"There happen to be a great many lawyers who actually care about the oaths they've taken."

Rachel stood up, dropping the towel to the ground. She marched into the hall, pulled her wet jacket from the coat rack, and opened the front door.

Len got up and followed. "Rachel . . ."

When she looked back, her face was stony. "Until I had Hannah, I thought I knew what love was." She blinked. "I didn't. And of course I felt it again when Janie was born, and Dusty. But what a parent feels for a special child—it's inexplicable. Hannah was so unique, so dependent, so completely defenseless. The thought of her being out there in the world without me . . . it still scares me to death. You, of all people, should understand."

Len felt his throat tighten. "I do. More than you know."

She stared at him for a moment, silent. Then marched out the door, slamming it behind her.

CHAPTER 27

"Cesspools in Eden"

—DEAD KENNEDYS

Two weeks into summer vacation, shopping bag knocking against her bare legs, Janie watched the city bus pull away as she approached the stop. Then, the bus slowed momentarily and, certain the driver had seen her, Janie broke into a run.

Bikini shopping could not have been more depressing. An hour and a half in front of a full-length smoked mirror designed to visually soften the jiggly bits that the glaring overhead lighting worked so hard to accentuate. She must have tried on every bathing suit in the store, finally settling for a racy black tankini, because the high-cut legs made her thighs look longer and the reinforced top might actually keep her chest from becoming its own personal flotation device.

The bus picked up speed. Janie ran toward it, shouting, "Hey!" and waving her free arm. But it blew right past in a cloud of exhaust.

Shit. That was the one forty-nine. Another bus wouldn't come for thirty-three minutes. She trudged down a short slope to cross under the roaring freeway overpass. It would be a long, dirty walk home.

At the bottom of a stairway, she spotted a few guys huddled over a hash pipe. She slowed for a moment, contemplated going back to the bus stop, but one of the guys looked up and saw her. Cody Donovan. How embarrassing. With no choice now but to continue, she held her chin high and debated saying hello—a daring move she'd never have attempted a month ago—or pretending to be fascinated by something in her bag.

"Hey, Berman," called Cody, waving her over. His friends looked up and grinned—quite possibly happy to see her.

"Hey." She sashayed closer, hiding her Island Bikinis bag behind her legs. "Are you having as shitty a summer as me?"

They all nodded, laughed, passed the pipe around the circle.

"My parents wanted me to go on a trail ride for the day," said Bruce Weiner. "That piece-of-crap flytrap along the freeway." The guys broke out laughing, nudging and bumping into Bruce. "Horses ready for the dog-food factory."

"Never mind," Janie said, "it would have been mostly girls there." She knew this for a fact. And if Tabitha hadn't announced she was staying home by the pool all weekend, Janie might have considered signing up for a ride herself.

Bruce thought about this. "This chick's a genius," he said, thrusting the pipe in the air. "Berman for student body president!"

Robert giggled. "I'll vote for that body!"

Janie's spirits reeled. Sure, they were guys. But not even a stray dog had paid her any attention all year. She'd forgotten how good it felt to be wanted again.

Cody moved her away from the others. "I have to apologize for my moronic friends. They're, uh, basically they're morons. A lady like you deserves a higher-quality guy. A man." With a sweep of his hand, he gestured toward himself.

"I better go before my mom drags the river."

"Wait," he said. "I'm having a weekend-long party later this summer. My parents are going away. You should come by. Seventy-six Denby Drive." He pulled a pen out of his back pocket and gave it to her, holding out his hand as a paper. "Give me your number and I'll call you when I know the day."

She smiled, trying her best to appear detached. Aloof. Like it wasn't the one and only party invitation she'd had all year. Dropping her bag to the ground, she took the pen with one hand and his sweaty palm with the other, to steady it, and scrawled the number. Not one of these guys realized how very badly Janie *didn't* want them. But none of that mattered. What mattered was that, finally, *finally*, someone seemed to want her.

Janie hugged her bag to her chest and smiled to herself as she turned to head home.

"Hey, Berman," Cody called. "Just don't bring that little upside down kid. You'll be too busy for super-heroing."

CHAPTER 28

Friday Night at the Galaxy Bowl

*Let's face it. Life can get distracting, especially for parents.
But time with a child is precious and needs to be guarded.
When faced with a distraction, remind yourself that your
child lives in the moment and needs all your attention alongside him.*

—RACHEL BERMAN, *Perfect Parent* magazine

Friday evening, as Mindy tiptoed into Rachel's office, an older woman carrying a desk lamp walked out. They both smiled and offered bumbling apologies for nearly colliding, and the older woman slipped into the hall.

Mindy plopped herself into a chair. "You did it?"

Rachel nodded. "The woman's been here thirty-five years, started out as my father's assistant, and I just let her go." Pulling out a handful of tissues, Rachel dabbed her eyes. "She must hate me. I gave her my dad's lamp—some compensation, huh?"

Mindy sighed. "Rachel, slow down."

Rachel sucked in a fluttery breath. "Everyone's going to be looking over their shoulders now. Wondering who's next."

"Monica was going to retire soon anyway. Everyone knows that," Mindy said.

"You don't understand. I haven't told anyone yet, not even my mother, but our holiday party, we can't do it this year. There's not enough money."

"Seriously? That's when—"

Rachel shook her head. "No bonuses this year."

"Wow."

The phone rang. Mindy reached across the desk and picked up. "*Perfect Parent*." Mindy twisted her mouth to one side to stave off a smile. "One moment, Mrs. Dearborn, I'll see if she's still in."

Rachel shook her head and picked up her car keys, jiggling them in the air and pointing toward the door.

"Oh, you know what?" Mindy said into the receiver. "She's just left for the day." She paused, listening, then, after mumbling in agreement a few times, Mindy hung up and looked at Rachel. "Apparently you should have left earlier. You're meant to be meeting Len."

"Shit! I had plans with him. We were all going bowling together." Rachel pulled her purse out of her desk drawer. "I forgot to cancel."

"Cancel?"

"Long story. I better call home and tell the kids to get ready . . ."

"You're too late for that too. Your mother's driving Dustin and Janie to the bowling alley herself. Otherwise, she said, Len will think he's being stood up and she didn't raise you to stand people up." Mindy raised one eyebrow. "She makes a good point."

"Whose side are you on?"

"She also wondered aloud whether Dustin should have this forced upon him. Apparently, he's not into 'this Len person' . . ."

Rachel shook her head and walked away.

Following her out of the office, Mindy flicked off the overhead lights. "Oh, she also said if she's going to drive all the way down there, she might as well stay and play."

Rachel paused just long enough to sigh before heading out to the parking lot.

The faded sign floating above the mall entrance was in the shape of a boomerang. GALAXY BOWL was scrawled out in pink neon along the top arm; OPEN UNTIL MIDNIGHT was in red along the bottom. For as long as Rachel could remember, it had buzzed as if full of flies, most of the neon tubing having burned out long ago.

Rachel drove through a deep puddle and pulled into a parking spot to find Piper climbing out of the white Range Rover right beside her and popping open an umbrella. Dustin and Janie shot their mother aggrieved looks from the backseat.

"This is a nice surprise," said Rachel, slamming her car door and flipping up her collar in defense against the misty drizzle. She kissed Piper's cheek. "You should have brought Arthur, we could have made it a double date."

"No chance of that," said Piper. "Arthur and I broke up."

"No! He sounded so good for you."

"He was. Until he reconciled with his ex. She's five years younger than me and her daddy owns the brokerage." Piper reached inside the car for her purse. "What can I say? Men, especially older men, are bastards."

"No argument here," called Janie.

"They're obsessed with youth and money, and the more hair they lose, the worse it gets. I'm absolutely done with them. I've got my health," Piper paused to smile bravely at the kids, "and my family. I'm happy if the rest of you are happy."

Rachel waved at Janie and Dustin to get out of the car. "Well then, let's head inside and get happy." The kids didn't budge. "Come on, guys. They're waiting for us."

Janie squinted through the windshield toward the entrance, where Len waited with Olivia, who was hopping on one rain-booted foot and clasping her hands to her heart. Janie shook her head and muttered, "She's going to be *all* over me."

"Olivia?" said Rachel. "Len says she adores bowling. She won't be bothered with you. Now hurry up. I'm getting soaked."

Groaning, Janie poured herself out of the car, pulled her jean jacket over her head, and trotted behind her grandmother toward the Galaxy Bowl doorway.

"Let's move it," Rachel said to Dustin.

"Uh-uh. Not if *he's* going to be there."

"It's a game, honey. Not a wedding."

"I'll wait here."

"Dustin, you're embarrassing me. "

"I can't stand him."

Len jogged up, having left Olivia wrapped around Janie's legs and Piper under her umbrella. His half-smile told Rachel he was no more sure than she was as to where they stood after her night in the rain. He kissed her cheek, leaned down, and peered inside the car. "Don't be intimidated, Dustin. My gutter balls are legendary at this place."

Dustin let out an unimpressed huff.

"Why don't the rest of you go ahead?" Rachel whispered to Len. "Dusty and I will join you in a few minutes . . ."

Len leaned against the car door. "I've been looking forward to bowling with another guy, for a change. Come on, Dustin. Help me out."

"Please, Dustin," said Rachel. "You and I will be a team."

Dustin turned just enough to expose his profile, and picked at his grandmother's leather seat. "Give me one week of skate camp, Mom, and maybe I'll come."

"I'm *not* falling for this . . ." said Rachel.

"Please, Mom! One week. Half a week. I won't even go on the bigger half-pipes and NO rails. I promise."

"Dustin . . ."

"You know," Len said quietly, "my client and his wife just opened a skate facility. They're running a summer camp with a real focus on safety. No big equipment. It's all about technique. Technique and hot lunches." He pulled the hood of his windbreaker over his head and studied her. "Not *too* hot. Warm, really. And peanut-free. Though I can't make any promises about the grapes being sliced."

"Mom?"

Len looked at Rachel. "The guy's wife is a pediatrician."

"Mom! You have to say yes . . ."

Rachel chewed on her lip, glancing from Len to Dustin and back again. Rain trickled under her collar.

"*Please*, Mom."

"Do they have a Web site?" she asked Len.

"It's www.safeskate.com."

"You're not serious."

"I'm not," Len said, grinning. "I'll give you their phone number later. You can talk to them yourself."

She leaned down and stared at Dustin. "I'm not saying yes. But I'm not saying no."

"Seriously? Thank you SO much!"

"I can't believe I'm even considering this . . ." she said, as Dustin leaped from the car, squeezed her tight, then jogged behind Len, buzzing with camp questions.

At the doorway, Piper collapsed her umbrella and awaited her introduction. After offering up her fingertips for shaking, and informing Len it was a delight to meet him, she hung back with Rachel. Then, pulling out her Chanel lipstick, Piper whispered, "I hope for your sake he doesn't work for his ex-father-in-law like Arthur." She slipped her arm through Rachel's and watched Olivia hop backward to the doors. The child's cheeks were flushed pink from the effort, her lips a just-licked red even Chanel couldn't replicate.

"The girl's striking," said Piper as they walked. "Something of a shame, isn't it?"

"Mom. Don't start."

"I'm just saying. All that beauty going to waste."

"They'll *hear* you . . ."

Len smiled back at them as he held the dirty glass door. Olivia ran inside first, tripping over the black entry mat. "You have to picture where you want the ball to go," she said to Dustin when she righted herself. "That's the only way to bowl a strike. If you don't actually picture it, you should just give up and go pick strawberries with your grandma."

Dustin dragged his feet behind Olivia with a pained expression on his face. He looked back at Rachel, wincing at the smell inside the building. She grimaced back at him. The air was a clammy fusion of rubber mats and rental-shoe deodorizer.

"I'm on Janie and Rachel's team," Olivia chirped.

"Then I guess I'm on Len's," said Dustin, leaping into an imaginary kick flip before venturing further inside.

Rachel looked at Len, who appeared to be every bit as shocked as she was. She wished she wasn't still stewing about Shannon, she'd have loved to push the wet bangs off his forehead.

Janie walked up from behind. "This is so embarrassing." She tucked her face inside her jean jacket. "If I see one person from school, I swear to God I'm leaving."

"Let me know if you need change for the bus, honey," said Rachel.

Janie exhaled and stomped off after her brother.

"Ah, yes," Len said. "This evening should turn out ju-ust fine."

"Don't anybody look at all the birthday parties," said Olivia. "Things like that are called distractions. Athletes like me have to stay focused."

Piper looked impressed. "Sounds like you really know your stuff."

"I better," Olivia sniffed. "I've been playing bowling for three whole years. Just keep your shoulders straight. If you don't, your ball will go in the gutter. And if the thumb holes in your ball are too big, just tell me . . ." She patted her back pocket. "I got triple-sided tape."

A few minutes later, huddled around Lane Five's table—orange laminated, amoeba-shaped, and speckled with cigarette burns—they split into two teams: Olivia, Rachel, and Janie against Dustin, Piper, and Len. After lacing up her bowling shoes—half-burgundy, half-navy, with neon-green laces—Janie caught sight of tenth-grader Kyle Winters and his friends from school, babbled something about Kyle being Cody something-or-other's cousin, and went into hiding. Out came her sunglasses and her brother's beanie. She huddled under their wet raincoats and all but made herself invisible, calling out, "You people have no idea how NOT here I am."

Rachel set a large pump-bottle of Purell hand sanitizer on the table. "We have one rule tonight, everybody. After every turn, you come and Purell your hands."

Piper stared. "You *can't* be serious."

"They've done studies on bowling balls, subway poles, handrails. They're covered in respiratory secretions, skin flora," Rachel paused and leaned toward her mother, "*fecal* emissions . . ."

"That's repulsive," said Piper.

"The truth isn't always pretty."

Olivia said, "Every team has a name, so me, Rachel and Janie are going to be the Six-pound Balls."

Dustin fell over giggling.

"I said, *I'm not here!*" said Janie.

Len laughed, explaining, "It's the weight of her preferred bowling ball. Let's just shorten it to the Sixers and leave it at that. What do you think for our team, Dustin? The Strikes? The Spares?"

"No way." He scrunched up his nose and thought for a moment. "The Grinding Rails."

Piper sat back in her plastic chair. "What?"

"Skateboarding apparatus," Rachel explained. "Much less lurid than it sounds."

"We'll just shorten it to the Rails," Len said, typing on the scoring keyboard. He turned to Rachel. "Should buy us some extra time before we get turfed out of here."

Olivia, having insisted the Sixers go first, clomped across the hardwood floor with her shoes on the wrong feet. She began shaking her hands. "Oh no. There's no lime-green ball. I need lime-green!"

Len jumped out of his seat and squinted down the lane next to them, where a group of unshaven guys in football jerseys huddled over two pitchers of beer.

"Try a seven-pounder, Olivia," said Rachel. "You won't notice the difference."

"I need a lime-green!" She melted into a puddle beside the ball return they shared with the frat boys.

Rachel stood up. "Let me try." This was a clear-cut case of a child needing to benefit from someone else's problems. Knowing they aren't alone gives children hope. This Rachel knew for a fact. She'd had several letters from readers who'd had great success with this technique. "I know exactly how you feel. When I was a young girl, I took riding lessons and was in love with a palomino pony named Jazz. I rode him every Saturday morning. Well, one day I got there and another girl was putting on his saddle . . ."

"I hate ponies!" Olivia shouted. "I only like LIME-GREEN balls!"

"Oh God," Janie said from beneath her camouflage. All that showed were her calves and feet. "Kill me now!"

"Come with Daddy," Len said, holding out his hand. "We'll find you a green one."

Olivia didn't budge.

Rachel touched Len's arm. "You go. I'll watch her."

Len looked hesitant.

"No pony stories," she assured him.

Len marched across the other lanes, approaching family after family, all of whom seemed hell-bent on hanging on to their lime balls. Olivia was down on all fours now, her watery eyes following her father like a lost puppy.

Dustin stood up, walked toward the ball return, and said to Olivia, "Dude, can you, like, relocate?"

Olivia shifted her weeping bones and cleared the path for the Grinding Rails' first ball. Dustin had absolutely no interest in the weight or color of his ball, just grabbed the closest one, which happened to be navy blue, and hurled it along the gleaming floorboards. The ball veered close to the left gutter, then saved itself and careened into the middle pin. The pins exploded in every direction.

"Yes!" he shouted, jumping up to high-five the ceiling-mounted monitor, which shuddered its objection over their heads. Dustin looked at Olivia, waggled his thumbs, and said, "Look, dude. No tape!" Olivia reddened with fury.

"Dustin!" said Rachel. "A little dignity, please?"

"Whatever. It's your turn, Mom. Or is it Janie's? *Jane dear, where are you?*" Dustin sang.

"SHUT UP!" said the coats.

Rachel chose a ball swirling with colors. She stared down the pins, took three steps, followed by an impressive slide, then lobbed the nine-pounder straight down Lane Five. Her shot was doomed from the start. It came down with a mighty crash. There, in the middle of the lane, it slowed, almost stopped, before gaining just enough momentum to drop into the gutter.

Len returned as Piper was coming back from her first strike of the evening. "There are no more six-pounders, Olivia," he said. "You'll have to make do with a seven."

The wail began low. It sounded as if it were coming from the parking lot or maybe the dog groomer next door. Growly and pulsating, like the distress call of a wolverine tangled in barbed wire. Then the pitch rose fast and feverish, where it remained until Olivia crawled out from beneath the ball return and threw herself, chest-first, onto the floor, arms reaching for the ball she'd never had the chance to love. Dirty fists pounding furiously, the child wept with abandon.

Trying to ignore the stares cast their way, Len said. "You'll barely notice the difference. Look." He picked up a pink seven-pounder. "It's light as a feather."

Olivia lifted her tear-stained face and, for a moment, seemed convinced. The sobbing stopped and she twirled her feet in the air, one untied bowling shoe dropping to the floor with a thud. "I don't want to do bowling anymore," she said with a sniff.

Len put down the ball, his shoulders sagging. Looking exhausted, he sat in a chair opposite Rachel. "Piper," he said. "Why don't you take your shot?"

As Piper tightened her laces and began to pick through the balls, Len caught Rachel's eye. "You okay?" Under the table, he trapped her ankle between his feet and squeezed.

Rachel pumped hand sanitizer into her palm. "I'm fine," she said, rubbing her hands together.

"Good." He took her fingers in his. "I was thinking, maybe after bowling, you and I—"

"I'm a bit tired, actually."

"Tomorrow then."

"Maybe."

He stared at her. "Rachel, I understand if you're still upset, but try to understand my position—"

She felt hot blood rush through her body. Pushing her chair back with a loud scrape, she forced her face into a false smile, looking at the kids. "Who wants candy?"

Olivia jumped up from the floor. "Me! Additionally, I want to pee."

"Okay. Put on your shoe and let's go."

"No. It smells."

Piper said, "I'll take her to the restroom, you get the candy." She walked past Olivia's discarded shoe and held out her hand. "Come on, Olivia."

"She has to wear the shoe inside the bathroom," Rachel said.

Piper sighed and led the child away, leaving the shoe on the floor. With a groan of exasperation, Rachel scooped it up and trotted after them.

"What? You think I'd let her step anywhere unsanitary?" Piper asked Rachel when she caught up. "I'd like to believe, after all these years interacting with my grandchildren, that you'd begin to trust me. A little."

The coat pile grunted. "Yeah, GOOD LUCK WITH THAT!"

It seemed, as they passed the snack stand, Olivia didn't need to go to the restroom quite as badly as she needed a Snickers. Still holding the cast-off shoe, Rachel peered through the scratched glass counter at the candy spread out beneath. The one remaining Snickers looked like it had been there since opening night, some forty years prior.

"How about chocolate raisins, Olivia? They look a little less . . . ancient."

Pressing her face against the glass, Olivia considered her choices. "Do they have chocolate peanuts?"

Piper repeated the question to the teenage boy behind the counter, who shook his head sadly. "We only got the raisins left. You want 'em?"

A family gathered on Rachel's right side. She glanced over to see a shortish couple in their early fifties, with a teenage girl. The daughter, plump like her parents, had gorgeous wavy hair, long and black. Then she turned around and Rachel saw her face for the first time.

One chromosome too many.

The girl had Down's syndrome. Rachel's pulse quickened. Of course, it wasn't. Couldn't be. Hannah would be sixteen, and this girl had to be . . . oh God, she could definitely be the same age. Rachel leaned over the counter to look closer at the parents, searching for some sort of family connection. The parents were gray, but even without knowing their original hair color, Rachel could see from their mousy eyebrows they'd never been dark-haired like their daughter.

If she was their daughter.

Olivia tugged on Rachel's shirt. "I don't want the raisins. I wanna go to the bathroom."

Piper said, "Take her in, Rachel. I'll buy candy for everyone." To the boy behind the counter, Piper pointed at a series of candy bars, which the boy began laying out on the counter.

Rachel was so busy noticing that husband and wife wore matching Scottish flag sweatshirts, she didn't answer her mother.

Piper nudged her. "I think someone's in a hurry." Rachel looked down. Olivia was dancing from foot to foot.

The family on Rachel's other side moved closer to the candy. "You take her, Mom," said Rachel, hoping to get rid of Piper before she realized what her daughter was up to and blew her cover. "I'll buy the candy."

"Come on, Olivia. Let's go." Piper took hold of the child's hand and turned away.

"Mom, wait," said Rachel, tossing Piper the shoe. "Go into the ladies' room with her. You know, so she's not in there alone."

"Oh, come on. We're in a bowling alley. What could possibly happen?"

"The same thing that happened to a nine-year-old girl at a St. Louis truck stop last month," Rachel called after her. "In the ladies' room." She turned to smile at the man with the flag shirt, who was now holding Olivia's Snickers bar. "You can never be too careful," she said to him.

"My wife still goes into public restrooms with our daughter," he said as the girl picked up the Snickers and smelled it.

"I want it," she said in a monotone voice.

"Is this your daughter?" Rachel asked. "She's lovely."

It was clear they'd rarely heard such a compliment. Believed it themselves, but probably didn't hear it much from strangers. The man placed a hand on his daughter's shoulder. He seemed to be assessing the girl, nodding with enough pride to rip Rachel straight down the middle. "Yes," he answered. "This is Molly."

Molly.

"Hi, Molly," said Rachel. "How old are you?"

Molly looked up, smiled, and looked back down at the candy bar. "I want *that*."

"Molly's shy," said her mother.

Rachel's heart thumped. "I have a fourteen-year-old daughter. And a twelve-year-old son. Both born in winter." She leaned against the counter and slipped her hands into her pockets, trying not to burst with exhilaration. "How about Molly? When was she born?"

"She was born at Hillsdale sixteen years ago," said her father.

Rachel tried to breathe. Hillsdale Hospital. It was where she gave birth to Hannah.

Molly's father pointed to the Snickers bar. "Were you planning to buy that?"

"Take it. It's paid for," Rachel said, plunking a twenty-dollar bill on the counter. "It's my gift to Molly."

"Thank you," he said. "Very kind." He turned to Molly and asked her to thank Rachel. Molly smiled her thanks as she carefully peeled away the wrapper, as if she was going to reuse it.

"Hillsdale is a great hospital," Rachel said. "I delivered there too. Nice nursing staff."

"Oh yes," said Molly's mother. Maybe adoptive mother. "The nurses were just wonderful."

How to wrench the conversation away from the nurses and back where it belonged—pinpointing Molly's exact date of birth? And what, exactly, would she do if Molly did turn out to be Hannah? It probably wouldn't be too brilliant to admit it. These two would never believe the coincidence. They'd think she was crazy. Maybe even a stalker.

Rachel smiled again. "I read somewhere that people born in December are luckier than others. Was Hannah a December baby?"

The woman crinkled her nose. "Who's Hannah?"

"Molly!" said Rachel. "I meant Molly."

Molly's father shook his head. "Cicely had Molly in April. But we don't go in for that astronomy crap."

Rachel's whole body shrank. Deflated. Molly was born in April. To Cicely. Of course. So stupid to have thought . . . sixteen years later, that she'd find her, here, in a dingy bowling alley twenty minutes from home. Molly wasn't Hannah. Or was it that Hannah wasn't Molly? Rachel laughed silently in misery as Molly and her parents walked away.

Molly was the lucky one after all. Whichever month she'd come into the world, no one even thought of giving her up.

Molly's dad was right. Astrology was crap.

Just then, Piper meandered out of the ladies' room, stopping to rifle through her purse. She strolled toward her daughter. "Are we ready?" Tucked under her elbow was Olivia's bowling shoe.

"You didn't make her wear it?"

Piper set it on the counter. "Olivia's absolutely right. It smells like cheap air freshener."

Rachel looked past Piper toward the restroom. "Where is she?"

"I thought she was with you."

"With me? You took her to the bathroom!"

"Calm down, Rachel. The girl isn't a toddler. She finished before me and left. I'm sure she ran back to her father when you weren't looking. Honestly, do you know how much unnecessary stress you bring upon yourself? You create your own problems. You always have."

Rachel smirked. "Right. You lose a ten-year-old girl and I'm the one who's creating problems. So typical! I should have taken her myself."

"Why didn't you?"

"Doesn't matter. And by the way, don't think I don't know about you letting Dustin watch *The Shining* last time you babysat!"

"I did not—"

"He had a nightmare about finding REDRUM written in blood on his closet door!"

Piper tightened her mouth. "He might have watched a bit. Half at the most. Do you know he's the only child going into seventh grade who hasn't seen it? It's considered a classic."

Rachel felt someone standing just behind her. She turned to see Len stretching out his fingers. "You ladies missed my strike. And my spectacular choice of following it up with a gutter ball." He glanced around with the untroubled demeanor of a man who trusts his girlfriend not to lose his child. "Where's Olivia?"

Rachel and Piper locked eyes, then turned back to Len. "She's not with you?" Rachel whispered.

In an instant, the color drained from Len's face. Eyes darting around, Len marched around the counter, then poked his head into both restrooms. "She's not here."

Galaxy Bowl was one large, open room with the snack bar and shoe rental in the center and a dozen lanes, two steps down, lining the back wall. If she wasn't hiding in the bathrooms, glued to the candy window, or gamboling around down by the lanes, there was no mistaking it—Olivia was gone.

But how? The child couldn't have sliped out the front door, the one that led back out into the parking lot. It wasn't possible, Rachel would have seen her.

Just then, the double doors connecting the bowling alley to the mall next door opened. Two couples strolled in, bringing with them sounds of the Woodfield Mall, one of the busiest shopping centers in the region.

"No," said Rachel. "You don't think she'd . . . ?"

Len didn't answer. He was already racing through the doors.

CHAPTER 29

Code Adam

The single most important thing parents can do to protect their children from predators is to supervise them at all times—even while playing close to home. In eighty percent of child-abduction murders, the victim is approached within a quarter-mile radius of where she was last seen.

—RACHEL BERMAN, *Perfect Parent* magazine

When a shopping mall issues a Code Adam alert over the speaker system, they rarely broadcast the child's name, for fear of giving the potential perpetrator too much information. Typically, the child's parent or guardian notifies a mall employee— a store clerk or, better yet, a security guard—and gives them a description of the child. Their gender, race, age, approximate height and weight, hair and eye color, and—if the shattered parent can remember—a description of their clothing and shoes. The mall employee then arranges for a Code Adam alert to be announced throughout the shopping center, along with a description of the child and where he or she was last seen.

So, while the parent goes into emotional freefall listening to his or her child's description read out over the PA system and tries to mentally block out words such as "abducted," "pedophile," and "murder," store employees rush to monitor entrances and exits, and hunt for the missing child. Employees are expected to abandon their customers and search for any child matching the description. Toy departments, parking lots, and bathrooms get special attention.

Piper stayed with Dustin and Janie at the information booth while Len and Rachel split up. By the time the somewhat garbled announcement was made, a minute or two after Len gave Olivia's description—right down to the missing bowling shoe—Rachel had already raced through three women's shops, calling Olivia's name, statistics swirling through her mind.

Fact: 74 percent of abducted children who are murdered are killed in the first three hours. Most missing-children cases aren't reported for two hours.

Fact: children abducted by strangers are three times more likely to be murdered than those abducted by family members or acquaintances.

Fact: it was all her fault. If she hadn't been mentally abducting Molly, Olivia would be eating a stale Snickers bar off the dirty floor back at Lane Five.

Rachel jogged into the food court, racing passed rows and rows of tables, slowing to peer underneath. Once she'd covered the eating area, she ran down the hall to the restrooms. Rushing past the lineup of women waiting for stalls, she shouted, "Olivia?" and bent down, checking each of the locked stalls for anything other than women's shoes, faced forward. She turned to the women in line. "Did anyone see a girl? Ten-years-old, pink sweatpants, one shoe . . . ?" Two of the women shook their heads, the other three looked around, as if the child might suddenly materialize from behind their pant legs.

In the men's room, Rachel's presence was met with a chorus of "Hey!" "What is this?" and "Gonna call security." She ignored the comments, checking stalls by banging the metal doors open, one by one. All four were empty.

"I'm looking for a ten-year-old girl," Rachel said. For the first time, she was aware of her chest heaving up and down. "Long reddish-brown hair. One bowling shoe. Pink sweats. Didn't you hear the announcement? A child is missing."

"Shit," said a guy at the sink, in his mid-thirties, maybe, but with a hairline that shouldn't happen until his mid-fifties. "She's your daughter?"

Rachel ignored the question. "You haven't seen her?"

The men all shook their heads. The bald one waved his hands and added, "Good luck."

Back out in the mall, she stopped. Should she go back the way she came—past the bowling alley and toward the Nike outlet, Victoria's Secret, and, way at the end, the candy shop? Or should she turn right, toward the big camping store and—

Oh God. The pet shop.

Sweeting's Pets was nestled between a heavily scented cinnamon-bun kiosk and a create-your-own-T-shirt shop that practically shook with a heavy-metal beat. When Dustin was young, Rachel had spent too many hours to contemplate hanging around the pet store while Dustin tortured himself by gaping at the tarantulas and black widows at the back of the store. As long as Rachel could remember, the front window had always been a gigantic plastic maze of see-through tunnels with hamsters scampering through it.

The front of the store was empty. As she raced toward the back, she knocked over a basket of rubber animal toys that squeaked in cheerful indignation beneath her feet.

A small voice was saying, ". . . worms, ants, beetles. Umm, spiders and lizards. *Rattus exulans* also eats fruits and maybe even actual birds . . ." There at the very back, between the lizards and the spiders, sitting cross-legged on the floor, with a hamster in an orange plastic exercise ball pressed to her cheek, sat Olivia with the glassy-eyed Sweeting's Pets employee—a tall, bony teenager with wispy tufts of facial hair. "*Rattus rattus* usually has about twelve nipples, but at the end of the day *rattus exulans* only has eight. I don't know why . . ." She was rocking herself back and forth in a way Rachel had never seen, her speech high-pitched and unusually fast. The girl was on the edge of panic.

"Olivia," Rachel breathed, dropping to her knees in front of the child.

Without removing the exercise ball from her cheek, Olivia leaped into Rachel's arms and molded her little body into Rachel's. Standing up, Rachel thanked the bored-looking teenager and waited while he extricated the hamster ball from Olivia's clutch.

"Sorry," said the teenager as he inspected the hamster inside, then set the ball on the floor so the animal could roam around. "She wanted to hug a rodent, but we have a no-touching policy with the smaller animals. Especially with kids. I figured it'd be all right if the hamster was in a plastic ball."

"Thank you," Rachel whispered. "Please call security. Tell them we've found the missing child and that she's fine."

"Whoa." His nametag said BRAD, but Rachel couldn't imagine anyone looking less like a Brad. "She's the Code Adam kid?"

Rachel nodded and followed him to the cash desk. After Brad hung up the phone, he reached out to tickle Olivia in the ribs and asked, "Are you happy to be back with your mom?"

Olivia didn't answer right away. Still in Rachel's arms, she lifted her head off Rachel's shoulder and stared at her face, her nose not two inches away. Those steely eyes, unblinking, were far too intense for Rachel. She flashed Olivia a nervous smile, then looked away, walking back toward the mall.

As they passed the hamster labyrinth in the front window, Olivia whispered, "Yes."

CHAPTER 30

An Awfully Nice Girl

If he'd been asked, before Friday, to name the very worst moment of his life, Len wouldn't have hesitated. There were several worthy contenders—his young wife dying half a block from home on a rainy Monday morning, being told his daughter would never achieve that ever-elusive status of normalcy—but no doubt, until Friday, the victor would have been that rubbing-alcohol-and-latex-glove-scented dark horse, the Diagnosis. Actually, that wasn't fully true. It wasn't the Diagnosis itself, it was the child-deserting aftermath that was certain to follow.

But now, sitting in Dr. Foxman's waiting room a few days later, Len would—without question—select Friday night at the Woodfield Mall. More specifically, the moment the police officer who'd arrived on the scene asked if Len had any recent photos of Olivia, and if he'd ever had his daughter fingerprinted.

There was only one use for a child's fingerprints.

Olivia was missing for a total of twenty-five and a half minutes. A lifetime. Even the lay-down-and-thank-the-heavens ending couldn't take away what Len saw, lived, and tasted in those 1,530 seconds. And the moment her father died, Olivia's Code Adam experience would begin for real. She'd be living in a world full of people who had no idea what she needed.

The waiting room was empty but for Len and a bearded fellow in a wheelchair, who appeared to be much closer to his medically predicted expiration date. The man's head was bandaged and his right hand lay limp in his lap. As if they were waiting for a routine cleaning at the dentist, the man began chatting about the weather—so-so; the Rangers' recent acquisition of Brian Simms—terrible; the shapeliness of Dr. Foxman's nurse's calves—very good. Len, feeling pressured to contribute to the conversation, complained about summer months passing much more quickly than winter months. It was the third week of July. Both skirted around the dismal reality of being in that particular waiting room of that particular building.

The man extended his limp hand, supporting it with the strength of his other arm. "My name's Chris." He reached into his jacket pocket for his wallet and pulled out a photo of twin baby boys he'd never get to see grow up. He pointed at one, then the other. "This one's Callum, the other one's Colt."

Len smiled, nodding his head. "They're handsome boys."

Chris handed him another photo, this one of a woman, a hearty brunette with shoulders that looked like they could handle whatever else life hurled her way. "Sandy," he said, tracing the edge of the picture with his fingertip. "My wife."

Len leaned closer and muttered, "Lovely," then dug through his pocket for his own wallet. "I have a picture of my daughter. It's not recent, but it's one of my favorites." He passed Chris a snapshot of a six- or seven-year-old Olivia squatting under a tree, setting up a croquet set. Smiling as if she hadn't a problem in the world.

"That's a good-looking kid," Chris said. He gestured toward Len's wallet. "You got a picture of your wife in there too?"

"No," Len said. "I don't. My, uh, my wife died when Olivia was much younger." Keenly aware of the implication left hanging in the air, Len slid the picture back into his wallet and chewed on the inside of his cheek.

Chris said nothing. He didn't have to. The horror of Len's situation was all over his bearded face.

After Len's appointment—whereupon he learned that wheelchairs could be had at a 20 percent discount in the lobby, for when he was so inclined, and that he was about to have the luxury of spending a few days in the hospital being X-rayed, jabbed, and prodded in the name of delaying his ultimate demise—he squeezed himself into the crowded elevator and turned to face the closing doors. He was certain that the nearness of his fellow passengers made his anguish palpable. If they hadn't read it in his face, certainly they could feel it pulsating from his body.

When the doors opened to the lobby, he bolted forward, determined to be the first one out, and marched straight into Tammy and Philip Peyton.

After mumbling quick greetings and moving aside to let people pass, Philip said: "I hope you're not in the building for the same reason we are." He held up a bandaged wrist. "Sprained it playing touch football."

"Tell him the whole story, honey," said Tammy.

"With my six-year-old nephew," he added.

"Phillip takes Michael out to the park every Saturday," Tammy explained. "My sister isn't married, so, you know, it's really nice for Mikey."

Len nodded and they paused, waiting, Len realized, for him to explain his own presence in the medical arts building. "I was just . . . dropping something off for a client," he said. "By the way, how did your meeting go with little Zachary?"

They looked at each other, uncomfortable.

"He is a sweet boy, really he is," said Tammy. "It's just that he loves to play road hockey and we live in a high-rise. He desperately wants to live in the country and ride horses and have cats and dogs, and Philip has his allergies. I just don't think we're the right people for him. The most we could offer him is a hamster in a cage."

Len nearly stopped breathing.

How had he missed it? *A hamster in a cage.*

Here, before him, stood the answer to his problem. This young couple who'd just lost out on a little boy, who spent their weekends trying to make their fatherless nephew happy, who were born to be parents, who were offering up rodents in cages, could not have been brought to him for nothing. Could they? They were young, strong. Healthy.

"Tammy," Len said. "Remind me again what you do for a living?"

"I'm a teacher."

A teacher. What else?

"Her students adore her." Philip took hold of Tammy's elbow with his good hand. "Anyway, we'd better get moving or we'll be late."

"Wait," said Len. He felt his heart pounding through his shirt. "I know of another child, a ten-year-old, who will be needing a good home. A special home." A rush of sweat dampened his shirt. "Have you ever heard of NLD? Nonverbal learning disorder?"

"I'm not sure . . ." Tammy said. "Oh yes! Three years ago, I had a student with NLD. A real sweetheart of a girl. Fifteen, but terribly misunderstood by her peers."

"Yes!" Len nearly shouted. He wanted to handcuff these two and keep them by his side until papers were signed. Hamsters were bought. "Exactly. Children with NLD are constantly misunderstood."

"The parents—are they living?" asked Philip.

"Yes. No. One is—the father. The mother passed away years ago. But the father is, well, the father's been told he has very little time. He's desperate to find—"

"He's dying?" asked Tammy.

"Well, he's . . . yes. He's dying."

Tammy's face crinkled up in sorrow. "That's so sad for the child. Is he a boy?"

"No. That's the thing. She's a little girl. Beautiful child. Just beautiful. Full of light, love. Her name is Olivia. I could arrange for a meeting. Maybe at the park or—"

Tammy and Philip were looking at each other, unsure.

"Or maybe in my office if you'd rather . . ."

"No, it's not that," said Philip.

Tammy explained, "She sounds awfully nice, this Olivia." She reached up and rubbed Philip's shoulder, smiling an upside-down smile. "But Philip and I have our hearts set on a boy."

CHAPTER 31

"1-2 Crush on You"

—The Clash

Sunday afternoon, while her mother and Len read on the back porch, Janie traipsed over to where Olivia sat in the mud, under the bush that refused to be pruned. She was digging a surprisingly deep hole.

"What's the hole for?" Janie asked, leaning over.

The girl shrugged. "Nothing. And it's not a hole, it's a grave."

How totally gross. "What for?" Janie asked.

"In case I ever have to bury a gerbil."

Whatever. This kid was bizarre. Janie stood up and saw Tabitha hanging around the pool deck with a tray of drinks. "I'll be right back," she whispered to Olivia. She climbed through the dogwood bush and made her way across Tabitha's backyard.

As she got closer, she could hear the conversation between Tabitha and the balding construction worker who'd been watching them in the pool. "Yeah, well," the guy was saying, "no one's teen years were as dull as mine. My parents knew about everything I did. I had no life."

"Try having no life in two separate houses. It's twice the misery and boredom. Twice the missed parties," said Tabitha.

"Yeah," he said, smiling. "You're going to have to resort to sneaking out with your friends. My brother was the smart one. His bedroom was over the garage; he came and went as he pleased. Any time of night. I guess that's what I got for choosing the bigger bedroom. Mine was right next to my parents'."

Janie walked up and helped herself to a glass of lemonade from Tabitha's tray. "My bedroom's next door, in purgatory," she said.

Tabitha laughed. "I was old enough to know better when we moved in." She pointed up at the large second-floor window opposite to Janie's house. "I chose the room farthest away from my mother's. I didn't want to know anything about her dating life, if you know what I mean."

The guy, whose legs were covered in dust, nodded and laughed, thanking Tabitha for the drink, waving to Janie, and returning to his pile of rocks.

"I like your sandals," said Janie, leaning down and inspecting the braided leather.

"Thanks. I *love* your flip-flops, all raggedy at the edges. Do they come in women's, too?"

Janie looked down at her feet. "These *are* women's."

"Oh, cool." Tabitha shrugged and dropped into a swinging chair.

"Going swimming?" asked Janie.

"Nah. I'm not in the mood. My dad just made his big announcement. He's marrying Kristina."

"No!"

"Yes. In August, at the Ritz-Carlton. He's booked the Ritz-Carlton Suite for his wedding night. Two thousand square feet overlooking the New York Harbor so he can finally nail her with a view. Chocolates and petit fours are complimentary, of course."

Janie brought the glass to her mouth too quickly, and lemonade dribbled onto her shirt. "The harbor view is for her benefit. Believe me, if your dad's anything like mine, the only view he gives a shit about involves his babe-chick's stubbly thighs wrapped around his head."

"Ech. That's disgusting."

"*Men* are disgusting," Janie said with zeal, seizing the opportunity to bolster her own creed by slamming the male of the species.

Tabitha said nothing.

"If it will make you feel any better, I might be able to arrange to sleep over that night. *If* you think it would help."

Tabitha looked up, her blue eyes dazzling in the water's glow. She sniffed. "Really? Would you do that?"

Janie swatted at a mosquito on her bare arm. "Totally."

CHAPTER 32

Lucky Charms

Set aside half an hour of personal time each day. Whether you take a bath, a long walk, or simply sit in the garden and stare at a single rosebud, use that time to nourish and regenerate.

—RACHEL BERMAN, *Perfect Parent* magazine

All your clothes are labeled," said Rachel, hauling Dustin's duffel bag out of the trunk. Campers of all ages prowled around the church parking lot, feeding skateboards and duffels into the belly of the Greyhound bus, doing their best to avoid their exuberant teenage counselors, offering up self-conscious good-byes to their parents. "So check the name inside before putting on your boxers. Things get strewn around in cabins and you don't want to put on someone else's underwear by accident."

Dustin hunched his shoulders and looked around to make sure no one heard. *"Mom."* For the past week he'd been locking himself in the bathroom with a jar of styling mud, masterminding a hairstyle worthy of skate camp. He'd settled on an oceanic tangle that hinted of rough weather. Looking around, Rachel noticed Dustin wasn't the only one who appeared to have been struck sideways by a rather nasty wave.

"And be careful in the pool," Rachel added. "These camp lifeguards are young. Hormonal. And they have a lot of kids to watch . . ."

"Nothing's going to happen to me!"

"I'm just saying—you can have as much fun in the shallow end as the deep end."

Rolling his eyes, Dustin hauled his bag over his back, staggering under the weight. He held out one hand, all business. "Bye, Mom. Try not to lose it. Seriously. I'm going to be fine."

Ignoring his handshake, she wrapped her arms around him and pulled him close, kissing his prickly hair. "I know, sweetie. This week will fly by and before you know it, it'll be next Monday and I'll be picking you up."

He pulled away and adjusted his hair, walking backward, grinning. "Can't wait."

She watched her son stumble away, dwarfed by his canvas sack. He hurled his gear onto the bus and, in one motion, swung himself inside. Shielding her eyes from the midday sun, Rachel leaned against her dusty trunk and waited until every last camper boarded, the engine started up, and the Greyhound lumbered out of the parking lot, leaving in its wake some fifty relieved-looking parents.

And Rachel.

As she pulled onto Montrose Avenue, somewhat proud of her dry eyes, her cell phone rang. She glanced at the display. Len. "Hey," she said.

"You survived the drop-off?"

"Barely."

"You did the right thing. I'm proud of you."

She didn't answer right away, having realized she'd just sent her son off on a four-hour journey without so much as a water bottle for hydration. "A football player in Arizona died during practice earlier this month. Dehydration. His teammates said he needed a drink but was too intimidated to tell his coach. Didn't want to seem like a wimp."

"Rachel . . ."

"I just hope these counselors give them water breaks. There's probably no shade over the ramps and pools—"

"Bowls," he corrected her. "And several of the half-pipes are covered by shade structures. Dustin will be fine."

"Right." She nodded to herself. "He'll be fine, I know."

"You can't shelter them from everything."

"Only sun. And only on *several* half-pipes."

"You're at your cutest when you get all worked up. Did you know that?"

"I'm not 'all worked up.' I'm just considering my son's electrolyte balance."

"Listen," Len said. "I'm going to take about four days for myself. To prepare for an upcoming trial. I just didn't want you thinking I'd disappeared."

"What about Olivia?"

"My parents are going to take her. Not quite the understanding backdrop she needs, but it's the best I can do."

"I have an idea," Rachel said, making a quick left on a yellow light. "I know I don't have a stellar track record, in fact I probably have the shittiest track record with Olivia that anyone could ever have, after the way I let her get lost in the busiest mall in the Hudson—"

"Rachel. Stop apologizing. It could have happened to anyone."

She sucked in a deep breath. Nothing about her past relation-ship with Olivia indicated she could handle the child for any lon-ger than the time it took to unwrap a candy bar. In fact, she was nearly certain she'd live to regret her words. "I'll do it."

"Do what?"

"Watch Olivia. Bring her to my house. I'll take a bit of time away from the office."

The phone hissed with Len's pause. "You?"

He didn't trust her. "I'm sorry. If you don't want me to, it's totally fine. I mean, she knows your parents. She'd be at home. It was probably a stupid idea—"

"You'd watch her? Seriously?"

"Actually, I shouldn't. I don't know what I'm doing and it wouldn't be fair to her to impose my bumbling—"

"Of course you can do it! You're a wonderful mother. Olivia lights up when she's around you." He paused. "You'd be just per-fect for her."

"Are you sure . . ."

"She'll be thrilled when I tell her. Of course, she can't know I'll be nearby working around the clock. You'll have to put up with me telling her I'm away. Far away. Los Angeles, maybe. Otherwise she'll beg to call me in the middle of the night." There was a crack-ling on the cell connection. "I know you're not into lying to kids, but it's the only way it'll work."

She thought of Olivia on the floor of the pet store, chattering deliriously and pressing the hamster ball into her cheek. "You do the lying. I'll do the rest."

Olivia arrived a few hours later. Twenty minutes into the visit, she sat at the kitchen table doing nothing but breathing. With every intake, her entire body puffed up taller, only to shrivel down again with the exhale, slumping all over the suitcase she held on her lap. Birthday Wishes Barbie lay, bare buttocks up, on the table. "How long is my dad going to be away again?"

"Only four days," said Rachel. "And you'll be having so much fun with Janie, it'll go by in a blink."

"Why can't I have fun with you too?"

Rachel poured dry macaroni into a pot of bubbling water. Lunch, if somewhat late, was all planned. Organic macaroni and cheese, baby carrots, and papaya-banana juice. The meal was, of course, completely monochromatic, unappetizingly orange and beige. She'd have to scare up some jazzier hues at dinner. "You will be having fun with me. I think we might even be having fun right now."

"No." Olivia shook her head. "We're not. Can I have my Lucky Charms cereal now?"

"We're having macaroni. And other stuff."

"But it's Monday and at the end of the day I always have Lucky Charms on Mondays for lunch in the summer. My dad brings it to my KidFun daycare. Every single, solitary, actual, complete Monday."

"Not this Monday."

"Every Monday."

"Except this one. I don't bring marmallowy cereals into the house. Especially those made with food dyes. Yellow is made from coal tar. And pink has been linked to thyroid tumors in rats."

Olivia's eyes lit up. "Rats?"

"Rats. Very little food coloring enters this house. It's kind of a rule I have."

Olivia's lips flat-lined. Her little nostrils flared and her cheeks burned with fury. She jutted out her jaw and growled, "When I don't get Charms, I don't eat until I get Charms. And that's a kind of a rule *I* have."

"My rules are my rules." At least Rachel hoped they were. With Olivia, she wasn't quite sure what to expect.

"I want Lucky Charms."

Okay. It was time to pull out a solid parenting technique. Something from the magazine. She thought about the situation.

Fact: the child was disappointed.

Fact: disappointment is part of life.

Fact: helping a child cope with disappointment will build her confidence by letting her see she can survive a situation as difficult as . . . as running out of Charms.

"Olivia," Rachel began. "I know you're upset because you can't have your favorite cereal. I'm wondering what you will do to make yourself feel better."

"Starve."

"Starving is not an option."

"YES IT IS!" she screamed. "I'M GOING TO STARVE AND YOU CAN'T STOP ME!"

"I'm going to have to send you to your room if you don't settle down," Rachel warned. As soon as the words were out of her mouth, she regretted them, mainly because she had no idea whether a time-out would work any better.

Without taking her narrowed eyes off Rachel's face, Olivia reached her arm across the table and held a pointed finger up to the side of the salt shaker. She paused for a moment, then stabbed the shaker, knocking it sideways and dumping salt all over the table.

"Now you've given me no choice. Go to your room, Olivia."

With her suitcase clutched tight in one hand and Barbie's hair in the other, Olivia stomped from the kitchen. Rachel stared into the steaming pot of macaroni. She'd always found with Dustin and Janie that time spent in their rooms, thinking about what they could have done differently, made them emerge thoughtful and cooperative. Defused. Somehow having a little alone time matured them. With any luck, Len would come to pick up Olivia on Friday afternoon and she'd be a calmer, happier, more settled child.

The front door slammed.

Rachel wandered into the hall to find it empty. She could see upstairs that Janie's bedroom door was shut. Peeking through the hall window, she gasped aloud. There was Olivia, dragging her suitcase down the driveway, halfway to the street.

"Olivia!" Rachel shouted, racing out the front door. "Olivia, stop!"

Gravel piercing her bare feet as she ran, Rachel caught up with the child near the edge of the road. "Where are you going?"

The girl squinted up at her. Birthday Wishes Barbie, still hanging from her ponytail, twirled, wide-eyed, helpless in the breeze. "To my room. Like you said."

Oh dear. "Not your room at home, Olivia. Your room upstairs. Here. In my house." She took the suitcase in one hand and Olivia's limp little paw in the other and led her back to the house.

She settled Olivia in the guest bedroom and ran for the ringing phone. Her heart caught in her throat as she read the display. Camp Black Pine. "Yes?"

"Is this Mrs. Berman?"

She could barely answer. "Yes."

"It's Jordana Stein, I'm the director of Camp Black Pine. Your son Dustin's counselor is here beside me. I'm afraid there's been a bit of an accident."

———————

By the time Rachel and Olivia reached the camp laneway, hours later, it was dusk. The car shuddered and thumped along a road so narrow branches scraped the windows. They passed under a CAMP BLACK PINE sign made of slender birch logs, and pulled into the parking lot.

One building appeared to be larger than the others, so she swung the car in that direction, her headlights illuminating a teenage boy—staff, most likely—sitting on a bench beside a huge duffel bag and a boy with tousled hair, one arm in a sling and a sheepish look on his face. Rachel shut off the engine and jumped out.

"I know what you're going to say," said Dustin as she marched forward. *"No skate camp ever again."*

Fighting the impulse to threaten to write the camp up in the magazine as a facility that broke children in record time, she kissed her son's head and forced a smile. The camp was, after all, owned by Len's client. She'd have to tread very carefully. "We'll discuss it when we get home."

The teenager extended his hand, which Rachel shook with unintended force. "Mrs. Berman. I'm Steven, Dusty's counselor. This kid's a total trooper. Didn't squawk at all when they reset the bone. It stuck right up, bulging under his skin. I thought I was going to die the way the doctor was jamming it back into place, but he's one tough little dude . . ."

Rachel grabbed the duffel bag. "I just want to get him home right now. Can you walk to the car, honey?" she asked Dustin.

"It's my wrist. Not my leg." He waved good-bye to Steven with his cast, which Rachel could now see was covered in signatures. "Bye, Stevie."

"Later, buddy. Come back when you're all healed."

Rachel let out a half-laugh, swung the bag into the trunk, and slammed it tight.

"Mrs. B., the director's inside. She wants to see you—"

She hurried to open the passenger door for Dustin and help him sit down, fasten his seat belt. "Tell her I'll call her in the morning," she said. "Right now, I have a long drive ahead of me with two tired kids . . ."

"I'm not tired," called Olivia from the backseat. "I want Lucky Charms."

"I want McDonald's," said Dustin. "I totally deserve some fries."

Steven stepped closer as Rachel climbed into her seat. He handed her a large square envelope. "These are his X-rays. Jordana wants you to sign some stuff and talk to you about how it happened. It'll only take a few minutes. It's camp policy."

Camp policy. After they break your only son, they have a policy about signing. She slammed the door and opened the window. "I'll call Jordana in the morning." As Dustin turned on the radio with his good hand, the car sped off into the trees.

"Hey! There's mosquitoes back here!" Olivia slapped her leg. "Hundreds."

"Mom," said Dustin. "It's not what you think . . ."

"If you'd gone to computer camp, you'd be in one piece right now," Rachel said. "That's it for skateboarding. We're lucky it was only your arm."

"Mom . . ."

"You could have taken up archery, sailing, soccer. What's wrong with soccer?"

"I love this song!" said Olivia, tapping her feet to the raging punk music playing on the radio. Then she whispered, "No mainstream bullshit."

Dustin spun around, then looked at his mother. "Did you hear what she said? I bet Janie taught her that!"

"Don't try to change the topic, Dustin. Karate—there's a safe sport." She glanced at his cast as they rambled through the trees.

"How much pain are you in? Did they give you any Tylenol? What time did it happen?"

"Three fifteen."

Rachel squinted. "Three fifteen? The bus wasn't even supposed to get here until three fifteen. And where were your wrist guards?"

"That's what I'm trying to tell you. It had nothing to do with skateboarding. I was so happy to get out of the bus, I jumped over a chain that blocks off the parking lot and caught my foot in it. I broke my fall with my hands."

Nineteen hours into her stay, Olivia was in full hunger strike mode. She'd consented to four glasses of chocolate milk, but not so much as a crumb of food. On the way home from camp the night before, Rachel offered her a Happy Meal. When they arrived home after midnight, a peanut butter sandwich. At breakfast, a blueberry muffin and a cheese string. To all selections Olivia turned up her perfect nose and announced she would only open her mouth for Lucky Charms. Nothing else would tempt the child. And Len had been quite clear with his "only if Olivia's on fire" instructions.

Sagging in front of her milk glass, Olivia already seemed to have shrunk. Rachel sipped her coffee and tried to work out a plan. The Charms weren't going away. They were only going to be shifted into the Tuesday lunchtime slot. This child had a will of marble. No, granite. Marble was too absorbent. There was nothing porous about Olivia's resolve.

Rachel had to give in. She was going to have to get in the car and go pick up a box of goddamned Lucky Charms before stopping by Dustin's pediatrician's office with the X-rays.

Twenty-one and a half hours into Olivia's sojourn, Rachel was back. She'd left Dustin and Olivia upstairs with Janie for an hour while she learned Dustin's injury was a clean one, requiring nothing more than six weeks in an autographed cast. Assured the country doctors had set the bone to the city doctor's satisfaction, Rachel had been free to traipse through three different stores in search of Lucky Charms. Original, not Berry.

With arms full of shopping bags, Rachel stepped into the house and called up the stairs. "Janie? You're off duty now. I'm home."

Janie whooped with glee and slammed her door.

Rachel called Olivia to come down for lunch. She pulled a bowl out of the cupboard, filled it with Charms, then turned around to set it on the island, knocking a bag of groceries onto the floor with a crash. Damn! That would be the bag with the olive jar. Almost immediately, a cloud of fine white powder billowed into the air. Unbleached flour. Coughing, she scooped up what she could and dumped it into the trash. The floor was a pasty mess of olive juice and flour. The more she wiped at it with the torn paper bag, the worse it looked. She reached for a tea towel and tied it around her nose and mouth so she could breathe, and remain conscious long enough to rid the floor of glass shards, then dropped down to the floor and began to scrub.

"Olivia!" she called. "Don't come in here yet. I'm cleaning a—"

"What?" the girl answered from behind her.

Rachel spun around and clutched her chest, her face still covered. "You scared me—"

Olivia's eyes bulged. Her mouth tripled in size. She screamed, running in place. Rachel lunged closer in an effort to console her, but the closer she came, the louder Olivia howled.

Janie tore into the room. "What's going on? Why's it all cloudy in here?" She waved her hands in front of her face, coughing. "Are we on fire?"

Dustin was next. "Man, that kid has some chords! Can't you shut her up?"

Rachel shouted through her tea towel mask, "I don't know how! Go open the windows so the room can clear out." She pushed powdered hair out of her eyes. "Olivia, sweetie, please stop!"

"YOUR MOUTH!" Olivia screamed, still hopping around. "WHERE'S YOUR MOUTH?"

Rachel ripped off the towel and smiled. "Honey, it's just me! It's Rachel." Olivia threw herself into Rachel's arms, the hysterical screaming giving way to gentler, quieter sobbing. Once she settled down, she grabbed her bowl of dry cereal and padded out to the backyard.

"Hey," huffed Dustin, waving his cast through the dust. "How come *she* gets Lucky Charms?"

CHAPTER 33

A Pretty Good Door
for Slamming

Under the lilac bush, Olivia perched her paws on the rim of the bowl like a rodent and wiggled her whiskers as she chewed. She thought about how much better the cereal tasted at Rachel's house, even when she forgot to cry for milk.

She heard a noise next door and looked up, using her whiskers to see because rats don't have very good sight. Janie's friend Tabitha was on her patio, looking under chairs and under cushions. Then she said the swear that sounds like duck but not quite. The one Dad said when he got real mad.

Janie's friend yelled, "Mom, I can't find your stupid keys!" and went inside the house and slammed the back door. It sounded like a pretty good door for slamming.

Lucky.

Olivia ate up the rest of her cereal, wiped a rainbow of marshmallow smears onto her Snoopy shirt, and ran back into the house to burrow into Rachel's couch.

CHAPTER 34

"Sitting in My Room"

—THE RAMONES

Friday evening, Janie wrapped a bottle of wine in a pillowcase and stuffed it into her backpack along with two of her mother's good wineglasses—each one wrapped in a winter mitten—and her Sex Pistols' *Never Mind the Bollocks* CD. "Bollocks" meaning scrotum or testicles, this particular CD would add just the right subliminal anti-male ambience to the evening.

Tabitha would spend all day Saturday at her father's crap wedding and should arrive home by seven. Janie wanted her arrival for the sleepover to coincide with Tabitha's changing out of her strapless dress and into her sweatpants. She figured she should probably show up at about 7:02, just to be safe.

The last things that went into the backpack, after the troll doll and a toothbrush, were Janie's brand-new nightie—hot pink like Tabitha's pool noodle—and a pair of plaid flannel pajama bottoms, in case the nightie seemed over the top.

Zipping up the bag, Janie plopped down onto her bed to wait. She tapped her foot and glanced at the clock radio.

5:57.

She thought for a moment. Twenty-five hours and five minutes to go.

CHAPTER 35

Improper Seaming

Know your limitations. We all have them.

—RACHEL BERMAN, *Perfect Parent* magazine

One hundred hours into Olivia's visit—almost time for another dreaded meal—and Dustin had accidentally soaked his cast in the bath, Olivia had finished off all the Lucky Charms, Janie had locked herself in her room, and Rachel was desperate for a shower. She winced as she pulled out the efficient ponytail she'd worn for two days straight.

Olivia lay sprawled across the sofa, watching *The Incredibles* for the fifth or sixth time that week. It seemed a good time to slip away and at least brush her teeth before Len arrived, so Rachel crept up the stairs to her room, where she paused at the sight of her rumpled bed. Perhaps just a quick rest—no more than five minutes—might do more to restore her spirits than toothpaste and washcloth combined.

She sunk down into her pillow and closed her eyes.

What seemed like moments later, she was awakened by a clattering at her door. She watched, dazed, as the knob turned and the door swung inward a few inches. More rattling ensued, followed by the door being bumped open all the way. Olivia lifted something off the floor, then stood in the doorway, sneezing into a tray full of clattering dishes.

"Bless you," said Rachel.

"I brought you some breakfast-in-bed for dinner," Olivia said, rubbing her nose on her shoulder. Rachel heard some sort of liquid slosh out of a glass and onto the tray. "That's what my dad does when I'm sick and you kind of look sick."

Rachel pulled herself up to a seated position as Olivia tiptoed toward her bed and, with her help, slid the tray onto Rachel's lap where she could finally see its wares. An apple with a bite taken out of it, a pile of fish-shaped crackers, and milk poured into a chipped measuring cup.

"Are you thirsty?" Olivia asked.

Rachel smiled, taking the measuring cup in her hands. "Yes. How did you know?"

The girl shrugged and tried to stop herself from beaming with obvious pride by squeezing her lips together into a frown. "Sometimes if you get so busy doing something else," she looked around the dimly lit room, scrunched up her face, and wiped her nose with her sleeve, "like sitting in the almost-dark, you think you're pretty good. But really you want milk. You just don't know it till you smell it."

Blinking back confusion, Rachel paused, unsure of how to respond. "Well, Olivia, thank you." She sipped from the cup, watching the child stare. "You're a very kind girl."

Olivia could no longer fight her grin, not even with her front teeth clamped down hard on her lower lip. Her small hands fluttered upward, stopping to allow her fingers to tap the center of her chest. Like she was playing a piano. She stared at Rachel for a moment, as if she were about to say something, then, much more quietly than she arrived, she vanished.

Rachel wrapped both hands around the wet cup and stared at the empty doorway, overwhelmed by the sweetness of the girl's gesture.

She'd never hated herself more.

Piper was right. After seventeen years of despising her mother for taking away her right to raise her own daughter, Rachel could finally see the truth. Even when faced with "breakfast-in-bed for dinner," she couldn't do it. Wasn't pinned and stitched the same way as people like Len. Extreme parenting called for a someone much more highly evolved than herself.

That moment—four days into what had to be the most trying week of her life—Rachel knew the truth. All these years, she'd tortured herself with what she should have done when it came to Hannah, when the reality was that she couldn't have done it—not for a year, a month, not even a week.

Buckling under a towering basket of clean laundry, Rachel tapped on Janie's door with her foot. "Janie? Open the door, please. My arms are full." She'd overstuffed the basket—socks and underwear on top of jeans, on top of a sleeping bag Janie had begged to have washed and specially dried with a scented dryer sheet for Tabitha's slumber party the following night.

"Janie?" She kicked the door this time, leaning the basket against the door frame. "Open up!"

She heard nothing but the warring and dogged beat of The Ramones' "Teenage Lobotomy." "JANIE!"

Swearing under her breath, Rachel let the basket slip slowly, painfully, between her body and the door. She opened Janie's door.

"Didn't you hear me?" asked Rachel.

Janie looked up from where she sat on her window seat and pointed to the music, smiling sweetly. "No." She shook a bottle of blackberry-colored nail polish and began painting her toenails.

Her daughter's tranquil aplomb was too much to take. No one in the house had the right to feel that good after the week Rachel had just had. "Well, do you think I could trouble you for a little help?"

"Sure." Janie screwed on the cap and leaped up. She knelt down and began picking up the fallen clothes. "Sorry, Mom," she sang. "You go rest. I'll put this stuff away."

Rachel was too stunned to speak. Never, in fourteen years, had such an offer been uttered in her house. Not by a child, anyway. Could it be that her careful parenting had finally paid off? Should she be telling her readers that if they were patient and waited a decade or so—that their efforts would bear fruit?

Janie pressed her face to the sleeping bag, inhaled, looked at Rachel and said, "Nice," then laid it on top of the overnight bag she seemed to have packed a full day early.

On the wall, just behind Janie's desk, was a poster Rachel had never seen before. A grinning Jessica Simpson in a red top and Daisy Dukes, looking back over her shoulder. It wasn't like Janie to display anything other than the most obscene rock posters and it *certainly* wasn't like Janie to display vampy photos of tabloid celebrities. "You got a new poster?" Rachel asked.

"Yeah. Dad got it for me on eBay. It's signed."

"By Jessica? Are you sure?"

"Yes!"

"Huh." Rachel walked over to the poster and reaffixed one of the thumbtacks. "Did you even see *Dukes of Hazzard*?"

"No, but I might rent it."

"Hm." It reminded Rachel of the Farrah Fawcett poster from the '70s, the grinning, feathered Farrah in the red bathing suit that must have been the last thing every boy on the planet stared at before dropping off to sleep.

Though she couldn't recall any girls pinning Farrah on their walls.

"Why did you get it?"

"I don't know. I like the way it looks, I guess."

"Because you want to look like her?"

Janie's cheeks burned red. "Either look like her or, uh, I don't know. Whatever."

"And why are you putting posters on the *wall* now? I thought we agreed on one place—the ceiling."

"There's no more room on the ceiling." Janie resumed painting her last toenail, then recapped the bottle and admired her feet before shuffling, toes in the air, to the clothes her mother had set on the bed and picking up a red tank. She pulled it on over her white tank, and looked down at her chest, where the red cotton had been slashed and was now being stretched into a shredded diamond shape. "What the fuck happened to my lucky shirt?"

"*Janie!*"

"Oh my God!" Janie pulled at the hole, getting wider by the second. "I planned my whole sleepover outfit around this shirt! It's my best tank top!"

Rachel sighed. "Sorry, sweetie. Olivia was doing a bit of arts and crafts while I was folding on the kitchen table—"

"Olivia? She did this? I'll slaughter her!"

"Janie, calm down! She's a little girl. And she worships you. I'll replace the shirt, okay?"

"But what am I going to wear tomorrow?"

"The white tank looks fine." Rachel's eyes narrowed. "Is there something you aren't telling me? Are there going to be boys over there?"

Janie pulled off the red shirt and kicked it under the bed. "No. Just me and her."

"All right. Len's coming to pick up Olivia. You should probably come down now. So you can be there to say good-bye."

Janie huffed. "Gladly."

Rachel looked around the room one last time, picked up the empty basket, and closed the door.

CHAPTER 36

Wading

Len pulled the Audi into Rachel's driveway and killed the engine. He sat for a moment, wondering if he'd be around to hear the raucous drone of the cicadas another season. It had become a sadistic game he played with himself: how many more hot showers, broken shoelaces, worn-out toothbrushes? Suddenly, the prospect of being around long enough to see the elastic waistbands of the underwear in his drawer pucker and fray seemed a personal triumph. He was always careful now to tumble-dry his briefs on high—though outlasting his underwear through heat manipulation was too pathetic to contemplate.

Four days of treatment and tests had done nothing to change things. Not for the better, anyway. The masses had, apparently, grown somewhat over the past few months. Not enough to worsen his prognosis—were it possible—but enough to make Len realize that not having a plan for Olivia was no longer an option.

Before being admitted to the hospital, he hadn't really felt the part. He'd had the headaches, nausea, the odd bout of dizziness, but the diagnosis hadn't really felt a part of him. This week, however, had stripped him of who he was. He'd taken to sleeping much of the day, walking unsteadily. He'd begun losing his words. Three times during his stay, his mind blanked while he was speaking to

his nurse. Well, not blanked exactly, his mind raced in circles trying to find the words "juice," "blanket," and "bedpan." These three
simple nouns dangled, heartlessly, just out of mental reach.

He glanced out the window and watched a black squirrel bounce
its way across a wooden fence. It was time to talk to Rachel, Len
thought. Not about Olivia. The last thing he would ever do was
beg and cajole someone into loving and caring for his daughter.
Olivia deserved better.

A damp chill drifted into the car and settled over his skin. It
was the death before the death. The end of one of the most sat-
isfying relationships Len had ever known. In his eyes at least, he
and Rachel were perfect for each other. How impossibly cruel was
life—benching Len what seemed like moments after he found her?
And the truth was, no matter how she reacted, whether she chose
to stick around or not, the flirtatious simplicity of the relationship
would be no more. Every glance, every joke, every touch would be
tainted with mortality. Until now, he'd only been "sick" to his parents, doctors, partners. The fucking disease had no heart. Tonight,
it would metastasize to the one adult relationship he never wanted
to hurt.

As he reached out to open the car door, he caught sight of his
hospital wristband, grabbed hold of it, and attempted to pull it
from his arm. It wouldn't tear. He preferred to think that the blue
Tyvek band was too strong—not that he himself was too weak.

His cell phone rang. "Len here."

At first there was no sound. Then crackling.

"Hello?" said Len. "Hello?"

"Len? Philip Peyton." The phone crackled again. "Listen,
Tammy and I have been doing some thinking."

"Yes?"

"We'd like to meet her after all."

Len barely dared to ask. "Who?"

"Olivia. The girl you told us about the other day."

Len said nothing. He squeezed his eyes shut and let the phone drop onto the seat between his legs. As Philip's tinny voice repeated Len's name over and over, Len let his head drop against his head-rest. Tears blurred his vision.

They wanted Olivia. This model couple, these consummate parents, ideal right down to their shoes, who understood NLD even, were willing to consider his daughter. Relief was so strong it was nearly liquid, bucketing over his body with precisely the same strength as the panic that slithered up his spine.

Olivia was in a deep sleep on Rachel's sofa when Len entered. He watched the girl's eyelids twitch, her chest rise and fall. He kissed her on the forehead, but didn't try to rouse her. Accidental naps too close to bedtime never ended well and Len wasn't entirely sure he could handle any tears but his own. The plan was to carry Olivia into the car and pray she slept straight through the night.

He paused to pull the extra quilt off his daughter, then looked at Rachel quizzically. She couldn't know it, but double-blanketing the child was something Virginia had been famous for. Two com-forters in Olivia's crib. Two blankets in the stroller on crisp days. *Instinct*, Virginia had said when teased.

"What?" asked Rachel, blushing from his stare.

"Nothing." He walked across the room to where she stood, kissed her hard, and pulled away. "I just missed you, that's all."

"Me too."

It was Rachel's idea to drag two Adirondack chairs to the land's edge and talk in the fading light. Clearly, she'd had a rough four days. Her hair was unwashed and dark smudges ringed her eyes.

Len had seen Olivia do that to babysitters after a few hours, and insisted Rachel rest while he brewed a pot of coffee. She didn't argue, just fell into the chair and laid her head back, closing her eyes.

By the time he stepped onto the back porch, the day's warmth had given way to a biting chill. In a matter of minutes, the evening had turned crisp, shifting from summer to autumn as an evening in late August can. Len watched the steam from the mugs scrabble skyward as he waded through the overgrown grass to Rachel, asleep, dark chocolate curls skittering across her face in the breeze.

As soon as Len sat, Rachel opened her eyes and blinked, pulling her sweater tighter around her body. "Sorry. I dozed off."

He reached down for her mug, placing it in her hands, and debated whether it was better to tell your girlfriend you were dying before or after she reached full consciousness.

Rachel wrapped her fingers around her coffee and sipped, staring at the scruffy bushes teetering at the bluff's edge. Some of the leaves were already streaked with yellow and brown. "Summer's going fast, isn't it? The leaves are losing their luster."

Len couldn't help but grin sadly. He was beginning to lose luster himself.

"Is Olivia still asleep?" she asked.

"Yes."

"I tried to keep her awake . . ."

"It's fine. She'll sleep right through."

"Did you accomplish whatever it was you were working on?"

"I did." He smiled. "You make little squeaking sounds when you sleep."

She blushed. "I squeak? God, how embarrassing. Sorry."

"That's my girl." He rubbed her arm. "As apologetic as ever."

"Yeah, well, some things never—"

"I bumped into Dustin and his cast in the house," Len said, shaking his head. "Tripped over the chain from a parking barrier. I guess neither of us saw that coming."

"No, we didn't."

"And he'd been there how long?"

"Five minutes. Maybe four."

"My client must feel just terrible."

Rachel shut her eyes. "I've been meaning to call them. I might have been a bit rude when I picked Dusty up."

"Olivia wore you out, didn't she?"

She laughed. "She did her best. She's one stubborn little being."

"Mm. Can't argue that."

"I was thinking, it probably wouldn't hurt Olivia to follow a few rules. Kids are actually more secure when they know the boundaries never change. Parents don't always realize this."

"I know," Len said. "I used to read the magazine, remember?"

Rachel smiled.

"She has boundaries about some things. But I've learned to be flexible about others, in the interest of getting through the day without tantrums and tears."

"It might work now, when she's a child, but what about when she's older? When she doesn't have you around all the time to make sure everything is to her liking?"

Len looked back toward the house. A gust of wind rattled a shutter against the stucco wall. "That scares me so much I can hardly see straight." He placed his hand over hers and leaned forward. "Rachel, sweetheart, I'm dying."

"Oh come on, things aren't *that* bad."

"I'm being serious. I have a year or two. Or less. The doctors aren't sure . . ."

She said nothing. Just listened while he told her about his head-aches, the hospital, the tests, the doctors, his options—or lack of them. He still couldn't say the dreaded C-word out loud, not even to himself. Calling his problem "it" instead.

Rachel looked out at the muddy waters of the Hudson and shook her head, shocked. "But there must be something you can do. There must be other doctors who have fixed this before. This is the twenty-first century, for Christ's sake. Someone must have an answer."

Shivering, Len pulled on the sweatshirt he'd brought from the car. "Maybe if I'd been diagnosed earlier, but not now. I'm beyond fixing."

"But you're so young. So strong. Maybe it's stupid to believe in miracles, but people have overcome things like this before, right? If anyone can handle this, beat this, it's got to be you."

It was natural for her to wish it away. He'd have done the same thing. You can't just sit there and listen to a person revealing their death sentence without grasping at any branch within reach. It was how she was comforting herself. What wasn't comforting to Len was that the best he had to hope for was an event so unlikely it was lumped under the same heading as walking on water.

CHAPTER 37

Despicable

You can't be everything to everyone.

—RACHEL BERMAN, *Perfect Parent* magazine

All the papers she'd seen scattered on his kitchen table a few weeks back—the will, the insurance policy, the file marked "urgent"—as was her instinct, Rachel had assumed the worst. Which was the safest thing to do. If your mind had already covered the gravest of scenarios, you were all but guaranteed to glide past them unscathed. It was how she kept terrible happenings from touching her family. But, this time, this one time, she'd veered away from her system.

The one time she was right. It was too morbid for irony.

Rachel watched Len disappear inside the house to collect Olivia's things. Olivia. How was he going to leave that child? How was he going to care for the girl as his health worsened? Suddenly her weekend with Olivia seemed nearly pleasurable. A few strewn blankets, a couple of bowls of marshmallow cereal—had it really been so bad?

God, she was a bitch.

She walked into the house and followed the sounds of footsteps to the guest room, Olivia's room, where Len was trying to cram a Dora the Explorer pillow into the overstuffed suitcase. She reached out her arm to stop him.

"Let her sleep," she said, taking the pillow from him and tossing it on the bed. "It's starting to rain."

"Are you sure? She's been here—"

She placed a finger on his lips. "I'm sure. You too. Stay for the weekend."

Len let the suitcase drop to the floor, where he watched it topple over and regurgitate its contents, spilling balled-up socks, rumpled T-shirts, and Birthday Wishes Barbie onto the rug. He glanced at Rachel, who smiled. Neither of them moved. Len said, "I didn't say anything before . . . I didn't want things to change . . ." He stuffed his hands into his pockets. "Where does this leave us?"

She stepped over the suitcase, threaded her arms through his, and pulled him close, laying her head on his chest. "I'm not going anywhere."

CHAPTER 38

"Janie Jones"

—THE CLASH

Being in Tabitha's bedroom was like being sandwiched between layers of a birthday cake slathered with pink icing. Frothy curtains matched a fizzy bed canopy. Pink shag carpeting drifted across the floor like sugar. A chandelier hung from the ceiling, dripping with cherry and spearmint teardrops, and matching bedside lamps were cloaked in pink leopard fabric.

Janie had been halfway brave enough to put on the fuchsia nightie. She'd pulled on her flannel bottoms with it. Maybe after the wine, she'd get brave enough to lose the plaid and the army boots.

"And then, my dad took off Kristina's garter with his teeth! He put his whole head up her skirt and bit into it." Tabitha plunked down on a raspberry beanbag. "Right in front of my grandma! It was sickening."

"Another vile display of men acting like primates," said Janie, wrestling with the corkscrew. "It just goes to show . . ."

"Show what?"

Half the cork broke off. Janie unscrewed it from the coiled metal and speared the jagged chunk still lodged in the bottle's neck. "That men have somehow missed out on the entire process of evolution. They're stuck somewhere between gorilla and caveman." The last piece of cork crumbled into small bits, so Janie hammered it inside the bottle and started to fill the glasses to the brims. They chinked their glasses together and said, "Cheers."

Tabitha pretend-sipped, then set her glass on last year's algebra book. Janie didn't care how bad the wine tasted, she held her breath and gulped down most of the glass. Right away her head spun.

Janie had waited a long time to be really alone with Tabitha. Whatever happened—or didn't happen—she'd remember this night, this room, her entire life. You couldn't officially call yourself a lesbian if all you'd ever had were thoughts, could you? It was the break she'd been needing to launch her gay career for real.

The thing was, Janie could never make the first move. It was too dangerous. Being rejected by the hottest girl in school was one thing, being rejected by the hottest girl who tells the whole school that you she-tongued her would be the social equivalent of being eaten by a swarm of Olivia's *rattus rattus* in an alley—one hantavirus-infected nibble at a time.

No. Tabitha would have to kiss first.

"I just hate Kristina," said Tabitha. "You know what she said to me after the ceremony? 'Now I'm officially your Evil Stepmother. So you better behave or I'll make you clean the chimney.' She thought she was being funny."

Janie took another drink. "This Kristina must be stopped," she said, wincing. "Do you have a candle?"

Tabitha reached onto her nightstand and pulled down a purple glass cup with a tea light inside. Then she pulled matches from her desk drawer and lit the wick. Janie placed it on the algebra book beside Tabitha's wineglass.

"Here's what you do," Janie explained. "You swirl your hands above the flame, but always swirling forward and out. Forward and out."

"Where'd you learn this?"

"From some New Age book of my dad's. It's Babe-chick's."

"Cool." Tabitha began swirling.

"Now imagine Katrina—"

"*Krist*ina."

"Kristina, floating far away and out of your life. When you've pushed her far enough away, visualize she's trapped in a bubble and blow it farther, until it disappears like a balloon. Then, pop! She's gone."

Tabitha squinted and looked toward the window, as if watching Kristina floating through the glass.

"Close your eyes!" Janie said.

With her eyes shut, Tabitha repeated Kristina's voyage away from the earth. Janie studied her friend's face as she wished her new stepmother into the next galaxy. Tabitha had on peachy-pink lip gloss. Maybe even a little blush. Janie liked to think it was a good sign, that she'd applied it specially for the sleepover. If she'd worn makeup for the wedding, it would have worn off hours ago, right? At least the lip gloss.

Tabitha opened her eyes and grinned. "Done. Kristina's history."

"Good. We should drink to celebrate."

"I want to play Million Trillion. Did you bring the Seer?"

Janie poured herself more wine and took the troll from her bag, setting him next to the candle. "Turn out all the lights," she said unsteadily. "The Seer prefers the candlebright. Candle*light*."

With the room lit only by the flickering candle, the Seer's pen-light having finally given out, Tabitha spoke first. "What would you rather do, Janie Berman? Never be allowed to shave your under-arms again or eat a million trillion prunes?"

Prunes. Janie loved prunes. It was a good thing Tabitha was hot, because the kid sucked at Million Trillion. "Eat the prunes." Janie downed her wine. "Why aren't you drinking?"

Tabitha took a tiny sip. "I am."

"Drink again."

"I just drank. *You* drink!"

Janie drank and set her glass down with a bang. "Okay. What would you rather do? Have sex with skinny Randy Rousseau and get pregnant and be forced to carry his demon spawn for nine months, then move into a musty trailer with Randy and raise the little brat for a million trillion years. *Or* kiss someone else in the room."

Tabitha sipped from her glass, spilling a little on her shirt. "That's so completely disgusting it should be a Hall-of-Famer!"

Janie leaned back against the pink wall and tried to look kissable. She shrugged. "I've been at this a long time." Hall-of-Fame Million Trillion Ultimatums. It somehow legitimated the whole thing.

"Yeah, I guess."

"The Seer is waiting."

"All right. Well, I'm definitely not sleeping with Rousseau, so I guess I'd kiss someone in the room—if there were anyone here to kiss."

Janie clutched her chest and pulled out an imaginary arrow. "Nice."

"You know what I mean. My turn . . ."

"No way," said Janie. "You have to kiss the kiss."

"Since when? We didn't have to follow through last time."

Janie glanced around the room, trying to think fast—no simple task in her inebriated state of mind. Her eyes rested on the wine bottle. "Alcohol," she said. "When alcohol's involved, the game heats up. Go ahead."

Tabitha laughed. "But there's no one in the room to kiss."

Janie did her best to appear frustrated by the tyrannical shackles of the Seer's rules. "You have to kiss someone, so you might as well go ahead and kiss me."

Tabitha giggled, looking away. "Right!"

"Rules are rules," said Janie. "The kiss *must* happen."

Tabitha narrowed her eyes and studied Janie's face. "Okay. But you have to swear, in front of the Seer of All Truths, that you'll never tell."

Janie crossed her heart and bowed down before the Seer, her hair narrowly missing the tea light. As her forehead rested on the shag, a wave of nausea washed over her, probably the only thing that kept her from grinning like a madman. Madwoman.

They leaned toward each other. Just as they got close enough to feel each other's breath, Tabitha backed up and took another drink of wine. "Wait," she said, swallowing. "I need sustenance."

Again, they moved together. When Janie got within an inch of Tabitha's mouth, she closed her eyes. Then it happened. Their lips met. Touched. Janie felt faint with pleasure and desire and alcohol.

Janie didn't know if it was the wine or Tabitha losing her balance, but Tabitha parted her mouth and pushed into the kiss. She wants this as much as I do, Janie thought. She moved closer, exploring Tabitha's lip with her tongue. She tasted the sweetness of cherry coughdrops mixed with the acidic bite of red wine.

Just as Janie felt the stiff stiffness of Tabitha's tongue against her own, Tabitha jumped, sitting back on her heels and wiping her mouth. "What the hell are you doing? You're making out with me?"

"No! I—"

"What? You think I'm some kind of a lesbian?"

Janie stood up and wavered for a moment, feeling she might throw up. "I don't think any kind of anything . . ."

Standing up, Tabitha kicked the troll doll across the room, then backed away, crawling over her bed and standing on the other side. She started to cry. "This sleepover's over. Pick up your stuff and go."

"Tabitha, relax. It's just a game. Besides, *you're* the one who kissed *me*."

She said nothing, just sobbed into her hands.

"It's not so bad . . ."

"Get out."

"You think I would have kissed *you* if it was my choice?" asked Janie. "I'd have chosen Rousseau!"

"I said, GET OUT!"

Grabbing for her bag, Janie marched toward the door. Halfway across the room, she stopped and turned. The Seer of All Truths had landed on his heels, leaning against the pink wall where Tabitha stood sobbing and clutching her shirt like some kind of fucking rape victim. Janie scooped up the grinning troll and stomped out of the house.

With a chair pushed in front of the door, Janie dug through her desk drawer for the Zippo lighter she'd stolen from her dad's house so she could burn her big panties once she lost ten pounds. If she ever lost ten pounds.

She swiped a pillar candle from a wall sconce and carried it over to her window seat. After lighting the wick, she sat down and closed her eyes, wiping away tears with the heels of her hands. She thought about three things: Tabitha Carlisle had kissed back,

Tabitha Carlisle was a total liar of a poseur bitch with a gap in her teeth, and the image of Tabitha Carlisle drifting across the sky in a pink bubble that disappeared over the horizon and popped.

Her bedroom door creaked, then opened a crack. A crazy halo of reddish hair appeared. "Janie?"

"Not now."

Olivia's whole body appeared. "Can you teach me the words to that song—'No Feelings'?"

"I said, *not now.*"

Olivia stumbled into the room and sat down under the Jessica Simpson poster, flopping her legs out in front of her. "I tried to know all the words, but Aly & AJ keep jumping into my head. The only word I know of your song is 'piss.' "

"Olivia, leave me alone. *Please!* I can't fucking do this right now . . ."

"Callie and Samantha don't believe you gave me the Sex Pistols." Olivia's arms pounded uselessly against the wall behind her. "I told them I actually actually actually really like Johnny Rotten and all they did was laugh at me." The pounding intensified with each "actually." "I hate their stupid guts!"

Janie called, "Mom!"

"They don't even know Johnny Rotten is the singer. And they say they're going to tell the teacher—"

"Olivia, I've *actually actually actually* had a really bad day. The worst in my whole life. And you're supposed to be in bed. If you don't leave me alone, I'm going to have to scream . . ."

"Did you know a naked mole rat is called a *Heterocephalus glaber?* And in a whole neighborhood of them, there's only one mother and father . . . ?"

"No!" Through the window, Janie saw Tabitha look at her, then yank her blind down.

Olivia stood up too fast, sliding up the wall. The sound of tearing confused Janie at first. She thought it was coming from Olivia's clothing or something under her nightgown. It wasn't until her beloved Jessica Simpson poster fell from the wall in strips that she realized what had happened. That Olivia's barrettes had sliced Jessica up the middle like a knife.

"Holy shit, look what you've done! You ripped right through her signature—do you know what this thing is worth?"

Olivia squinted at the torn paper. "Are you still going to come to my birthday party . . . ?"

"NO! Get the hell out of my room! You never get the hint, do you? Wait, I'll teach you some of my own words. Can you remember this: 'You drive me fucking crazy.' Now get out!"

Olivia's lower lip quivered and she raced out of the room. As soon as she was gone, Janie slammed her door and fell on her bed, her body heaving with sobs.

CHAPTER 39

The Bat's Eyeball
Winks in the Grass

The house was quiet. Olivia crawled back into Rachel's guest bed, scratched at her pajama bottoms, and wondered where her dad was sleeping. Maybe in Dustin's room. Or Rachel's. Outside the sky still looked like night—all starry and black. She fell back onto her Dora pillow and closed her eyes. But sleep didn't come. She needed her dad but Janie was the only person who was up. And Olivia wasn't going into Janie's room. Maybe not ever again.

She sat up again, then crawled along the foot of the bed to her suitcase. From deep inside her case, Olivia noticed a tiny sparkle peeking out of a bag. Her treasure box!

While her dad was busy packing up her things and he said, "You're going to stay at Rachel's house for a few days," Olivia had snuck out to the backyard with a soup spoon. If she was going to live at Rachel's house all week, there was no way she was going to leave Georgie Boy behind.

Now, digging through her sweatpants and underwear, hurling them to the floor, Olivia saw more and more of the plastic bag containing the glittery treasure box and, right next to it, the muddy spoon. She clapped her hands. With the flashlight from under her pillow, she took the spoon and the twinkling box and tiptoed down the stairs, out the back door into the darkness.

The grave was harder to dig here. The dirt was packed down hard and the spoon kept flicking muck into her eyes. Finally, once the hole was big enough, Olivia poured the gerbil into it. She couldn't just pick up Georgie Boy with her hands, because part of his tail wasn't even attached anymore.

As she spooned dirt and grass clippings over the hole, she heard a noise from the backyard next door. She looked up.

There was a man standing beside Tabitha's pool. The same one who talked to Tabitha on the days she wore her bathing suit. His beard looked like the prickly kind and the top of his head was shiny in the moonlight.

The man took something out of his pocket and used it to unlock the back door, which meant the something was a key. Tabitha and her mother went out a few minutes ago; Olivia saw them drive away. The house was pitch-dark. The man opened the door, then shut it again, and locked it. Then he did it all over again. Unlocked the actual door, opened it, and shut it again, locking it.

When he was all done, he put the key into his pants again and lit a cigarette with his match. Olivia watched. She liked the way every time the man sucked the cigarette, the end of it burned orange. Like a bat's eyeball.

She stayed very still. The man didn't see her and it was probably a good plan to make sure the man kept right on not seeing her. Then he threw the cigarette into the grass and left. Olivia didn't move. Not even a finger. She waited until the cigarette started winking, then burned itself out, before spooning more dirt on top of Georgie Boy and sneaking back to bed.

CHAPTER 40

Empty Shelving

Back-to-school shopping can be stressful for your children. Plan carefully so you shop at a time of day when they are neither hungry, nor tired. Make them feel this is special time with you.

—RACHEL BERMAN, *Perfect Parent magazine*

There's nothing left," wailed Janie, hunting through the bin of damaged binders. Rachel sighed. She didn't know whether Janie's recent foul mood had been driven by teenage hormones or back-to-school frustration. The girl had been impossible to deal with since early August.

"What about this one?" asked Piper, holding up a pink binder with flowers on the spine.

Janie grimaced. "Would *you* carry that thing around?"

Piper tossed it back onto an otherwise empty shelf.

"Oh, come on. Does it really matter what your binder looks like?" asked Rachel. The belly of the plastic shopping cart was fully occupied by Olivia, sitting cross-legged, wearing a combination SpongeBob toque with attached SpongeBob pencil case. In spite of Len's repeated offers to unhook hat and case, Olivia insisted on wearing them as a set.

The last-day-of-summer-vacation celebratory dinner with Len and Olivia—and Piper—had taken slightly longer than expected. Olivia's meal was switched three times, owing to chicken nuggets that refused to look exactly as they did in the picture on the menu. By the time the check arrived, Olivia was nearly fainting from hunger. Rachel and Len had been forced to stop at McDonald's before their trip to the drugstore to pick up back-to-school supplies.

Janie examined a plaid binder and rolled her eyes when the zipper jammed. "I'll be the only kid in high school without a binder tomorrow. Or click pencils, even!"

"Never mind, Insanie," said Dustin, who had just returned from the perfume area, reeking of men's cologne. "That Cinderella glitter pen makes more of a statement anyway."

"Dustin," called Piper, holding up a dictionary. "Come and look at these. They're bound in leather." She looked closer, then dropped it in a bin. When Dustin reached in after it, she tapped his hands. "My mistake, darling. It was vinyl."

"I'm tired," said Olivia. "I want to go home."

"You're going to Rachel's house," Len said. "Just for the night. And you're riding the school bus with Janie and Dustin in the morning. First day of school, remember?"

Olivia shook her head, making the pencil case jiggle across her face. "I don't want to go on the bus with Janie and Dustin. I want to go in a car with you."

"You'll have much more fun on the bus," Len assured her.

"I'll have much more fun IN A CAR!"

"We'd better hurry," Rachel whispered to Len. "They're exhausted and you'll end up driving all night."

"It's less than three hours to Amherst. I'll check in by two, sleep a few hours, and meet up with the Peytons for breakfast. They'll drive me out to Tammy's parents from there."

"I should come with you. Help with the driving."

He kissed her head. "I'll be fine."

"Can't you go later in the week? Or meet her family later in the day tomorrow? You need your sleep."

"I don't want Olivia getting to know Tammy and Philip before I've checked out the whole family." He sniffed, looking at Rachel. "I don't want to waste time incase anything . . . goes wrong in the meantime."

She put a hand on his back, rubbing softly. "You're sure they're the right ones, babe?"

It was barely perceptible, but his gaze lowered slightly and lost its focus. He drew in a long breath. "They are." Then he clapped his hands and rubbed them together. "Who wants to come look for lunch boxes?"

The parking lot was nearly empty by the time both families filed out of the store with their scanty purchases. Janie and Dustin grumbled and shoved each other as they raced for Rachel's car. Olivia tumbled out of the shopping cart and ran toward the front door of her father's car, shouting, "Called it!"—like Janie and Dustin.

"Wrong car, sweetie," Len said to Olivia. "You're going with Rachel and Piper."

"Is Janie coming?" asked Olivia.

"Absolutely."

Olivia's shoulders sagged. She sucked in a deep breath and glanced toward Rachel's Saab. The passenger seat was a writhing snarl of adolescent arms and legs.

"Daddy, I don't want to go with them . . ."

"Of course you do," Len said. "Janie's your special friend, remember?"

Olivia didn't answer.

"It's my turn, assface!" Janie grunted from the car.

"I have squatter's rights!"

"Language, darlings," called Piper, opening Rachel's trunk and setting her bags inside.

Len gave Olivia a gentle shove toward the backseat of Rachel's car. "Go on . . ."

Once all three kids were strapped in, Len kissed Olivia good-bye, telling her he was off to an evening seminar. Rachel followed Len to the driver's side of his car, leaning on the door after he'd climbed inside. He opened all the windows. "I'll call you in the morning. You have enough Lucky Charms?"

Rachel grinned. "Yes."

"Good." He glanced back at her car. "I can hear them squabbling from here. Are you sure you're up for this?"

"They're off to school in . . . what?" She checked her watch. "Less than ten hours. I can handle any amount of squabbling for less than twelve."

"Olivia seems a bit clingy."

"I noticed."

"Probably school nerves." He kissed her nose. "I love you, babe, but I should probably get—"

"Wait. I've been thinking."

His eyebrows inched upward as he waited, arms resting on the steering wheel.

"About the whole Leaside thing," she said, tilting her head. "I know you don't want to discuss it, but I think I have the answer. What if I hired you as my lawyer? Then you could request Hannah's file, right?"

"Rachel," he started to say.

"The whole thing would be perfectly legitimate—"

"I still couldn't do it. We'd need a court order and no judge would ever rule in your favor, not if the adoptive parents are good people."

"Please."

"It's unethical."

She stood up, taking her hands off the door. "You won't do anything unethical? You just lied to your daughter—you told her you're off to a seminar when really you're going to meet her new, her new . . ."

"That's not fair. You know I can't tell her the truth. Not until it's . . . imminent, Dr. Kate said."

Rachel spun around to find her mother directly behind her. Piper handed Len a forgotten shopping bag and returned to the Saab without a word.

CHAPTER 41

"Jigsaw Feeling"

—Siouxsie and the Banshees

Janie walked to the end of her driveway and paused. She squinted toward the bus stop. It was the first day of school and Tabitha was already there, talking to Arianna as if life was just perfect. Janie guessed that if you were Tabitha Carlisle, it pretty much always was. She bent over and pretended to tie her shoe while Olivia followed Dustin to the stop.

She'd been praying that, by some miracle, Tabitha would have transferred to public school and Janie wouldn't have to face her blue eyes ever again. She hadn't seen Tabitha since the Night, mainly because she hadn't ventured outside other than putting out the trash cans. The risk of bumping into the Goddess Herself had kept her on high alert the last few weeks of summer, causing her to abort her plans to go to Cody's party—her one and only invitation all year—and seriously establish herself as one of the cool kids. Cody had left several messages urging her to come, then, after the fact, urging her to call him. Not only that, but because Tabitha might see her, Janie had given up getting a sun-kissed glow lying out by the river. Under her mother's authoritarian regime, tanning by the river involved a half-mile hike down the road. Past Tabitha's very exposed corner yard. So here Janie was, on the first day of her freshman year, looking as bloodless as a cadaver.

And it didn't help to be showing up with Olivia Bean.

When she reached the stop, Tabitha and Arianna fell silent. Olivia was humming The Ramones' "We're a Happy Family," and, still humming, she went over to Tabitha and stood too close. Tabitha stepped away. Olivia moved closer.

"*Mus musculus* pee glows in the dark, you know," said Olivia. "Like glow-in-the-dark bowling balls."

Arianna said, "What the fuck are you talking about?"

Olivia blinked. "A mouse."

Arianna and Tabitha turned away from her, laughing.

"I saw someone at your house," Olivia said to Tabitha.

Tabitha rolled her eyes and grunted.

Undaunted, Olivia continued, "It was your special friend."

Tabitha's eyes darted from Janie to Arianna. She laughed nervously, before saying, "I don't know what you're talking about, kid."

"Your friend. The one you talk to by the pool."

Tabitha flashed Janie a look. "I wonder who *that* could be?"

"Me too," said Olivia. "Your friend sure likes your house."

"Oh, really?" Tabitha folded her arms and shifted her weight. "Better keep your windows closed, Arianna. Berman just might climb inside. And while you're at it, cover your mouth. Berman likes to lock lips."

Dustin snorted and looked at Arianna. "Sorry. Ain't gonna happen, dude."

"Not you," said Tabitha. "Your *sister*."

Janie noticed Olivia had clamped one hand over her mouth. "Olivia, you can let go of your mouth, it's okay," she said. Olivia ignored her and moved closer to Tabitha.

"I'd keep it covered," Tabitha sneered. "You could get a disease from *her*."

Olivia smiled at her new friend before covering her mouth again.

Janie removed Olivia's hands from her face. "No, Olivia. She's teasing you. That's what Tabitha does best—tease."

"You're a sicko," said Tabitha. "You and your stupid Million Trillion."

"Shut up," said Janie.

"Hey!" Dustin looked at his sister. "That's a secret!"

Tabitha grinned. "Oh, I'll tell you a secret . . ."

Janie lunged forward and shoved Tabitha's shoulders, knocking her backward into the dirt. "I said, *shut up!*"

The bus roared around the corner and pulled to the side of the road. Tabitha picked herself up, dusted off her pants, and reached for her backpack. As she pushed past Janie to board the bus, she stopped and whispered, "You're fucked, Berman."

Janie swung into the fourth last seat from the back and scooted right over to the window to make room for Olivia. Not her first choice of seatmates, but the bus was nearly full. She pushed her book bag down between her feet and watched Olivia stumble along the aisle, saying hello to all she passed. Some kids burst out laughing, others didn't bother to look up.

Assholes.

When Olivia got to Janie, she started to say hello, then stopped herself. Janie half-smiled, but Olivia walked straight past and plopped into the seat behind Janie. A surprising move when you considered Janie was the only one on the bus who acknowledged the girl. Whatever.

Tabitha's hair looked too dazzling to be naturally sun-bleached. She'd obviously had it colored since the almost-sleepover. As the bus roared through traffic, Tabitha looked back at Janie and grinned wickedly. Then she leaned over her seat back and whispered into Jeffrey Greenblatt's ear. Jeffrey's head whipped around. Once he located Janie, he started laughing. Then he whispered to the boy next to him.

Janie's stomach took a dive. Tabitha wouldn't. She wasn't that cruel. Was she?

"Janie," said Olivia, tapping the back of Janie's head. "Is it my birthday today?"

"No," Janie said, watching the other side of the bus.

The kids behind Jeffrey were whispering now. And leaning forward into the next row. Soon half the bus was throbbing. Janie slumped down in her seat, propping her knees against the seat in front of her. Robert Charing ducked into the aisle and whispered into Olivia's ear.

"What did he say?" Janie asked when he'd gone.

"He said you're either-way gay."

Janie felt her insides go liquid in horror. She shrank down in her seat, willing herself to disappear. The laughter on the bus sounded distant. Muffled. For a moment, she thought of getting off at the next bus stop, looking for a field, a forest, anyplace she could lose herself.

She'd hidden her feelings so well, for so long. And now, just like that, her life was over.

Olivia tapped her. "Janie, what does you're either-way gay mean?"

"Nothing."

"It means you're nothing?"

She turned to look out the window. "Pretty much."

The bus pulled over again and a handful of kids piled on, including none other than the gloriously bronzed Cody Donovan. He lumbered along the aisle, pointing at people as a cooler-than-you ninth-grader. As he passed Janie, he didn't point or grin or make some lame sexist remark. He just raised his eyebrows in mock amusement and sauntered past.

He knew.

CHAPTER 42

Shannon

Encourage grandmothers and grandfathers to get involved.
They can play a magical role in your child's life.

—RACHEL BERMAN, *Perfect Parent* magazine

Monday, the following week, Rachel looked up from her desk to see her mother stomp across the office, pumpkin-colored purse in one hand, McDonald's bag in the other. She fell into the chair in front of Rachel's desk. Piper's layered bangs, usually artfully swept to one side, had splattered over her forehead and her face was taut. And, Rachel couldn't be certain but Piper's eyeliner might have been smudged ever so slightly.

Rachel didn't know what was more shocking—that her mother may have been crying or that she'd set a loafered foot in McDonald's.

"Hello, dear," said Piper, after clearing her throat. Her eyes darted across Rachel's desk.

"Is that your lunch?" Rachel asked, incredulous.

"Ours. I'm treating you."

"*You* are going to eat French fries and a, a . . . ?"

"Double Quarter Pounder. With cheese."

Rachel glanced at the crumpled bag, then back to Piper, unsure of what to do. Piper looked thoroughly unglued. "Well, I *was* going to skip lunch today," Rachel said. "I've got a lot of financial things to figure out. But I suppose . . ."

Piper picked up the papers on Rachel's desk. "Is this your payroll?" Her eyes widened and she looked at Rachel, surprised. "It's enormous. How can you stay afloat with expenses like these?" She scanned the statement. "Look here, Michael Singer in sales is making nearly as much as your father did."

"Michael's been here for more than twenty years. Plus there's inflation. And commissions."

"You don't need so many salespeople, Rachel. If you don't downsize, you may lose the business."

Piper set the sheets down and picked up a pencil, crossing out name after name as she went through the list. When she'd finished, she slid the paper back to Rachel and laid her hand over her daughter's. "I'm only telling you what your father would have."

Rachel stared down at Piper's neat graphite strokes, marveling at how easy it would be to eliminate her problems. With one hand, she crumpled up the paper and hurled it at the trash can. "When I took over this business, I swore I'd do everything in my power to keep this company, this family, intact. When Dad and I discussed—"

"I just left Leaside Adoption," Piper blurted out, sitting back in her chair.

"What?"

"I wanted her file. For you."

Rachel was too stunned to move.

"I called in advance," Piper explained. "I wanted to find out the best time of day to arrive. I learned they open at eight, and most of them break for lunch at eleven. Except for the receptionist." She stared hard at her daughter. "Shannon."

The reception area had been nearly silent but for a tinny radio. Behind the long desk, the wall was covered floor-to-ceiling in color-coded files. Shannon wasn't quite the vixen Rachel had made her out to be, Piper thought. About forty pounds overweight, with multiple piercings up one ear and a wrist full of clinking bangles, she could not have been less appropriate for Len.

Shannon looked up from her desk and smacked her gum. "Can I help you?"

"Yes." Piper dug through her quilted leather purse, pulling out various items and laying them on the desk: first her wallet, then her car keys, then her lipstick case. Finally, she produced a torn piece of paper. "I've forgotten my reading glasses," she explained. "So I'm not quite sure I'm in the right place." Piper stared at the paper. Squinted. Held it farther away. "I can't seem to read this address . . ."

"Let's see?" Shannon stood up and reached for the paper, examining it. Under the fluorescent office lights, Piper could see her face was slick with perspiration. Shannon pushed her sleeves up to her elbows and said, "Oh, no. You're looking for 301 Eastern Boulevard. This is *31* Eastern."

"Oh dear." Piper fluttered her lashes. "I should really keep those glasses hanging around my neck. At my age, I'm absolutely lost without them."

Shannon sat back down again. She smiled, holding up a finger as she reached for the ringing phone. "Leaside Adoption, how may I help you?"

As Shannon dictated the mailing address to the caller, Piper swept her things back into her bag, snapped it shut, then—perhaps

a shade too dramatically—swooned, pitching forward and clutching the desk.

Shannon jumped up, told the caller she had an emergency, and
rushed around to Piper's side of the desk. "Are you okay, ma'am?"

Piper lifted a feeble hand to her brow. "I'm, I'm just a little
dizzy," she breathed. Shooting a sideways glance at Shannon, Piper
congratulated herself at the look of panic on the poor girl's face.

Shannon took her by the arm and guided her to one of the
ancient sofas in front of her desk. Lowering Piper down onto the
crumbling black leather, she said, "Should I call 911? Or a family
member?"

"Heavens, no," Piper said, forcing a brave smile. She reached for
a magazine and fanned her face with it. "It's just my blood sugar
acting up again. Don't ever get old, dear. It's a terrible thing."

"Oh, I'd never consider *you* ol—"

"If it's not too much trouble . . ." Piper interrupted, touching the
girl's arm. "I could really use a drink."

"Sure thing." Shannon disappeared down a hall, cheap metal
bracelets chattering.

"If you have juice or a small carton of milk, that would be perfect!" Piper called after her. Then she jumped up and darted over to
the files, which were labeled with the first three letters of people's
names. Just as she located the Ds, all of which were coded in red,
Piper heard the bracelets jingling back toward reception and flew
back to her fainting couch.

"Here," said Shannon, slightly out of breath. She handed Piper a
glass of tepid tap water. "It's all we had. I didn't wait for the water
to run cold," she explained. "Just in case."

"You know, I don't think water is going to do it." Piper set the
glass on the side table and pulled a five-dollar bill from her bag. "I
hate to trouble you . . ."

"Not at all!"

"I noticed a convenience store just down the block. If you could pick me up a bottle of orange juice, unsweetened, it might be enough to stabilize my insulin."

Shannon hesitated. She glanced toward the phone and crinkled her nose. "I don't know if I should leave; I'm the only one here."

"Oh, I'll be fine on the couch by myself."

"No. I meant my coworkers are all out and the phone might ring. Or someone might come in."

Piper leaned back and closed her eyes for a moment. "Oh dear, you stay then. God knows I don't want you to get in trouble." Then she reached out to pat Shannon's hand. "Just promise when the ambulance arrives—tell the attendants I'm allergic to Erythromycin."

Shannon snatched the money, pressed a few buttons on the phone, and headed for the door.

The moment the girl had gone, Piper jumped up and returned to the red-coded files. She ran her finger along the shelf, and slowed when she reached the DEs. There were several files with the code DEA, and Piper pulled them out, one after another. Deacon, Deakos, two Deans, Deangelis, Deangelo, Deappollonia, Dear— Piper stopped, sucked in a breath, scanning the file to make sure it wasn't an abbreviation for Dearborn. It wasn't. Dearden-Myers. Wait—she'd gone too far. She pulled them out again, rifling through the contents of each, then pushed them back into place, her heart thumping.

The file was gone.

Now, Rachel just shook her head in disbelief. So many emotions were doing battle inside her, she could barely breathe. That her mother—*Piper Dearborn*—had gone from pretending Hannah didn't exist to trying to steal her file was incomprehensible. Through a fainting caper, no less. It had been Rachel's one and only shot at finding her lost daughter, and by some barbed twist of fate, the file wasn't even there.

"What made you do it?" Rachel asked quietly. "After all this time . . . why?"

Piper pulled a burger out of the bag and unwrapped it. "My silence about Hannah wasn't born of cruelty, despite what you might think. You'd just been so quiet about her until this Olivia came into your life. I thought it best not to stir it up."

Rachel said nothing.

"I regret it now."

"It's all right, Mom. You tried today."

"I wasn't talking about that. I regret forcing you to give her up."

Rachel looked up. "What?"

"You were nearly eighteen. Almost a woman. I should never have interfered." Piper balanced her burger on her knees and reached out to pat Rachel's arm. Then, as if not knowing what to do with her hand, she went back to her Quarter Pounder.

"But . . . how long have you felt this way?" asked Rachel.

"Since Janie was born."

Rachel closed her eyes and exhaled.

"It was Janie . . . holding my own grandchild for the first time."

"Mom, that was *fourteen* years ago. Why didn't you say something sooner?"

Piper pulled out a compact to check her teeth for sesame seeds. "I regret that too. I'm actually considering hiring a therapist. Stifling one's emotions is very unhealthy."

Rachel laughed.

"That's so funny?"

"Just that you regret it for *your* sake. Not mine."

"What? Loving one's grandchildren is suddenly reprehensible? Unforgivable?" Piper blinked at her daughter. The thing about Rachel's mother was, no matter how misguided, how insensitive she may have been when it came to Hannah, she truly loved her grandchildren. And if Hannah was now being considered one of her grandchildren, well, it was a considerable evolution.

"No, Mother," Rachel said, lips twitching. "It's sweet." She reached for her ringing phone. "Rachel Berman."

"It's Len." He sounded exhausted.

Rachel felt a muscle in her back tighten. Since the night in the dark parking lot, she'd only spoken to him once—when he picked up Olivia after school. His meeting with Tammy and Philip's families had gone even better than he'd hoped and today, Tammy and Philip were to go to Len's office early that afternoon to meet Olivia—who was being allowed to skip school for the day—and, ultimately, sign papers.

Olivia's future would be secure. And Len's future, well . . . she couldn't think about that right now. She'd just lost her daughter all over again. "Hey. How did your meet—",

"Rachel." She could hear busy office sounds behind him. Phones ringing, people's voices. "Rachel?"

"I'm here, Len. What is it?"

"Write down these directions."

As she scrawled down his instructions, a prickly chill spread down her shoulders, her arms, her chest. Her eyes darted up to her mother's and she mouthed, "Get your purse."

CHAPTER 43

Through the Chain-link Fence

Most of all, there will be moments to treasure. No matter how brief, how seemingly insignificant, some of these moments will feed you forever.

—RACHEL BERMAN, *Perfect Parent* magazine

They parked the car under the shadow of a mature elm in front of the fenced playground. Brighton wasn't a particularly large high school, just the original red brick building, about seventy or eighty years old, with a long, low stucco addition that ran around the back of the playground. A school janitor stood in the center of the grassy field beside a cement shed, painting over masterful graffitied prose that read, "Brighton can bite my hairy . . ."

The recipient of Brighton's bicuspids, mercifully, had been covered over and would, from that moment forward, remain a mystery.

Opening the paper bag, which she'd grabbed from Rachel's desk at the last minute, Piper pulled out a handful of cold fries. "You should eat now, before the recess bell rings. Your food's cold, but soon it'll be soggy, too."

Rachel shook her head, unable to take her eyes off the front doors.

From two sets of double doors, teenage girls spilled out onto the school grounds. As soon as she saw them, Rachel realized picking Hannah out from this sea of white blouses, tartan skirts, knee socks, and clunky black shoes wasn't going to be simple. Girls of every height, width, hair color, and ethnicity broke into clusters, where they stood around laughing and whispering. Gone were the carefree days of playing tag or four-square on the tarmac. That clearly went out in grade school. These girls were working hard to achieve a look that was both cool and poised beyond their years.

That was it.

That was how she'd know Hannah. Hannah wouldn't care much about how thin her legs looked in her hiked-up skirt. Nor would she care about being seen talking to the right kids at lunchtime. Hannah would be a free spirit, her movements more childlike and uninhibited. Rachel squinted her eyes and tried not to focus.

Then she saw it. The loose fluid movements of a much younger spirit, jogging across the lawn. Rachel focused her eyes and saw a girl with long, curly, very nearly black hair, more animated and smaller than most of the others, looking back and waving for someone to join her.

Her cheeks were rounder than Janie's, but her mouth was the same tight little red rose just beginning to bud. Rachel's breath caught in her throat as she somehow got out of the car. Suddenly her face felt the cool chain links of the fence and she sensed Piper close by, on her right.

Two other girls, both of them with Down's syndrome, joined the dark-haired girl, racing her across the grass but stopping just short of the tarmac and letting her win.

She had friends.

The image of Olivia sneezing into the measuring cup flashed before her.

A teacher walked over to the grass and called out, "Chloe!" The girl's face lit up and she raced toward the older woman, who put something in the girl's hands.

Rachel glanced at Piper for a moment. They both had to be thinking the same thing. The girl was happy. Loved. Safe. She was brimming with joy, overflowing with people who cared.

Something struck the fence at Rachel's feet. She looked down to see a small turquoise ball lying in the grass. The dark-haired girl ran after it, dropping onto her hands and knees in the grass. Rachel sank to the sidewalk, her face just above the girl's, and threaded her fingers through the cool links of the fence. As the girl scooped up the ball, she rose up on her knees and stared at Rachel.

Chills spread across Rachel's body. Tears stung her eyes. Her breath came in ragged gasps, but she smiled. The face looking back at her, the silver, almond-shaped eyes that looked like shards of burnished steel, the dark lashes—double thick—the upturned nose . . . it was Hannah.

"Hi," said Hannah, grinning shyly.

Rachel smiled, silently sobbing at the same time. Her body shook as she laughed, cried, whispered, "Hi."

A wisp of hair blew across Hannah's eyes. Narrow fingers, like Janie's, pushed it away.

Rachel squeezed the chain links and moved closer. She almost blurted out the truth. Said, "I gave birth to you and don't for one second ever believe I didn't want you, didn't love you," but stopped herself. Olivia was wrong. Hannah didn't need to hear it. It was Rachel who needed to say it.

Hannah rose to her feet and was gone. She disappeared into the sea of uniforms, followed by a group of friends. As hard as Rachel tried, she couldn't find her. She and Piper walked the length of the fence and back again several times without luck. There were simply too many girls, too many white blouses.

For a long while, Rachel didn't move. The bell rang and the girls filed back inside, not one of them possessing Hannah's life force. Just before the doors closed, something blue rolled through them and down two cement steps. Hannah burst back outside, picked up the ball, and glanced at Rachel. She waved and dashed back in.

Neither Piper nor Rachel spoke once they got in the car. They stared through the windshield for what seemed like hours, but could only have been a few minutes. "She's beautiful, don't you think?" asked Rachel.

"Like Janie."

"And fine. More than fine. She looks like she's thriving."

Piper, who had finished her own meal before the girls came outside, poured half of Rachel's fries onto her lap. "If only I'd had it so good as a child," she said. "I might have had the confidence to help run your father's magazine instead of staying home, scooping up cat shit from your father's Himalayans."

Rachel bit into a small fry. She half-smiled. "Please. Olivia prefers the word 'droppings.'"

Olivia.

Since the Code Adam night, one of the worst nights of her life, she'd been haunted by two things. The guilt of being too distracted by her own fantasy to pay attention to the reality of the little girl in her care. And, in the pet store, the warmth of Olivia's body bundled snugly around her own, that soft, fleshy cheek glued to Rachel's neck, those dimpled hands clasped behind Rachel's head, lost in the tangles of her fallen ponytail. She remembered the child's hair tickling her cheek.

God, Olivia had smelled good.

The polarity of Hannah's and Olivia's worlds was almost too much to consider.

Hannah had everyone. Olivia had . . . Olivia had the Peytons, or she would once Len was gone. Rachel checked her watch. They were probably signing right now.

The child would be living in their condo. They planned to buy her a hamster.

Rachel's heartbeat quickened and the smell of Olivia's shampoo filled her nostrils again.

The girl's words came back to her, from the breakfast-in-bed-for-dinner night. "Sometimes if you get so busy doing something else," she'd said, "like sitting in the almost-dark, you think you're pretty good. But really you want milk. You just don't know it till you smell it."

"Oh my God," Rachel said out loud. Her mouth went dry. "What have I done?"

"What?"

Rachel's heart pounded as she fumbled through her purse.

"What's wrong?"

Rachel pulled out her cell phone. It was dead. "Damn it!" she wailed, hurling it into her lap. "Give me your cell phone."

"I don't have it. I left it—"

"We have to get to Len's office."

Piper started the car and pulled out into traffic, waving her arm out the window to mollify the honking drivers. "Rachel, what is going on?"

Rachel stared through the windshield. In the tiniest movement, she shook her head. "I've been sitting in the almost-dark too long."

———————

The elevator was taking too long. Rachel raced through Len's lobby, the soles of her shoes slapping against the polished marble floors. She tugged open the heavy fire door that led to the stairwell and took the steps two at a time, barely noticing that she was gulping air, swallowing, and gasping instead of breathing.

She burst onto the seventh floor and into the tranquility of Standish, Bean and Roche, her footsteps silent now. Marching past Len's assistant, who was filing something in a drawer behind her desk, Rachel kept her eyes on Len's closed door. Just as she reached for the handle, his secretary called out, "You just missed him. He finished early and went home for the night."

Somehow Rachel wasn't prepared for Olivia to open the door. The whole way over, she'd rehearsed what she was going to say to Len. First, about his sudden decision to help her find Hannah. Second, about Olivia's eventual guardians. She'd so perfectly blown her chances, for the zillionth time in her life, that she'd elevated lost opportunities to an art form. Still, she was hoping, praying, that maybe there'd be some way Len could work Rachel into the signed guardianship agreement, at the very least as someone with regular visits. Perhaps a feeble sort of too-little, too-late codicil that would never be good enough for Rachel, but would be a whole lot better than the alternative—never seeing Olivia again.

It wasn't even three o'clock in the afternoon, but Olivia was wearing bright red pajamas and matching slippers. Her hair was still wet from the bath, slicked back and brushed smoother than Rachel had ever seen.

Olivia blinked fast when she saw Rachel.

"Whoa." Her right hand held Birthday Wishes Barbie by the foot. Her left fluttered up and pattered against her chest. "I didn't even *know* you were coming over. Is it my birthday?"

She smiled, giving the child a gentle poke in the stomach. "No, sweetie. Not today."

"You could come in anyway. Even if you didn't bring a present." The door opened wider and, as the child looked past her, Rachel saw there were bubbles in her ear. She pulled out a Kleenex and wiped Olivia's ear clean. The girl was surprisingly tolerant of all the fussing, and when Rachel finished, Olivia looked up. "Were you just taking care of me?"

Rachel whispered, "I think I might have been." She pulled Olivia into her arms and held her close enough to smell her shampoo. The girl's stiff little body relaxed, and she allowed herself to be rocked from side to side. When Olivia's hands came to rest on Rachel's stomach, tapered fingers tapping the rhythm of maternal effervescence, Rachel closed her eyes and willed herself not to cry.

CHAPTER 44

"Anarchy for Sale"

—DEAD KENNEDYS

J anie sat cross-legged on the gritty wooden stage floor, eating a tuna sandwich. The heavy velvet curtain, the only thing separating her from the cafeteria, draped against her back like a hug. It seemed the entire school had divided itself into two teams: Team Carlisle and Team Berman. And Team Berman had substantially fewer members.

Since her bus-stop fight with Tabitha the week prior, Janie had faked sick twice. Her mother took her to the pediatrician, who chalked it up to high-school-newbie stress—although he hadn't quite used those words.

One thing was certain. She had to do something. She'd been using her solitary lunch hours on the darkened stage to plan. Her first instinct was to destroy Tabitha's Golden Girl reputation. But how? Send Tabitha's best friend, Charlotte, a pair of lacy black panties by mail with an anonymous note saying "I found Tabitha with your boyfriend in the back of my garage. Be a doll, won't you, and return these to her?"

But that wouldn't undo the crippling damage Janie's reputation had suffered. No. She needed to focus on herself.

Do something that would clear her name.

In other words, she needed to lose the whole virginal debutante lesbian shit and fuck some guy's brains out.

She walked along the second-floor hallway, lunch bag pressed to her chest.

"Don't even think about it, Berman," said Samantha Ewing as Janie passed. "I'm off limits . . . to you!" As if Janie would ever, in a million *trillion* years, touch her twelfth-grade sack of bones. What kind of moron goes to L.A. for Christmas holidays, returns three cup sizes larger—with a note to excuse her from gym for the next month—and expects everyone to believe she had a "gush of hormones?"

When Janie reached her locker, she stopped and stared. The words I LIKE GIRLZ were scrawled across the metal door. Janie quickly unlocked the door and with her face pushed inside, she wiped her teary eyes and took a few deep breaths. Then she slammed the door shut.

Cody Donovan was on the other side, sucking on a marker. He smiled, pulled the pen out of his mouth, and flicked off the cap. He blacked over the graffiti and grinned. "Not everyone thinks it's a bad thing," he said, his breath stinking of cigarettes. "I'm all for girls on girls." He put an arm around her shoulders.

"Shut up, Donovan," Janie said, trying to slip away.

"Seriously. I'll cheer you up."

"Thanks, but I'm doing fine."

He ran his finger down the neck of her blouse, laughing when she knocked it away. "Come on, Berman. You're killing me here."

Maybe Cody was exactly what she needed. A guy who'd strut around with his feathers spread and blast his conquest to the whole school. Nobody would believe a real lesbian would sleep with a guy like him. People might think Tabitha made the whole kiss thing up.

What other choice did Janie have? As terrible as it might be, she had to do it. "Okay," she whispered.

He tilted his head, opening his eyes wide. "What did you say?"

"I said, okay," she repeated, knocking his arms off and stepping backward.

"Well, fuck me."

Exactly what I plan to do, thought Janie. Out loud, she said, "Saturday night. Midnight. You know where I live, right? Next door to Tabitha?"

Cody nodded, speechless.

"Good," Janie said. "Meet me on the bluffs behind my garage."

CHAPTER 45

Straining Paint for
Watermelon Seeds

Len hurried down the hall, buttoning his shirt. Rachel should be home by now and he wanted to be the first one she spoke to about . . . her road trip. As he headed down the stairs, he could hear Olivia speaking to someone in the kitchen.

"My dad's getting changed," said his daughter. "Having said that, if you feel like doing something you could get me a drink. I'm not allowed because of spilling. We keep our drinks in the fridge mostly. That's because my dad likes cold stuff. One time I snuck the milk out and hid it in the closet so it wouldn't be so cold but it got all clumped up and smelly and my dad yelled about it."

"Olivia, honey, did your dad take you to his office today, to meet some people?" It was Rachel.

Len paused in the doorway to see Olivia's head in the fridge. She was hopping from one foot to the other, humming. Rachel stood behind her in jeans and a white shirt, heeled boots, her hair loose and falling down her back. She hadn't seen him.

"Sweetie," Rachel said, placing a hand on the child's back. "Did you meet a nice man today? And a nice lady? What was her name . . . Randi? Candy?"

Len stepped forward. "Tammy."

Rachel spun around. There was a quietness, a stillness about her he'd never seen before. She looked at once gratified and serene, but also sorrowful. The corners of her mouth twitched, just a fraction.

He raised his eyebrows in question—had she seen her daughter?

Over Olivia's head, she nodded and mouthed the words "thank you."

After settling Olivia on Len's bed with a plate of apple slices and a DVD, they were alone. Wordlessly, Rachel followed him into the kitchen, kicked off her boots, and hopped onto the counter while he uncorked a bottle of white wine. His day could do with a bit of blurring around the edges and he didn't doubt hers could as well. As he filled two glasses, she told him about Hannah. About her school, her uniform, her friends, her little turquoise ball, but mostly the air of contentment and joyousness on Hannah's face.

They carried their drinks into the living room and settled on the window seat, each leaning against cold window panes, facing each other, feet touching. Suddenly, Rachel sat up taller, pointing across the room. "What's that?"

Dr. Foxman's secretary had arranged for a brand-new wheel-chair, a long-term rental, to be delivered to his house. When he'd found it that afternoon on his porch, all gleaming metal, red vinyl, with wheels so clean the white rubber shone, he'd heaved it inside, hoping the neighbors hadn't seen it, and given it a good shove, just hard enough to send it sailing into the living room wall, where it would remain until Len was ready to give in. Or, if he never felt ready, until his depreciating sack of traitorous cells eradicated any other option.

"I don't need it," he said. "Not yet."

She stared at him for a moment, then picked up his hand and kissed it. "I've been wanting to ask you all day—why now?" she asked. "After all my begging and pleading—why did you send me to Hannah now?"

"I don't know. I guess I finally understood that until you saw for yourself that Hannah was safe, happy, you could never open yourself up to . . . other things. That it was worth the risk."

"And what about you?" she asked. "This was as big a day for you."

He sipped from his drink, then wrapped his arms around his bent knees, cupping the glass with both hands, as if for warmth. He stared into the liquid. Nothing about his day had wound up as he'd intended. Had it turned out as planned, he and Olivia would have been touring the Peytons' condo that very minute. "A big day it was."

"I've been doing some thinking," she said. "I know I have no right to request this, and I know it's probably far too late, but I was wondering if maybe a codicil to your agreement could be added, something that ensures that I can still see Olivia once—"

Len looked up. "There is no agreement."

"But I thought . . ."

"I couldn't do it. There we were in my office, Tammy pulled out coloring books for Olivia. Philip brought her a real paintbrush, for painting houses, and asked Olivia if she'd like to come over and paint a whole wall at their condo."

Rachel smiled. "I'll bet Olivia was into that."

"She said she'd only do it if the paint was watermelon color. Then she told them the paint didn't have to smell like actual watermelons and it should be seedless because she hates the seeds. Apparently, even in paint." Len stroked the side of his glass with his thumb. "So there we were talking about straining paint for watermelon seeds—and I believe this couple would have actually done it . . ."

"What? Paint their walls the color of watermelon, or strain their bucket of paint?"

"Both."

Rachel moved closer until their knees were touching. "So, what then?"

He stared at her for a long time, unsure how to begin. How do you tell someone that the only way you can possibly leave this world is if she takes on your daughter? Not only takes her on, but *wants* to take her so badly it hurts?

He stared into Rachel's eyes, partially curtained by loose curls. If he couldn't have this woman for a lifetime, Jesus, please let Olivia have her. He'd *give* what remained of his life to let his daughter have Rachel. Finally, he spoke. "Without a doubt, I am the worst dying parent on the planet. I had a lovely, idyllic situation for my daughter. Tammy and Philip were perfectly appropriate. They'd have done a great, no, a terrific job with her."

"But?"

"But neither one of them is you."

She looked as if she'd been slapped. Her face blanched and she stiffened. "But you never said . . ."

"I couldn't ask you to do it." Tears welled up in his eyes. "Because you might have said yes for the wrong reason. I decided I'd never leave her that way—with someone I had to ask, persuade."

"Len . . ."

"And I'm still not asking. But you wanted to know why and I guess," he paused, looking down and laughing, "well, I guess I decided to be like you for once. Totally honest. Whatever happens now, if you decided to walk out of here this moment and never—"

"*Len.*" She set her drink down on a nearby table and did the same with his. Crawling closer, she pushed him back on the seat cushion until she was lying on his chest, her hair falling forward. "Len. I don't want to be Olivia's mother." Her tears spilled onto his cheeks. "I *need* to be."

CHAPTER 46

Not as Much as Rats

Take time to celebrate small moments. When you are old and gray, you will realize these snippets of time were what mattered most.

—RACHEL BERMAN, *Perfect Parent* magazine

Linda Haas slid her black glasses down her nose Tuesday morning. "I'm sorry, Rachel. But the news is not good." She motioned toward the reams of spreadsheets on Rachel's desk. "Our accounts payables are multiplying each month. They're astronomical." She folded her arms. "I don't know what to tell our creditors."

Rachel stared at the figures. "Maybe we could speak to the bank again?"

"We're way past that. Unless you've got a revival plan that can wow them, they're not going to be too patient. I'm afraid you've got two choices, both lousy ones. Shut down and sell off the assets, or lay off staff. Fast."

Rachel remained silent. She took a long, deep breath and pulled out a red pen. "Okay. Let's go through the names together. We'll make the announcements next Monday. I need time to prepare."

Brad wiggled his finger in some sort of Sweeting's Pets salute to the hamster he'd just placed into a cardboard animal transport box. He'd sworn to Rachel it was the very same teddy-bear hamster Olivia had been holding to her face the night Rachel and Piper lost her at the bowling alley.

"So you say it's a . . . a boy hamster?" she asked.

"He's a buck alright."

"And the feeding and care instructions are inside the bag?"

"Yup. It's all there. Our card, too. You call if you need any more info."

"How old would you say it—he—is? Olivia's already had one rodent die this year, I just want to be sure this one will last awhile."

Brad closed one eye and stared at the cardboard box as if hoping the hamster inside would help him out. "He's a coupla months, I guess. Maybe four. But he'll live another two and a half years or more."

She paid and arranged all three Sweeting's Pets paper bags along her forearms. The heaviest sack held the hamster habitat. The bag next to it contained the all-important hamster food, and the lightest bag held the male lead in this production, the little buck himself.

"So this is for that little girl who got lost that day? When we had the Code Adam?"

Rachel nodded, smiling.

"I remember that kid. She was pretty cool."

She felt her chest swell. "Yeah. She is."

"You should call him Adam."

"Who?"

"The hamster."

"Oh. Maybe. We'll probably just let Olivia name him."

Rachel turned to leave. As she neared the doorway, Brad said softly, "Your daughter's going to love this."

She stopped and smiled. "Yes. She is."

Propped against the wall, Len stretched out his legs and sighed. The guest room, having been stripped of its lacy curtains and yellow-tulip duvet, and painted with watermelon-colored paint—seedless—was now Olivia's room. The week prior, Len and his daughter had officially moved in, partially so Rachel could help shoulder Len's workload at home, partially to make Olivia's ultimate transition smoother. But mostly because Rachel wanted them close.

"Is it three forty-five yet?" asked Len with a yawn. The poor guy could use some rest. Since the moment, two hours prior, that Rachel arrived with her load, she and Len had been sitting on the floor hunched over the setting up of the habitat, a perplexing achievement that had included snapping a plastic tunnel in two, dumping cedar shavings down the heating vent, and losing the buck himself for about twenty-five minutes after he chewed his way through his ventilated carton.

"Any minute now. Remember, you promised to nap after she settles."

He nudged her leg with his toe. "I promised to go to bed. No one said anything about napping."

Smirking, she threw a yogurt treat, hitting him in the stomach. As he dug it out of his shirt and tossed it back, the front door slammed.

"Olivia? Janie? Dustin? Come up here, Rachel has something to show you," Len called out, motioning for Rachel to stand in front of the habitat so Olivia wouldn't see it right away. Rachel couldn't wait to see the look on the child's face.

Olivia and Dustin tore up the stairs and into the room. "Where's Janie?" asked Len.

Dustin shrugged. "She went straight to her room. She's in another mood."

Rachel turned to face Olivia and bent down, smiling. "Sweetie, you like hamsters a lot, don't you?"

Olivia shrugged. "Not as much as rats. Rats come when you call them and know when something is funny."

"But if you could have a hamster of your very own . . ." Rachel said.

"I'd cry and trade him in for a rat. Because I actually want to tell a rat a joke and see if he can laugh. I really want a rat. At the end of the day."

Len said, "Assume there are no rats, the pet store is all out—"

Olivia thought about this. "Then I'd go to another pet store."

"All the pet stores, everywhere, are all out of rats," Rachel said, feeling her blood pressure rise. "The only pets left are hamsters."

The child scrunched her mouth to the left. "No puppies?"

Len looked at Rachel and shrugged. She stood up straight, pushed her hair behind her ears, and stepped away from the cage. "Well, this is for you. It's the teddy-bear hamster from the mall that day."

Olivia's eyes tripled in size. "That hamster?" She lunged forward and skidded down to the carpet on her knees, fingers tapping her chest. "I love that hamster!"

Dustin moved closer. "I thought you only love *rats*."

"Dustin," warned Rachel.

Olivia ran her hands along the labyrinth and bounced up and down with excitement. "Did you access to water him?"

"We gave him *access to water*, yes." Len pointed to the water bottle he'd wrestled into position.

"Can I hug him?"

Rachel laughed. "Of course you can. He's yours now."

Olivia beamed at Rachel, then at Dustin. She turned back to the hamster and let out a small squeak. Then she threw her body around the habitat, closing her eyes and resting her cheek against the plastic. "I love you, Jojo," she whispered.

"No, Olivia." Rachel pulled the child off the maze of tunnels and rubbed her arms. "You can take him out and hug him for real this time. No pet store rules here."

CHAPTER 47

With Silver Buttons
All Down Her Back

Friday at school, Olivia stared at the girls with the skipping rope. Samantha and Jada swung the pink rope and sang "Miss Mary Mack" while Callie Corbin jumped, her pretty blond braid slapping her in the back. The faster the girls turned, the faster Callie Corbin jumped.

Dropping her stick, which she'd been using to draw rodents in the sand, Olivia moved closer to the girls, mesmerized by the rhythm of the rope smacking against the pavement. Bits of sharp gravel flicked up from under Callie Corbin's feet and struck Olivia's bare shins like needles. Some tumbled down into her boots. She'd dressed extra special for class pictures today, in a white blouse that buttoned up the back and navy skirt that her dad said made her look like a proper young lady. Olivia didn't care much about looking like a lady. All she knew was that the skirt made her legs itch and she was never wearing it again, not ever.

The class wasn't supposed to get filthy dirty at lunchtime, the teacher said, since pictures were right after. So far, Olivia thought, she looked pretty good. She stayed off the grass so she wouldn't forget and roll down the hill. Her knees got kind of dusted-up from the sand but the rocks in her boots didn't count, since no one else knew they were there.

Olivia had never skipped before. She once begged her dad to buy her a purple skipping rope, but when she brought it to school the next day, none of the girls would hold it for her. When she tried again next recess, a boy yanked it out of her hands and used it to swing from the big tree behind the jungle gym. It snapped in half on his very first try.

Sidling up beside Samantha, Olivia waited until Callie Corbin jumped out before getting brave enough to ask, in the smallest of voices, "Can I have a turn?"

Jada pretended to retch into her hand, while Samantha laughed. Callie Corbin turned her back and grabbed the rope before walking away. "Get lost, Bean," she said. "We don't play with geeks who dress like librarians." She nodded to her friends. "Come on girls, let's find a better spot to skip."

Olivia trudged back to her stick and dropped down into the sand, this time settling cross-legged, her skirt flopped all over the dirt. She picked up the twig and started to draw a guinea pig, which was actually a rodent—not a pig, like some people thought. The guinea pig's face got messed up by a rock and she stomped the whole thing out with her boots.

"Olivia?" It was Callie Corbin wearing a big smile. "We've changed our minds. We've decided, since you look so nice today, since it's picture day, since we feel bad for not letting you skip, that we'd like to invite you to our party this weekend."

Olivia dropped the stick and gaped. "Me?"

"Sure," said Samantha, unzipping her hoodie and tying it around her waist. "We want you to be our friend."

Olivia stood up, her heart pounding with excitement. She smiled so wide her bottom lip cracked. She tasted blood. "*You* want to be friends with *me*?"

Callie Corbin backed away, still showing her teeth. "You know where I live?"

"Next to that apartment building?" Olivia asked. "In the big white house?"

Callie Corbin nodded. "That's right."

"What are you doing here anyway?" asked Jada.

"I don't know," said Olivia, "drawing my new hamster." She pointed at her earlier sand sketch. "See, this is his nose . . ."

"Nice," Samantha said, laughing.

"Be at my house tomorrow around four," said Callie. "We'll play in my fort out back."

CHAPTER 48

Informed Consent

"Please, Daddy!" Olivia hopped from foot to foot, shaking her hands. "I have to go! They invited me—Jada, Samantha, and Callie Corbin. They're my new best friends."

Len could scarcely believe it. Could it be that his daughter was finally making friends?

"Is it almost Saturday, Dad? Is it? Is it?" The child's eyes danced with what was, to her, the invitation of a lifetime.

Rachel scraped cookies from a metal tray onto a plate. Chocolate chip. Olivia's favorite. "It's still Friday, sweetie. Is Callie's mother going to be home?"

Olivia screwed up her mouth and reached for a warm cookie. "I'm not going there to play with her mother . . ."

Len got up from the kitchen table, blood rushing to his head. Turning away from Rachel so she wouldn't see, he grabbed hold of the table's edge and breathed through the dizziness. Once steady, composed, he turned around and reached for an overbaked cookie for himself.

Rachel's eyes were on him. "Next time ask me," she said softly before nodding to the wheelchair in the corner. "Or use the chair."

"I don't need the chair."

"I do!" Olivia trotted across the room and plunked herself onto the vinyl seat, wheeling herself into the cupboards, the wall. "Please can I go to Callie Corbin's?"

"These girls picked on you last year, didn't they?" Len asked.

"But now they're my *best* friends," Olivia argued. "They said I looked nice for picture day and then actually said they wished I played skipping with them. They even said my hamster drawing was good."

Len nodded. It was possible that the girls had matured enough to accept Olivia's differences, wasn't it? Maybe the teacher had spoken to the class again. After all, kids didn't invite kids they disliked to play after school, did they?

Rachel handed Olivia another cookie and leaned closer to Len, whispering, "Maybe I could take her and stay awhile. Keep an eye on things."

"That would be the kiss of social death."

"What do we know about this family? Have you met the mother?"

"I've seen her around, at different school events. Seems nice enough. Her father's an accountant in the city."

Rachel pursed her lips, deep in thought.

"The house is only two streets over," said Len.

"*Please*, Dad," Olivia said with her mouth full. "Callie Corbin has a fort!" She wheeled the chair backward, then paused a moment. "What's a fort?"

"It's a playhouse in the yard," he said. "Like a very tiny house for kids to play in. You know, Olivia, when you go visit someone at their house, a friend, you need to be on your best behavior. Treat her things with care, say nice things about her house . . . or her fort."

"What's a fort again?"

"A very tiny house. So if she's showing you her fort, for instance, you might say, 'Your fort is very pretty.' Something like that."

Olivia thought about it. "Okay. Can I go?"

He glanced at Rachel. She would be Olivia's sole guardian. More than that. Her mother. It was time to start trusting her with this kind of thing. "What do you think, honey?"

"Please, Rachel!"

Rachel drew in a slow breath and folded her arms. She was quiet for a moment, then raised her eyebrows. "It's sixty minutes . . ."

Len nodded.

"A lot can happen in sixty minutes."

"Yes, it can."

"Then again, it's important for a child to have a social life," she said. "I've written about this very thing."

He said nothing.

"I think it's okay. But just for an hour." As Olivia spun the wheelchair around in happy circles, Rachel looked back at Len. "It's a risk worth taking."

CHAPTER 49

Your Tiny House Is Pretty

On the patio, Olivia pulled Rachel's container out of her back-pack and held it out to the girls, who snatched it away and began gorging on chocolate chip cookies, finishing them off without leaving so much as a crumb for Olivia. When they were done, Jada tossed the plastic container onto the grass. Olivia to pick it up, but Callie Corbin linked arms with her and led her down the wide steps of the wooden deck, toward the fort in the far corner of the backyard. Olivia thought her dad was right. The fort was a very tiny house.

"It's party time," said Callie Corbin. "You like parties, Olivia?"

She began to skip. "Sure!"

Jada took Olivia's other arm, and Samantha took Jada's. They moved through the yard as a foursome.

"You're one of the cool kids now," Samantha told her. "One of us."

Olivia looked at Callie Corbin's tanned arms, then at Jada's pink-sweatered arms. As they stomped toward the back of the yard, Olivia thought of the last time two people linked arms with her, attached themselves to her like this. It was Mommy and Daddy and they were taking Olivia to see her first movie in a theater. Her parents made their way across the parking lot, picking her up and swinging her every few steps. The movie was *Stuart Little 2*, it was about a mouse, and the theater was freezing cold.

At the door to the very tiny house—fort—the girls dropped Olivia's arms and, bending down low, scurried inside, one by one. They all dropped to the dusty floor in the center of the room, which really looked like more of a crate than a house once you got inside. Olivia glanced at the wooden boards around her, not certain if she liked the sameness of the floor and the walls and the ceiling. She thought if she spun around too quick, she might not know which way was up, which way was down, which way was out.

Remembering her father's advice, Olivia said, "Let's come here every single solitary day after school. It can be our clubhouse and our most favorite kids and teachers can come here."

"Yeah," Samantha said, poking Callie Corbin in the leg. "Let's invite Mr. Lee and old Mrs. Antonio. They'd be a *blast*. Maybe Mr. Lee could bring his calculator and we could even do math."

"And we'd bring the librarian!" said Callie Corbin. "You can't have a party without the librarian. That would suck!"

"She could bring books," said Olivia, thinking maybe she'd ask the librarian to bring *Charlotte's Web*, one of her favorite books in the library.

Jada and Samantha laughed, then scooted closer to Olivia and took hold of her shoulders. "Ready to start the party, Cal?" asked Jada.

"What are you doing?" asked Olivia, moving back but hitting a wall. Or a ceiling. "It hurts."

"I thought you liked hugging," said Samantha. "We're just getting you back for all the hugs you've given us."

Callie Corbin grinned a nasty kind of grin. She lifted up her T-shirt and pulled out a pair of shiny scissors.

Olivia laughed nervously, tucking her legs in closer to her body. "What's that for?"

Samantha gripped her arm tighter, her fingernails piercing Olivia's flesh. She held Olivia's head still by grabbing her by the hair. Olivia tried to pull away by looking from side to side, but she was trapped. Tears stung her eyes and she blinked furiously to hold them back.

Callie sat cross-legged in front of Olivia, gnashing the blades open and shut. Olivia's breath came in terrified puffs now, she looked at Callie and tried to smile a smile that wouldn't come. "C-Callie? You're my friend, right?"

Callie laughed, then climbed onto her hands and knees, crawling over to Olivia. "We're getting a little sick of looking at that ratty hair of yours. We think you'd look a lot better if we cut it."

Jada hissed, "But you're going to tell everyone you did it yourself or we'll sneak into your new house and steal that hamster."

"Don't!"

"Then promise you'll say you did it . . ."

"I will!"

"Say I promise!"

"I *promise!*"

Callie reached for a thick clump of hair and pulled it in front of Olivia's face.

"Don't touch it! *Please*," Olivia shouted, kicking her legs toward Callie. Samantha straddled her, pressing her legs down, while Jada wrapped her in a hug that was anything but. Trapped, Olivia gulped in sharp breaths, tears blurring her vision. "Callie!" She thought of her father, of Rachel, sitting in the kitchen so far away. "Your . . . your very tiny house is pretty!"

Someone's sweaty hand clamped over Olivia's mouth and, other than the sound of her own muffled screams and pounding heart, all Olivia heard was the sharp rasp of the scissors sawing through her hair.

CHAPTER 50

The Least Perfect Parent

New parents may doubt their decisions at first. This is completely normal. Your confidence will improve with each choice you make.

—RACHEL BERMAN, *Perfect Parent* magazine

Eleven thirty had never felt so late. Rachel's head ached, her body felt shattered. Neither she nor Len had had the emotional fortitude right away to consider retribution, so consumed had they been with pacifying Olivia after the "party." Cocooning her in blankets, tempting her with uneaten snacks. Rachel reeling with her own guilt. Len, too generous with her, saying no one was to blame but the three monsters who did it.

They both lay with Olivia, wrapping themselves around her in an effort to undo the damage they'd enabled. Finally, two hours later, the child fell asleep; eyes nearly swollen shut from crying, hair knotted and chopped to the earlobe on one side. Her perfect little face blotchy and wretched with grief.

The only words the child had spoken were, "I promise I cut it myself."

Dustin and Janie had no idea, thank God, their grandmother having picked them up for pizza and a movie before Olivia left. By the time they returned, Olivia and Len were asleep.

While the rest of the family slept, Rachel stumbled around the house in a stupor, locking doors and windows. Janie's green canvas army bag was lying on its side, covering the floor vent, so Rachel reached for it, accidentally dumping its contents. She quickly began shoving uncapped pens, lip gloss, and change back into the bag. A folded paper lay on the floor. She flicked it open.

It was a magazine article from—Rachel scanned the bottom edge of the paper—*Seventeen* magazine and, judging from the way the paper fuzzed around the creases, it had spent a fair amount of time at the bottom of a purse. "How to Snare the Guy Next Door." But the word "Guy" had been crossed out with a black marker, replaced with the word "Goddess."

Without question, it was from Janie's magazine. April issue. Rachel had given Janie a subscription to *Seventeen* for her birthday this year.

Of course it was possible Dustin had gotten hold of one of Janie's magazines, flipped through it in hopes of checking out the cute girls, and decided he could make use of such an article himself by changing the pronouns. Possible, but not likely.

Dustin wasn't the one devastated by the ruin of a pouty poster.

Dustin wasn't the one obsessing over which swimsuit to wear to Tabitha's pool.

Was it possible for a fourteen-year-old girl to be gay?

Stupid. Of course it was. She'd read somewhere that some people knew from childhood.

But *her* daughter? Rachel's mind raced back through time, searching for any possible thing she might have done to cause such a life choice. Was it the time, when Janie was much younger and refused to let her mother comb her hair after a bath, that Rachel took her to the salon and had her hair cut short? Had she not been emotionally available to her daughter? What if she hadn't been so pushy?

My daughter is gay.

What did it mean? Would her life be tougher? Would friends be harder to come by? What about jobs? Love?

Love. Rachel traced the page with her finger. What was Janie thinking and feeling? Was she confused, ashamed, maybe even scared of what her family might say? The child must feel completely alone. Was she angry that Rachel hadn't figured it out on her own and somehow figured out a way to help her cope?

Or, worse, had Janie tried to tell her?

She thought back to the night she noticed Janie's new poster. Now it made perfect sense, but back then . . . back then she'd missed it. And when she'd asked Janie if she hung it up because she wanted to look like Jessica Simpson, Janie had definitely blushed. Then replied, "Whatever."

How could she have missed such a blatant sign? Janie didn't tack the poster to the wall because she wanted her feelings to remain hidden. She did it because she wanted someone to know. For her mother to know.

If only her mother had been listening.

Suddenly, Rachel needed to see Janie. As she bounded up the stairs two at a time, she passed a series of framed magazine covers from *Perfect Parent*'s very first issues. She paused a moment, staring at a faded, dated cover from 1963, feeling every bit the fraud that she was.

There couldn't be a less perfect parent on earth.

CHAPTER 51

"All Wound Up"

—CIRCLE JERKS

Lying under the covers in her tartan mini, knee socks, Doc Martens, and shrunken sweater, Janie had been waiting nearly an hour for the hall light to go out—the only sure sign that her mother had gone to bed. She glanced at her clock radio.

11:41. Nineteen minutes to Cody.

Friday afternoon, while Janie had been sitting at her desk in science, doodling on her binder, her cell phone vibrated from inside her bag. It was a text message from a number she didn't recognize. Looking around, she saw Cody grinning at her.

"Can't wait till tomorrow," it read.

Feeling sick, she slipped her phone into her pocket. She couldn't look at him.

She'd opened her binder to find a note, wondering how Cody managed to get it *inside* her binder. Cody had turned to face the teacher, so Janie pulled the tiny paper down onto her lap. It wasn't from Cody at all. It was from her mother.

J.R.W.L.Y., was all it said. *Just remember who loves you.* Rachel had been slipping the odd cryptic notes in Janie's lunch bag and books for years. It had started after Janie's best friend, Mandy, dropped her in third grade for the new girl from Rhode Island.

Rachel started leaving "chin up, sweetie" notes on a daily basis right up until Janie landed herself a replacement buddy.

Janie tucked this note further inside her binder. Her mother would die if she knew the plan for Friday. She'd tell Janie that sleeping with Cody wouldn't accomplish a thing. She'd say the best thing, the most mature thing, was to hold her head up and ignore the taunting because eventually it would end. And she'd probably be right. Eventually people would lose interest in Janie Berman.

Anna and Michelle had snuck past, trying to slide into seats before the teacher noticed and sent them to the office for late slips. Michelle knocked against Janie's desk as she passed. "Ugh," she giggled. "I bumped her desk. I hope it's not *catching*." They both collapsed, laughing silently as they sat down.

Fuck maturity, Janie had thought. She pulled Cody's note from her pocket, typed, "Me too" and hit send.

The clock read 11:42. Janie glanced at the gap between her door and the floorboards. The hall was dark. Just as she began to throw back her blanket, her door creaked open. Rachel. Janie closed her eyes and froze, willing her mother to go away.

In the silence, she heard a faint click as her digital clock added another minute.

She cracked open one eye, just enough to see the shadow of her mother leaning against the doorway. Watching her.

Rachel never did this. Not since Len and Olivia moved in at least. She was usually so exhausted at the end of the day, she could barely make it to bed.

The clock clicked again. 11:44. If she didn't show up, Cody would go back to school Monday and squeal. They'd all say it was because Janie Berman was gay.

Her mother came closer. Janie's heart thumped wildly. She prayed the tip of her boot wasn't poking out from under the blanket. Rachel smoothed out the covers and pulled the sheet up closer to Janie's chin. Then, so softly Janie wasn't entirely sure it happened, Rachel whispered, "Janie?" When Janie said nothing, her mother leaned over and pressed a kiss to her trembling cheek.

The clock clicked again and her mother was gone.

Ten minutes later, the house was silent. Janie tiptoed to her bedroom door and turned the handle without making a sound. Her mother's room was dark—a good sign, since Rachel usually read until she fell asleep. Janie made her way to the staircase, testing each floorboard for squeakiness before putting her weight on it. Halfway to the stairs, she heard humming from the bathroom, then a flushing toilet. *Shit*. Olivia. Janie ducked into the upstairs study and held her breath while Olivia slipped and skidded back to her new bedroom. She was missing a big chunk of hair on one side.

More arts and crafts, no doubt.

Janie had no choice but to tiptoe past the girl's room. Light poured out from under the door. Cody must be outside by now, but Janie couldn't help herself. As quietly as she could, she cracked open the door and peered inside.

Olivia was sitting on the floor, legs sprawled out wide, plunking stones into her old milk bottle, one by one, and listening to bubblegum music with the volume way down low. Janie recognized it as that Aly & AJ song . . . about sticks and stones or something. Softly, tunelessly, the child hummed along.

Listening to the lyrics, Janie looked at the stones on the rug, then back to Olivia. Sticks and stones. *Sticks and stones*. Oh God, the song was about being bullied. No wonder the kid was so stuck on it.

Janie had told her to forget about this band. This song. Wrote it off as sugary pop crap and burned her an anarchistic Sex Pistols CD. Worse, she'd yelled at the kid and told her to get the hell out of her room.

The child stopped singing and stomped on a pile of rocks, then rammed them into the bottle with force.

"Brandon." Plunk.

"Jada." Plunk.

"Samantha." Plunk.

Olivia fumbled around for another stone and hurled it into the bottle, which was much more full than the first time Janie saw it, months ago. Nearly to the top.

"Callie Stupid Corbin," Olivia muttered, touching her hair. She reached for a smooth charcoal pebble near her foot and held it close to her face, examining it before dropping it in with the others and whispering, "Janie."

Janie leaned against the doorframe. She felt sick with guilt. Olivia hadn't a friend in the world and Janie had humiliated her, both in public and private.

A quick glance at her watch told her it was midnight. She pulled the door shut and ran down the stairs.

CHAPTER 52

Dead Things That
Don't Stay Dead

Olivia hated going pee in the middle of the night. It was cold, spooky dark and the floors in Rachel's house squeaked. She ran back to her room but forgot to go to bed. Her bully stones needed counting and she could only count them if she played Aly & AJ. But when the song ended and she remembered to climb into bed, her foot kicked something over—she leaned down the side of the bed and gasped. Jojo's cage was knocked right over onto its side. She jumped down to the floor, got on her hands and knees, and peered into the cage. Uh-oh. This was bad. Jojo wasn't moving. He wasn't moving his nose or his ears or even his legs.

She'd killed him.

Olivia felt something wet on her foot. She pulled her foot out of her liner and saw blood, red blood. She poked at it with her finger and brought her finger up to her face. Licked it. Yup. She wiped the blood on the rug and opened the cage door.

Jojo didn't move, so Olivia scooped him up to get a better look at how dead he was. She squinted at the little hamster. He was just as dead as Georgie Boy, even before she dug him up the second time. And Georgie Boy's spirit was with Mommy, so that must be where Jojo decided to go when Olivia kicked him.

This was *very* bad.

Olivia sat back on the carpet. Her dad got real mad when she didn't keep dead things in the ground. And if her dad caught her holding another dead rodent, he might think she dug it up. She needed to bury Jojo beside the broken Georgie Boy parts under the bush.

She looked around the room for something warm to wear, something without buttons or zippers, because buttons and zippers were too hard to do. Spying her dirty orange ski jacket under the bed, she set Jojo down on the cage and pulled the jacket over her pajamas. Then she picked up the hamster and headed down to the kitchen for a spoon.

Outside it was dark and cold, and sticks on the ground pricked Olivia's bare feet. She found a big spoon on the counter beside the oven and put her pet in it. It was a pretty good spoon for digging because the tip was sharp. She walked across the yard and crawled under Georgie Boy's bush, setting her hamster down on the dirt. Then she looked for the popsicle stick that marked the gerbil's grave and began to dig right beside it. At least they could talk to each other . . . no, actually they couldn't. Dead rodents don't talk.

The ground was a little bit wet, so it was easy to dig the hole. Once it was deep, Olivia picked up Jojo and kissed his nose. "You're a good boy," she whispered as she lowered him into the ground. After a couple of shovelfuls of dirt, she heard a squeak and a scuffle. Then Jojo jumped out of his grave and raced across the grass into Tabitha's yard.

He didn't stay dead! And if he didn't stay dead, that meant he wasn't dead. Because only dead things stay dead.

Which meant Olivia hadn't killed anybody.

"Jojo," she called, crashing through the bushes and chasing after him in the moonlight. "Jojo!" The hamster slowed down for a moment in a small garden near the patio and she caught up with him, diving into the autumn flowers and scooping him up in her hands. She made a sack out of the bottom of her jacket and dropped Jojo in it, closing the hem over the hamster's head in case he tried to escape again.

As Olivia turned back to Rachel's, she heard a noise at Tabitha's house. No lights were on and it looked scary, so she started walking backward. The patio door swung open and a man stepped outside, dragging something with him.

It was the man from the other night . . . the one with the cigarette. But the something he was dragging wasn't a something. It was Tabitha.

Tabitha was bent over, trying to pull herself back toward the house, but he was too strong and got her out onto the patio. She jerked herself back and he almost let go; he only had her by the wrists now. "Little bitch!" he said and yanked her closer. He looked mean and Olivia didn't want the man to see her. She crouched in the garden. Tabitha kicked the man in the legs. The man grunted and yanked Tabitha's face upward by the forehead.

Tabitha's mouth was gone.

A cloth was wrapped around her face and Olivia couldn't see her mouth—not even one single solitary part of it.

As loud as she could, maybe louder than ever before, Olivia screamed.

———————

She screamed until she ran out of breath, then screamed again. The man looked up and said, "What the fuck?"

Lights turned on in Tabitha's house.

Lights flashed from Rachel's house and another neighbor's house.

Janie appeared out of nowhere.

The man dropped Tabitha and started to run and suddenly people were all around Olivia, all around Tabitha.

Her father picked her up and, still, Olivia screamed. She tucked her knees close to her chest so her father wouldn't squish Jojo, and then Rachel pulled the cloth off Tabitha's mouth. There was her mouth and her whole face. Her mouth started talking to her mother and Rachel and then Tabitha's eyes and mouth started crying.

Curled in a ball in her father's arms, Olivia didn't need to scream anymore. Tabitha had her mouth back.

CHAPTER 53

Monday in the Boardroom

Abandon any fantasies of the perfect life. Perfection is vastly overrated.

—RACHEL BERMAN, *Perfect Parent* magazine

Rachel stood at the head of the boardroom table next to the wilted fichus tree and watched as her staff filed in. All the excitement over the weekend—with Olivia wandering outside, and her exquisite scream stopping the abduction, and the police milling around the two houses all day Sunday, meant she'd had no time to prepare for this meeting, other than a quick breakfast with her bank manager.

Some employees sat in boardroom chairs, others leaned against the walls. All wore the same expression. Dread. To most of these people, losing their jobs meant much more than losing a paycheck. *Perfect Parent* employees, many of whom had never worked anywhere else, were like a big, grumbling, extended family.

They griped about whomever was spiking the air-conditioning. They complained when someone else got a raise. The women moaned about the men pouring the last cup of coffee and walking off without making more. The men complained about the women never emptying the dishwasher in the lunchroom. But they never missed each other's weddings and baby showers, bachelor parties, or family funerals.

Linda Haas nodded to Rachel that everyone was present.

Rachel breathed deeply and began. "Change is never easy. In fact, studies have shown that whether it's good or bad, people experience an equal amount of stress until they adjust."

She opened a folder and took out a stack of papers, handing them to Mindy and motioning for Mindy to pass them along. "It's no secret that *Perfect Parent* has been going through some rough times. So rough that I've been forced to consider taking significant measures, like cutting the size of the book again. And, as many of you have suspected, layoffs."

People shuffled miserably. Some whispered, others nudged.

"Both of these things would help push our numbers back toward profitability." Rachel pulled a sheet of paper off the easel behind her. The words PERFECT PARENT were written in large block letters. "But we're not going to do either."

Linda looked over her glasses. "What?"

"We're switching direction. I want you all to write down every parenting issue that's come up in your household, your sister's household, your neighbor's household. Because that's what this magazine will cover. I want learning disabilities, ADHD, autism, anxiety, and depression. I want gay teens, self-esteem issues, and eating disorders. Forget average parenting for average kids. I want us to cover the issues our readers are really dealing with. Our advice will no longer focus on the optimal number of strokes of the toothbrush at bedtime. Real parenting doesn't work that way. Real parents think it up as they go along. Real parents don't have time for perfection." Rachel dropped into her chair and kicked off her shoes, tucking her feet under her. "We'll need a new title."

Mindy shook her head and laughed.

"What?" asked Rachel.

Mindy stood up and wove her way through the crowd, stopping in front of the easel. After pulling the cap off the marker with her teeth, she crossed out PERFECT and wrote REAL in front of the word PARENT. "We have one now."

CHAPTER 54

Olivia's Army

*Be prepared, in an instant, to drop what you've learned as
a parent—even your most tightly held convictions—and give
your child what he or she needs most.*

—RACHEL BERMAN, *Perfect Parent* magazine

Monday after school, Janie stood on top of a kitchen chair,
affixing a foil streamer to the living room wall. "You better
hurry up with those balloons, Dustin. People will be here soon."

Dustin's legs were barely visible from beneath a mountain of
inflated blue latex. He rubbed his jaw and groaned. "I can't even
feel my cheeks. I'm *so* done." He held up his cast and wiggled
his fingers. "I wonder if the doctors would consider this child
abuse . . ."

Janie pulled a roll of tape from her pocket and tossed it to her
brother. "Mom wants you to start sticking the balloons all around
the house."

He groaned. "Everywhere? All the bedrooms, too?"

"You really think the guests want to see your reeking lair? The
balloons are for the main floor."

Rachel walked into the room, her fingers covered in icing. "Looks wonderful," she said as Olivia tore past, her hair now shorn into a cheeky chin-length bob, tangled with ungovernable waves, and thicker than it was long. The child craned her head around to watch her fluttering cape—a threadbare towel Janie had safety-pinned to the back of her shirt when she got home from school. "Not so fast in those socks, Olivia. We can't have our hero slipping and bumping her head. Put something else on your feet."

The girl skidded from side to side for dramatic effect before racing out of the room.

"I don't think she gets this whole hero party thing," said Janie, waving toward the decorations. "She just wants to look like one of *The Incredibles*."

"That's okay. We're doing it anyway."

"Whatever," said Janie.

Rachel sat down beside her. "Sweetie, I know it's been a crazy day and a half, but I think we need to talk."

"Can we do it later? I didn't get much sleep this weekend."

"The weekend is what I wanted to discuss. When we were outside Saturday night, I saw Cody Donovan out by the bluffs."

"I don't want to talk about that."

"Well, we're going to talk about it. My daughter, sneaking out of the house when I think she's in bed? To meet a boy?"

"What can I say? We were young and we were crazy and we were in love," Janie recited with all the enthusiasm of someone reading the fiber content on a box of cereal.

"I don't think so."

"Our feelings could not be contained."

"Janie . . ."

"Nor could the fire in our loins."

"Janie, I'm trying to have a conversation with you."

"Okay. I met Cody and Olivia screamed. I came back. End of story."

"That's not exactly the end of the story."

"It isn't?" Janie asked.

"I don't think so. First of all, he's not your type."

"How would *you* know?"

"Honey." Rachel laid a hand on her leg. "I know."

Janie looked away.

Rachel pushed the hair off Janie's face and leaned closer to see tears rimming her daughter's eyes. "I really should have clued in earlier. Here I was, so worried about you being with boys, and all the time it was their sisters I should have been watching. I feel like such a . . . such a terrible parent."

"I didn't want you to know."

"Maybe you did, just a little."

"I didn't want anyone . . . I didn't want *you* to look at me all different. I couldn't handle that. I figured you'd think I was just going all 'Fuck mainstream' on you."

"*Janie.*"

"Or that I wasn't me anymore. That I was suddenly all butch and tough . . ."

"Not for one moment since I found out have I thought of you as 'butch' or 'tough.'"

"Or a perve," Janie added.

Rachel smiled to herself. "Or a perve."

"I'm still the same old me."

"Same old you. Same old me."

"Oh God! You aren't going to write about me in the magazine again are you? Like the time when we drove to visit Dad's college and I saw all the cows in the field and took my juice bottle out of my mouth and said—"

"Fucking cows!" called Dustin from the next room.

"Dustin!" said Rachel. "Don't repeat it in front of Olivia."

He sighed out loud. "I wish I'd been born earlier. I missed the trucker-mouth toddler years."

"That's our Janie," said Rachel. "It was an article against washing kids' mouths out with soap."

"What were the parents supposed to do instead?" asked Janie.

"Reason with the child. And if that didn't work, take away television for an afternoon." Rachel gazed out the window, narrowing her eyes. "I probably should have tried the soap."

"Wouldn't have worked," called Dustin. "For her mouth you'd need turpentine. Hey look!" He and Olivia appeared in the doorway. He rubbed two balloons in her hair and held them over her head. Olivia's bob exploded like a hairy display of rusty pyrotechnics. They both giggled and disappeared, balloons billowing in their wake.

"That brother of yours is going to drive her crazy." Rachel turned back to Janie. "There'll never be another article about you. I promise. But there will be articles about gay teens in general." She took Janie's hands in hers. "Sweetheart, I love you no matter what. You'll be you no matter what. Nothing's going to change."

Janie leaned into her mother, burying her face in Rachel's shoulder. She didn't move, didn't speak for a moment.

"Mom, it's worse than you know. I was so stupid with Tabitha. I trusted her and now everybody at school knows . . ."

"Shh. It's okay. It'll pass. In a couple of weeks they'll be on to something else."

"I should have realized it was never going to work with her. Anything you have to work that hard at is going to suck." Janie sat back. "Want to hear the craziest part?"

"Sure."

"I was pretending to be you."

Feigning insult, Rachel fell against the couch cushions. "I'm offended and grateful at the same time."

Len wandered into the room, wearing a burned oven mitt. He dropped down onto the couch and closed his eyes. "Something in the microwave is smoking and the oven timer is buzzing."

"I'm sorry, love." Rachel smoothed his hair, letting her hand rest on the back of his head. "I left you in there all alone." She looked from the kitchen to Janie and back again, and called to Piper. "Mom? Would you mind turning off the oven and pulling out the lasagna? Just set it by the window . . ."

"Already done." Piper came out of the kitchen, pushing the shiny wheelchair. She looked at Len. "You're going to swallow that pride of yours and use this today. Otherwise you'll exhaust yourself."

Len didn't open his eyes. "I'll be fine in a minute."

Piper winked at Rachel. "*Stubborn* man."

He opened one eye, his lip twitching. "Interfering woman."

Olivia galumphed back into the room, not only caped, but now booted. On her feet were a pair of black, unlaced army boots that could only have come from Janie's closet.

Len winked at Janie. "First you, now Olivia. Have you girls *no* concern about the scuffmarks on these floors?"

"They were my first Docs," said Janie. "She thinks they're just as comfy as boot liners." She stopped to watch Olivia, who had paused to pull her tube socks over her knees and admire the effect in the hall mirror—now, caped, work-booted, and well-socked, the child appeared to be prepared for anything. "They'll look a whole lot cooler than winter boots at school, don't you think? More of a statement than a fashion catastrophe. I didn't want them going to just anyone. I was saving them for a . . ." she looked at Len, "a special person."

Len's face seemed to liquefy. He stared at Janie, smiling. He took her chin in his hands and kissed her young forehead, whispering, "Thank you."

Another buzzer rang in the kitchen.

Rachel shook Janie's knee and jumped up. "We'll talk later, sweetheart." When she reached the kitchen, she called back, "Sorry Janie, but could you be a doll and run out to the end of the driveway and drag the trash cans back to the garage?"

"Right now? We have this big . . . *moment* and you send me out for the trash?"

"I know. But people will be here soon. We'll talk later. I promise."

She heard Janie stomp out the front door.

In the kitchen, Piper dumped a store-bought Caesar salad into a large bowl, tore open a package of dressing, and squirted it over the greens. She put it in the fridge and said, "If anyone asks, I made it from scratch." She turned around and saw Olivia dancing past. "Olivia, you must be quite proud of yourself. You saved that girl's life."

Olivia scratched her toweled neck and stared at a plate of cookies. "Can I have one?"

Rachel watched in the reflection from the microwave door as Piper checked to see if anyone was looking. Assured they were not, she handed the child two rather large cookies and shooed her out of sight.

When Olivia was gone, Piper said, "I feel responsible for Janie's . . . issue."

"You?" said Rachel.

"Ever since Arthur left me, I've done nothing but insult the dignity of men. You know what sort of influence I've always had over the child. I've turned her off the entire gender."

Rachel looked from Piper's gleaming patent loafers through the window to Janie's unlaced Docs, "God Save the Queen" T-shirt, and plaid pajama bottoms. "It's sweet of you to look inward, Mother. But it's pretty safe to say Janie knows her own mind."

Piper wasn't convinced. "Still, I think I'll just have a few words with her. Tell her about a few of the decent men I've known . . ."

Watching her mother leave, Rachel shook her head. "Maybe I won't ground Janie for sneaking out. This might just be punishment enough."

Len pulled a spinach lasagna from the oven and set it on the island to cool. He looked at her with questioning eyes.

"I'd give it about fifteen minutes, then slice it up," Rachel said, winking. "Please. And thank you. Dearest."

"Into smallish pieces, I presume? Party-sized?" Len said.

"You're pretty handy in the kitchen."

"Mm. So now you kind of wish I was sticking around?"

She wrapped her arms around him and whispered, "Not if you tell a single guest I didn't do every bit of this myself."

"I should warn you. Spinach makes Olivia throw up. Or at least spit up. Something about it being too slippery and green, she says."

"Duly noted." Rachel tore open a package of wieners. "Where does she stand on veggie dogs?"

"Fairly safe bet. But only if the bun doesn't split into two, putting the wiener in danger of dropping onto the plate. Should this occur when you have no more buns to offer her, pull out five toothpicks and turn it into a wiener dog. She'll get a kick out of the tail and the legs will hold the bun in place."

Rachel dumped the wieners into a pot of boiling water. After turning down the heat, she turned to look at Len and said quietly, "I'm scared I'll never be what she needs."

He reached up to tuck a strand of hair behind her ear. "You have wonderful instincts with her. Just trust them."

The phone rang. Len turned to pick it up. "Hello?"

Through the kitchen window, Rachel spotted Janie dragging the garbage cans back toward the house with her grandmother in tow. Rachel hated to do it, but she had to ground the girl for sneaking out. It didn't matter that she may have been confused or feeling peer pressure. A child who snuck out needed to feel the consequence.

"She's busy right now," Len said into the phone. After a series of "mm-hm" and "I'll tell her," he scribbled something on the back of an envelope and hung up.

"What was that about?"

"That was a girl from Janie's new French class. Sidney. She's having a few kids over to study after dinner. Wants Janie to come. You better make that grounding decision quickly."

"A new friend who studies? I like the sound of that." Rachel reached into the crisper for a container of green grapes and set it in the sink, turning on the tap and running the fruit under water. "I have an idea. Why don't you make the grounding decision? You're going to be a big part of her life for the next . . ." She stopped herself and looked down for a moment. "Do you want to ground her?"

"From studying?" asked Len. "Never."

Len watched as she sliced each grape in half and arranged them on one end of the fruit platter. "I don't suppose one can stop them from making unwise decisions. Especially when kids don't seem interested in staying within the barricades we create to keep them safe," Len said. Rachel reached past him for the bag of carrots, which she dumped into a bowl and ran under water. He added, "Kids tend to leap right over the chains."

"Mm-hm."

He watched her pick up a knife and judiciously quarter each carrot lengthwise. At the same time, Dustin walked over, leaned on the counter, and stuffed a carrot stick into his mouth. His cast clunked hard against the wooden chopping block. Olivia trotted up behind him and surveyed the activity.

"It's impossible to plan for every catastrophe no matter how many precautions you take," Len said. "Life doesn't make things that easy. Look at me, I was worried about eating mussels. Real life is what happens when you're busy . . ." He paused. His goddamned words had disappeared again.

"Cutting the carrots," said Olivia.

Rachel dropped the knife and looked up, a wave of realization washing over her face.

"Mom, what are you doing?" Janie called down the edge of the bluff. "The guests will be here any minute."

Rachel climbed back up to the top with the help of a thick rope she'd tied to a chestnut tree at the edge. "Just go grab a handful of balloons, we'll tie them to the tree so people can find the path."

"Grandma's going to climb down here in her new loafers?"

"Grandma's driving the food over to the stairs with Len. They'll meet us at the bottom."

"She's driving me crazy with her man propaganda . . ."

Rachel tried not to smile. "Don't forget to stick a note to the front door saying we're at the river."

"What about me and Dusty? And Olivia? Are you driving us down the road to the stairs? Because it'll take us ages to walk all

the way back here and I'm already tired from setting up and dragging the garbage cans from the road. And anyway, I don't want
Olivia to miss her own party . . ."

Rachel scrambled to the top, wiped off her pants, and smiled.
"Janie, honey, take a breath." She placed an arm around Janie's
shoulder. "You're climbing down the bluff."

Janie widened her eyes. "Seriously?"

"Seriously."

"We have our beach back?"

"You have your beach back."

"Dustin and Olivia too?"

Rachel considered this. "Dustin can climb down on his own,
but we'll make sure we're there to help Olivia. Those new boots of
hers are a bit clunky."

Janie raced to the edge and started to pick her way down.

"Janie!"

"You said I could . . ."

"You can, sweetie. But you waited all summer to sunbathe by
the river. You can't do that without your bathing suit."

Janie squinted, looking around at the fallen leaves. "But it's Sep-
tember. Aren't you worried about us getting sick?"

"Bring a cover-up."

Janie raced back to the house.

A gray mist had settled over the rocky beach, bringing with it a
chilliness that seemed to Rachel to dampen even her insides. Shivering in maillot and rubber boots, she zipped her soggy red ski
jacket to the chin and drank in the air. It had been at least a year
since she'd been at the water's edge and had forgotten how peace-
ful it was to just sit, in the here, in the now, and listen to the river

flow. Len stretched out beside her on the plaid blanket, dressed in bathing trunks and David's forgotten hunting jacket, with a wool cap warming his head, and a scarf wound around his neck. He nudged Rachel's thigh and pointed to where Dustin stood in the river, legs red from the aching cold, showing his grandmother how to skip stones with his bad arm.

The party had been surprisingly portable. Balloons strung from bushes flapped in the wind; platters of party sandwiches and cold lasagna rested atop driftwood and rocks. Napkins and paper plates sat anchored by stones, awaiting their call to duty.

Janie held Olivia's hand, helping her navigate the lower half of the ridge. Olivia had been distracted halfway down by a dead squirrel and had stopped to explain, at great length, with Birthday Wishes Barbie by her side, that squirrels were just as much a part of the rodent family as gerbils or mice or even the renowned *rattus rattus*. Janie had parked herself on the path and listened with unusual patience. Now, trotting down onto the beach, they looked like sisters with their winter jackets, bare legs, and matching army boots.

"Whoa!" Rachel heard Olivia say as she looked around at the stones at her feet. "Look at all the pebbles here! I can actually use these for my bully bottle . . ."

Rachel watched as the child leaned over and scooped up a handful, kneeling down on the blanket. Her head appeared too weighty for her slender neck as the humid river mist terrorized her new bob. "Look at all of these!"

Before Len could answer, Janie leaned over Olivia, dark hair licking her face like blackened fire. She took the stones out of Olivia's hands and hurled them toward the river. "You don't need those anymore. They can say what they want to me, but no one bullies Janie Berman's sister."

Olivia's fingers tapped her chest, her face split into a smile.

Rachel looked over at Len for his reaction—that Olivia had her very own, if anarchistic, one-woman army was news that would surely assuage his fears for her future, at least at school. But his head had dropped onto his chest, his stubbly chin lost in his scarf. He snored softly.

Rachel tugged a second blanket over his legs and tucked it close to his body.

As Piper and Dustin joined them on the blanket, arguing over who got the most skips, Rachel pulled out a juice box and handed it to Olivia, who dropped her Barbie and snatched it up, sucking until the box caved in and crumpled. Once she'd sucked it dry, the child gulped in a breath and wiped her dripping mouth. She sat still for a moment, blinking at all the sets of feet stretched out on the blanket, looking for all the world like she might burst with joy.

Piper turned to Rachel. "I suppose this will exacerbate the erosion."

"I guess some things are beyond even *my* control," said Rachel.

"Hey," Olivia said, looking up the bluff. "There's somebody coming!" She got up on her knees and pointed. "See Rachel? There's people climbing down the mountain! There's Grandma and Grandpa. And there's Tabitha and her mother. And policemen . . . *real* policemen!" She pointed down the beach. "And those girls over there . . . are those girls from school?"

Rachel laughed. "Yes. And your whole class from school is coming. You're a celebrity, Olivia. The whole town's talking about you. You're a real hero."

"But why are they all coming *here*?"

"You saved Tabitha," said Dustin. "You're a hero."

Olivia twisted up her face. "But Tabitha doesn't get bullied."

Piper said, "A hero does more than stop bullies. A hero does something very brave and saves someone else from harm."

"What's harm?"

"Danger," Rachel said.

"Hey, there's Theodore! And Alex! And Brenda!"

Rachel laughed again. "Yes. And they're all coming to see you, Olivia."

Olivia's eyes tripled in size as she came to a realization and began to bounce in place. "You mean it's my birthday? They're coming to my birthday party?" She shook her hands wildly. "All these people are coming to my birthday party? Is today my birthday?"

Rachel glanced at Len, unsure of what to say. The child's birthday wasn't for another few months. But in spite of all the commotion, he hadn't stirred.

This hero business meant nothing to Olivia. Throwing her a party for being a hero was having no more impact than ironing her T-shirts or folding down her bedsheets. She wasn't able to make the connection between Tabitha losing her mouth and herself being brave.

"Is today my birthday?"

All the honesty in the world wasn't going to change that.

"Is it really my birthday?"

In the soft fog, Rachel could see that Olivia's gray eyes weren't gray at all. They were a kaleidoscope of shapes and colors, shards of blue with flecks of green, copper, even violet.

Olivia blinked. "Is that why they're here?"

To hell with honesty.

Rachel pulled the child onto her lap. "Yes, sweetheart," she said, her cheek touching Olivia's. "Today is your birthday. And everyone is coming to your party."

ACKNOWLEDGMENTS

Huge thanks to Connected Parenting's Jennifer Kolari, R.S.W., M.S.W., for sharing her wisdom, parenting model, and great love for children with nonverbal learning disorders. Thanks to Gillian and Pat, Michael Palmer, M.D., Alyson Pancer, Dr. Gary Shapero, John Lindsay, Michael Borum, Josh Getzler, Zeke Steiner, Genevieve Gagne-Hawes, Ricki Miller, Patry Francis, Bridgette Mongeon. At HarperCollins, Jeanette Perez, Alison Callahan, Carrie Kania, and Christopher O'Connell. At HarperCollinsCanada, Iris Tupholme, David Kent, Kate Cassaday, Rob Firing, Deanna McFadden, Miranda Snyder, Jennifer Lambert, and Lindsey Love. My film agent, Kassie Evashevski, at UTA, and all the film folks in Los Angeles for their continued support. My wonderful literary agent, Daniel Lazar, at Writers House and his assistant, Josh Getzler, as well as Maja Nikolic for foreign efforts. Finally, Steve, Max, and Lucas, because "there's also this."

Insights,
Interviews
& More...

About the author

About the book

Read on

Meet Tish Cohen

Pete Gaffney

TISH COHEN is the author of *Town House*, as well as the Zoe Lama series of children's novels. *Town House* is in development as a feature film from Fox 2000. Cohen has contributed articles to some of Canada's largest newspapers, such as *The Globe and Mail* and *The National Post*. She lives in Toronto. For more information visit www.tishcohen.com.

A Conversation with Tish Cohen

❝ Like Janie, I used humor to distance myself from my peers at school. ❞

How would you describe your childhood? Was it more like Janie Berman's or Olivia Bean's?

I'd have to say both. To different degrees, Olivia and Janie go through childhood somewhat alienated from their peers. Janie copes by using humor as a protective shield. When she laughs at herself the other kids feel safe from ridicule, prompting them to, if not encourage, at least tolerate her company. Also, the more self-deprecating Janie's humor, the more she makes herself undatable—which deflects any attention that might otherwise be shed on her utter disinterest in boys.

Like Janie, I used humor to distance myself from my peers at school. I had more than a healthy interest in boys, but used irreverent behavior to mask the pain of my parents' divorce and my own loneliness. The funnier I was, the greater chance I stood of keeping my truth a secret.

Olivia is not alienated by choice. She is bullied almost constantly and aches for a friend. A very real distraction for her is her obsession with rodents. Whatever else in life may be beyond her control, she can control her interest in learning more than any human really needs to know about the elimination habits of the *Rattus norvegicus*.

My social isolation wasn't nearly as dramatic, but I, too, found solace in a passion for animals—dogs being my creature of choice. By age six, I knew which breed was unable to bark, which had a black tongue, and which was the most likely to eat his own feces. I guess, like Olivia, I eventually found comfort in poop. ▶

3

A Conversation with Tish Cohen *(continued)*

Rachel Berman, your protagonist, feels like something of a sham running **Perfect Parent** *magazine. How would you describe yourself as a parent?*

I think, as parents, we've all felt like frauds at some point. After my first son was born, I remember strapping him to my chest in a baby carrier and taking him out for his first walk. I was twenty-seven years old, had made it through nine and a half months of pregnancy, had survived nineteen hours of labor, and hadn't slept in more than a week. I'd certainly earned the right to call myself a mother. Even so, I wandered down the street certain I glowed with incompetence. It didn't help when, while I waited at a crosswalk, a woman about my mother's age commented that my son, who was napping peacefully in his Snugli, had his head craned too far to the left and would surely wake up injured. The moment she climbed aboard a bus, I woke up my sleeping baby. He didn't wake up injured, he woke up hungry. I learned something that morning. That I actually had some maternal instincts, and not trusting them could leave me nursing an angry infant on the floor of the nearest bus shelter.

You seem to write about children to a large extent. Why?

I'm the mother of two boys, and my house and life are largely populated by children of all ages. I'm immersed in a child's-eye view of the world. My own thoughts are saturated with their worries, their triumphs, their quirky charms. I'm especially enjoying watching my boys navigate the preteen

> 66 I'm the mother of two boys, and my house and life are largely populated by children of all ages. I'm immersed in a child's-eye view of the world. 99

and teenage years. These are years I remember well.

As to why I tend to crowd my books with children, I think I'm one of those people with unresolved issues from my own childhood. In painful detail, I remember every joy, every ache, every wonder, every fright. How could I not write about it?

Olivia Bean, the Inside Out Girl, lives a life colored by bullying. Were you bullied as a child?

I was something of a peripheral child, but was lucky to avoid being the target of bullies. I was bullied only once; it was a death threat sent by sixth-grade messenger. I barely survived the anxiety, which lasted only until I fractured a finger playing European dodgeball the next day. Thankfully, mine was a bully with a heart.

My children have been lucky in that they haven't faced much in the way of harassment, but I will say, as a parent, there is very little as upsetting as knowing your child is being bullied. It's a huge problem in our society, one without a simple solution.

Rachel's daughter, Janie, likes to think she lives by a punk philosophy. What inspired this?

Janie is a headstrong character who doesn't do anything halfway. Her crush on Tabitha Carlisle is all-consuming, as is her insistence that her mother's parenting techniques will never work on her. So it made sense that if Janie saw herself as something of an ▶

A Conversation with Tish Cohen (*continued*)

iconoclast, an outsider, she might be into punk music as I was. But, being Janie, even her love for punk has parameters in that she only listens to what she considers "true punk," punk from the seventies and early eighties. Despite her desire to present a somewhat impenetrable exterior, Janie is a tender soul who loves hard and falls harder.

Do you have any writerly quirks?

Nowadays, I write in fits and starts. I tend to peck like mad for a few hours, then step away from the computer in search of chocolate or coffee. Always in the name of creativity.

Name a few jobs you've had.

I've worked as a pizza maker, an Icee stand girl, a glass art gallery manager, a media buyer, a receptionist, a decorative painter, an illustrator, a freelance writer, and an editor.

Your debut novel, Town House, *is being made into a movie. How is that experience?*

It's very exciting. Fox 2000 optioned the book and Ridley Scott's Scott Free Productions is producing. John Carney, director of the award-winning Irish indie film *Once*, is directing. The screen adaptation was done by Doug Wright (*Quills, Memoirs of a Geisha*).

There's something about my *Town House* characters being brought to life on screen that feels like the "ultimate" experience for me as a novelist. Rather than feeling apprehensive

66 Nowadays, I write in fits and starts. I tend to peck like mad for a few hours, then step away from the computer in search of chocolate or coffee. 99

about the involvement of other writers
and creative minds, I love that the story
is being reinterpreted. Of course, it helps
that *Town House* is in the hands of people
I truly respect.

What are you working on now?

I'm working on my third novel for adults and a
novel for young adults. ◞

A Life in Books

Favorite little-known novel?

I loved *Me & Emma* by Elizabeth Flock—
no one I know seems to have read it, but it
was a poignant story about the resilience
and terrifying vulnerability of children.

Favorite bookshop?

Book Soup in West Hollywood

Best film based on a novel?

Rebecca

Best short story you've ever read?

"The Lovely Leave" by Dorothy Parker

Any authors you'd like to have dinner with?

Jane Austen, Alan Hollinghurst, and
Joan Didion

Favorite little-known children's novel?

I don't know how little-known it is, but
I adored *The Railway Children* by Edith
Nesbit. When I mention it to people, no
one seems to remember it.

Books on your nightstand?

Twilight by Stephenie Meyer
Middlesex by Jeffrey Eugenides
84, Charing Cross Road by Helene Hanff
Look Me in the Eye by John Elder Robison
Digging to America by Anne Tyler

All time favorite literary character?

John Irving's Owen Meany

Book you wished you'd written?

This changes by the day. Right now, I'd say
Madame Bovary by Gustave Flaubert. ❧

Forever Young
The Inspiration for *Inside Out Girl*

MY GOOD FRIEND is a family therapist, and once mentioned that her favorite clients are children with nonverbal learning disorders or NLD, a condition often confused with Asperger's syndrome. While many of us are not familiar with NLD, we've probably known someone who has the condition. Have you ever met a child who constantly does, says, or wears the wrong thing? Someone who is fairly uncoordinated and takes things too literally, who never gets "the joke," or—in those rare cases this child *does* get the joke—repeats it so many times in succession that the other kids groan and scatter? Do you remember a child who wore cartooned sweatpants and rain boots in middle school or, worse, high school?

NLD is a neurologic condition that can prevent a person from understanding anything that is not verbal. A child with NLD will comprehend your words, but might miss any underlying subtext or sarcasm. If a child with NLD was playing baseball, was up at bat and happened to whack the ball into the outfield (not a likely event for a child with this disorder!), and the coach was to yell, "Run home!" the NLD child might very well turn around and race down the street to his bedroom. This overreliance on words tends to vary in severity—in its extreme form, NLD can prevent a child from recognizing her own mother until she hears her mom speak. It was this fact that inspired Olivia Bean's panic when unable to see people's mouths. The mouth is her only path to any sort of real understanding.

> ❝ Do you remember a child who wore cartooned sweatpants and rain boots in middle school or, worse, high school? ❞

The similarity with Asperger's syndrome lies in, among other things, the NLD child's inability to recognize social or facial cues, and the resulting social ostracism. But what often distinguishes the two conditions is that children with Asperger's (as is common with most forms of autism), tend to exist within their own reclusive bubble—they may have little desire to make social connections with peers and can be quite content to be left alone. Children with NLD have the very same need to connect with other children that most children have. They may be devastated by their undesired social isolation—they know they're being ostracized and usually want nothing more than to be accepted, to be loved. NLD can present differently from one person to the next, but for many children the social isolation is severe. Imagine never enjoying the simple childhood pleasure of attending a birthday party, or being invited to a sleepover. But, for the life of you, you cannot figure out why.

Now add in the emotional trauma that comes with being bullied. A child with NLD is often her own inadvertent enemy in that, being somewhat oblivious to social rules, she might march straight up to the nastiest clique of girls on the playground and ask them to play. What is clearly a socially fatal move to the rest of us can seem perfectly reasonable to the child with this condition. And as time passes, the other kids grow more and more sophisticated in terms of nonverbal social cues, inside jokes, and innuendo. Social rules grow ever more perplexing and the NLD child might be left out and bullied even more. Middle school can be a particularly rough time, because the other children are jostling for social positioning and are quick to lash out at those who don't conform. The NLD child typically doesn't understand what she ▶

> **Imagine never enjoying the simple childhood pleasure of attending a birthday party, or being invited to a sleepover. But, for the life of you, you cannot figure out why.**

Forever Young (*continued*)

is doing wrong; she just sees that she's unwanted.

What makes many children with NLD so endearing to my therapist friend, and to me, is that they can be completely naïve—they're such innocent beings. They love big and fall bigger when things don't work out as they'd hoped. Their rawness often gets them into trouble. Doughy and not athletically inclined, they may have little spatial awareness—they may lean too close to others and suddenly jump up in enthusiasm, accidentally injuring whoever may be nearby. In a school they've attended for most of their lives, they may get confused trying to find the office. Although they may be very gifted in certain areas such as reading, they may have severe disabilities with other subjects, such as math. But given the desire, a child with NLD can excel at a beloved activity—one boy was determined to make a local skateboarding team. Skateboarding is not an easy sport for most NLD children, but this fellow was determined and worked hard until he made the team. Having NLD is difficult, but does not preclude children from success in a given area.

I did extensive research on the condition, but through my therapist friend I was able to spend time with a darling thirteen-year-old girl with NLD who informed *Inside Out Girl* in a big way. I saw firsthand how a lifetime of being bullied and misunderstood had saturated her entire existence. Nearly every experience she had was tainted by cruelty from other kids. It allowed me to see just how isolating the condition can be, as well as how excruciating it would be for parents to watch their child live with this emotional pain day after day. As mothers and fathers,

> 66 I did extensive research on the condition, but through my therapist friend I was able to spend time with a darling thirteen-year-old girl with NLD who informed *Inside Out Girl* in a big way. 99

we want many things for our kids. Perhaps most of all we want them to be happy and well-adjusted socially.

Nonverbal learning disorder can be heartbreaking. Autism gets much attention in today's world and it's very much deserved. But NLD is terribly poignant in that it's an emotional trap in which children can feel tangled nearly every moment of their lives. It warrants having some light cast upon it as well. Because we typically see autistic or learning disabled characters as males in literature and film, and because parents of girls with these conditions face multiple layers of worry, I felt it was only right to build this story around the life of a feisty, whimsical, and utterly irrepressible girl I hope readers won't soon forget. ∾

Author's Picks
Favorite Female Characters in Literature

Emma by Jane Austen

Emma Woodhouse is perhaps the greatest heroine of all time. She's complex, opinionated, and meddling. In other words, charmingly human. If she wants something badly enough, Emma is fully capable of imagining her wish to be true; and if what she deems best for others *happens* to benefit her own situation, well, it's a coincidence she'd rather we ignore. And just when her wicked little ego has us completely smitten, she shows herself to be capable of self-examination, honesty, and remorse. Who but Jane Austen could accomplish all this in one high-minded young lady?

Anne of Green Gables by Lucy Maud Montgomery

This book didn't survive my childhood. There is a point, apparently, where paper simply gives up. Each time I read this novel, I *was* Anne Shirley. I pulled cows out of neighbors' gardens, ogled Gilbert Blythe, giggled with Diana Barry, and despised my rusty hair, which dictated that I couldn't wear red. Or maybe it was pink. Whatever. I even had a winter hat with thick braids for ties and loved the way the Anne-like braids swished against my cheeks when I tossed my head. I still carry with me a love for the name Anne, but only when spelled with an e.

“ This book [*Anne of Green Gables*] didn't survive my childhood. There is a point, apparently, where paper simply gives up. ”

To Kill a Mockingbird by Harper Lee

Scout Finch is the ultimate tomboy, a feisty little six-year-old who rubs the penniless (and lunchless) Walter Cunningham's nose in the dirt because sticking up for him meant getting her hand smacked with a ruler on the first day of school. In spite of her lack of mercy for those she defends, she has a heart big enough to feel for the very teacher who punished her. Too smart for her own good, Scout suffers no illusions. She knows the jingle in her brother's pocket means only one thing. He had to be paid to walk her to school.

The World According to Garp by John Irving

Jenny Fields, T. S. Garp's mother, is to be loved for her extremism, her passion for the Ellen Jamesians, and most of all, her deep-rooted suspicion that lust is the source of all evil. It is this very suspicion that drives her, when ready to have a child, to impregnate herself by having sex with a wounded but perpetually aroused gunner who is dying backwards—by returning to a fetal state. Once born, her young son's well-being drives her every life decision, even compelling her to attend classes to ensure they're worthy of her Garp's time. Jenny Fields is as powerful as they come.

Rebecca by Daphne du Maurier

The unnamed narrator of *Rebecca* has a vulnerability that captivates from the first page. Plucked from her position as travel companion to a nightmarish society woman, she has no difficulty enlisting our sympathy. But happiness evades the future wife of widower Maxim de Winter. Manderley, ▶

Author's Picks *(continued)*

Maxim's colossal and renowned estate,
is still haunted by the aura of his "perfect"
deceased wife, Rebecca. I don't know that
any character has ever given me more worry
or strain than the timid and self-doubting
young Mrs. de Winter. ⁓

Have You Read?
More by Tish Cohen

TOWN HOUSE

Jack Madigan is, by many accounts, blessed. He can still effortlessly turn a pretty head. And thanks to his legendary rock star father, he lives an enviable existence in a once-glorious, now-crumbling Boston town house with his teenage son, Harlan. But there is one tiny drawback: Jack is an agoraphobe. As long as his dad's admittedly dwindling royalties keep rolling in, Jack's condition isn't a problem. But then the money runs out . . . and all hell breaks loose.

"For someone who can't leave the house, Jack Madigan is a heck of a guy. *Town House* is everything you could ask for in a novel: touching, wry, bewitching, eccentric, and riveting to the end. I love this book and eagerly await Tish Cohen's next."
—Sara Gruen, *New York Times* bestselling author of *Water for Elephants*

Town House
Tish Cohen

"A constellation of characters whose idiosyncrasies make the family of *Little Miss Sunshine* look like *Ozzie and Harriet*." —*Kirkus Reviews*

A NOVEL

P.S.
INSIGHTS, INTERVIEWS & MORE...

The bank is foreclosing. Jack's ex is threatening to take Harlan to California. And Lucinda, the little girl next door, won't stay out of his kitchen . . . or his life. To save his sanity, Jack's path is clear, albeit impossible—he must outwit the bank's adorably determined real estate agent, win back his house, keep his son at home, and,

Have You Read? *(continued)*

finally, with Lucinda's help, find a way back to the world outside his door.

"[T]errifically written; Cohen's affinity for her nut-job characters is infectious and will keep readers involved."   —*Publishers Weekly*

Don't miss the next book by your favorite author. Sign up now for AuthorTracker by visiting www.AuthorTracker.com.